SOUTHERN CROSS

A John Marshall Tanner Novel

STEPHEN GREENLEAF

BANTAM BOOKS
NEW YORK • TORONTO • LONDON • SYDNEY • AUCKLAND

This edition contains the complete text of the original hardcover edition. NOT ONE WORD HAS BEEN OMITTED

SOUTHERN CROSS

A Bantam Crime Line Book / published by arrangement with William Morrow and Company, Inc.

PUBLISHING HISTORY
Morrow hardcover edition 1993
Bantam Paperback edition / March 1995

ISBN 0-553-56817-5

Published simultaneously in the United States and Canada

PRINTED IN THE UNITED STATES OF AMERICA

RAD   0 9 8 7 6 5 4 3 2 1

SOUTHERN CROSS

ONE

Maybe it was because it was one of those foggy San Francisco summer days that suggest the sun will forever shun us. Or maybe it was because I'd earned less than a thousand dollars the previous month and my banker had giggled like a geisha when I hinted I might need a loan to tide me over the rest of the recession. Or maybe it was because my banker was thirty-six and gorgeous, I was forty-eight and overweight, and she didn't even bother to blush when I flirted with her. Whatever the reason, I rejected the idea from the moment I learned of it.

After the mail deposited the first of what would become a dozen increasingly brash and artlessly imploring announcements on my desk, my primary reaction was dismay—that so much time had passed; that such a dread and distant milestone was suddenly upon me; that I had actually become one of those persons I'd formerly regarded, from within the brassy shell of youth, as comically obsolete and borderline pathetic; that I had truly toppled, suddenly and definitively, onto the dismal side of middle age. As with most idylls of introspection, the more I thought about it, the worse it got.

A more reasoned response, formulated that evening during a silent soliloquy at Guido's, was to shun the event on more exalted grounds: that the underlying sentiment was immature, reactionary, and possibly injurious in some gerontologic aspect; that at my age the only worthy focus was prospective—nostalgia was a crutch for the developmentally arrested or professionally unaccomplished, and I of course was neither; that memory was too perverse to mess with— the good times hadn't been that good, and the bad ones had been worse. All of which was reason enough to let bygones stay long gone and the dead stay deeply buried.

But philosophizing only maps your options; at some point you have to act, and then it's pretty much a dice roll. In this case, the fact that seemed determinative was that in my current fiscal state I couldn't afford to make the trip even if I wanted to. So I checked the box marked "Do Not Plan to Attend," and refrained from supplying biographical data beyond my name, address, and, after an interesting internal debate and a review of appropriate euphemisms, my current occupation. When I turned away an unctuous emissary, who materialized in my office to dun me for an absurdly monu- mental contribution to the development fund with far less tact than his mission warranted, I figured the issue was closed.

Yet somehow, six months after my last best pledge of noninvolvement, here I was, two thousand miles from home, lolling in line in an inadequately lit gymnasium on the cam- pus of a diminutive liberal-arts college in the heart of the Upper Midwest, waiting to receive my name tag and T-shirt and schedule of weekend activities, poised to dive headlong into the celebration of the twenty-fifth anniversary of my graduation from that selfsame institution. If I had to pick a reason for my change of heart, I'd say part of it had to do with wondering how a bunch of doctors and lawyers and insurance executives would react when confronted by a real live private eye.

But a more essential impulse had to do with age. Fifty loomed before me like the Matterhorn; I would need a boost to get beyond it. If I could recharge my psychological batteries, replenish my store of hope, find further reason to keep doing what I did, then the reunion would serve its purpose. But I wasn't optimistic.

As the registration line shortened imperceptibly, my heart was as aflutter as if someone held a gun on me, my nerves as frayed as if drunken revelations and compulsive camaraderie lay behind me instead of dead ahead. My eyes were as skittish as sparrows—I didn't want to seem aloof, but I didn't want to come face-to-face with someone I didn't recognize but should have, either. The stance I finally seized upon was to pretend I didn't know what the commotion was about; I was just there to read the meter. That bit of burlesque only got me through the next three minutes.

Such real and imagined dilemmas were tumbling through my mind like socks in a dryer when a hand landed on my shoulder with the subtlety of a sack of cement. "Tanner, you asshole. How come you never answered my letter?"

"The one I got back in '72? That said you'd be in San Francisco for a day and wanted to get together? The one that came a week after you were supposed to arrive? Because you didn't include a return address, you moron."

I had finished most of my declamation before I turned to greet the object of the exercise, to wit: Gilbert Huxley Hayward, one of my best friends in those years, at once the most endearing and maddening man I've ever known.

Although I was prepared to greet him warmly, when he was fully focused in my bifocals, I was afraid I'd been mistaken. The white hair, the bloated body, the jowls overgrown with Santa's beard, all suggested my radar had misfired.

"Gil?"

His smile was as big as his belly, which he patted like a pumpkin at the point where his belt was eclipsed by his bulge. "At your service."

"What the hell happened?"

To his credit, his ego was still intact and his laugh was

unrestrained. ''The same thing that happened to you, douche bag. I guess you don't have mirrors in your house, so you didn't notice you look more like Tom Foley than Tom Cruise these days. I hate like hell to be the one to break the news.''

I laughed to cover my boorishness. ''Good to see you, Gil.''

''Yeah. Been a long time and all that shit. Assume the appropriate clichés have been exhausted.'' He looked around the gym with more revulsion than reverence. ''Remember when I passed out behind the wrestling mats and got locked in all night, and Dean Antley called the cops 'cause he thought I'd been abducted?''

''Remember when you put Man Tan in my shaving lotion and I thought I had the pox?''

''Remember filling Janson's shoes with glue?''

''Remember the detergent in the pool?''

''Remember Susan Willoughby's tits?''

I remembered all of that and more, and Gil did, too, and we took a moment to take pleasure in the exercise. The swelling in my chest surprised me.

''So what keeps you busy these days?'' I asked when the memories dimmed.

''Same as always—getting rich and getting laid. Not that tough to do either in New Jersey.''

I detoured around his sex life. ''What are you doing for a living?''

He disdained an answer more elaborate than a shrug. ''Whatever.''

''Bring the wife and kids?''

Gil shook his head. ''Claimed they'd never heard anything about the joint that made them want to see it, plus the youngest had tickets to Kris Kross. Whatever that is.'' He looked at me more closely, as though he'd heard a nasty rumor but couldn't quite remember what it was. "How about you? Got family milling around somewhere?"

"Not here; not anywhere."

"You telling me you never married?"

"Correct."

"But you've lived with someone, right?"

"No longer than a three-day weekend."

Gil shook his head. "Jesus. I know you're not queer, not unless they got something in the water out there that turns the sex thing inside out, which come to think of it they should probably check out if they haven't already." Gil's look turned crafty; the elbow in my rib was sharp. "I know someone who'll be glad to learn you're still roaming the range, cowboy."

My stomach fluttered, then folded, then soared. "Not Libby, I hope."

His grin turned demented. "Looks good enough to eat, too. It's worth money if I can watch the good parts."

I tried to calm him down, although calm and Gil Hayward had ever been strangers. "I'm sure she brought a spouse along; she got married the year after we graduated."

Gil shook his head. "She's between husbands two and three, and number three hasn't put in an appearance yet. Her words exactly—you're free to take your shot."

"Great." My stomach opted for a second loop.

"Come on," Gil urged, slapping my back again. "Get the paperwork taken care of and follow me. We're over in Milton, same floor as freshman year. Hartman is already there, trying to figure out how to open his suitcase. Got a car?"

I nodded. "Rental."

"Good. We can cruise the strip if our classmates are as boring as they used to be. Remember the townies we picked up at the pizza place that time?"

"I try not to."

"Come on, Tanner; they were good sports."

"They were pitiful; if it happened today, they'd call it date rape."

Gil clouded over the way Texas clouds over—with mounds of black and rumbles of thunder. Sudden violence had always been one of his trademarks, and I thought for a moment he was going to slug me. But the fists at his side soon melted and he settled for a dismissive epithet. "Just because they didn't issue an invitation doesn't mean they didn't want it. Townies *lived* to fuck college guys."

"I seem to remember it took a long time to get yours to stop crying," I said stiffly, then regretted it. That I hadn't had sex with the girl I'd inherited that evening had more to do with being too drunk than too noble, and anyway the past was ineradicably past. Still, even if our behavior had been less unilateral than I'd suggested, the episode had been one of those excesses of youth that leave a splinter in your mind, something you hope never happens again, something you can't believe you did.

Something you need to atone for.

"It seems weird to have a car up here," I said on the way to the parking lot, referring to one of the numberless rules that, along with compulsory church on Sundays and coats and ties at dinner, had made the institution a comforting shawl of *in loco parentis* to the parents and a prickly anachronism to their children.

"Yeah," Gil groused, his enthusiasm already on the wane. "It would have almost been tolerable if we'd had wheels."

I opened the car for Gil, then tossed my jacket in the back and got in the driver's side. Before starting the engine, I opened my packet of reunion materials and glanced through the schedule for the day. Although my perusal was only cursory, the entertainments seemed to begin with a sing-along in the new theater and climax with a dance in the old gym and conclude with a meeting of Alcoholics Anonymous in the basement of the school chapel.

I had a feeling things were going to stay at least that weird through the weekend.

TWO

The drive to the dormitory was brief—a drive to anyplace on campus was necessarily brief—but it took long enough to confirm an enduring impression: The grounds of my alma mater were among the loveliest spots on earth. Broad swaths of grass; mammoth oaks and elms and maples; majestic buildings; blooming gardens; hills and vales and lakes and streams. Inspiring, all of it, then and now, yet at the same time deceptive and perhaps beside the point.

For one thing, it was summer, so the flora was on its most verdant behavior rather than curled in the scruffy somnolence it suffered during most of the academic term. Tempers had flared and moods had plummeted during those dull gray months of winter—loves were lost, friendships severed, studies neglected, often irretrievably. The tardy lift of spring never quite made up for it, not even the year the baseball team went 26 and 5 and Gil and I were named all-league.

More troubling than the intemperate cycles of botany and meteorology was my sense—grounded in resentments I didn't know I had until I boarded the flight that morning—that the attentions lavished on the grounds and buildings, as well as on the pursuits that pulsed within them, contrasted markedly with the neglect of more essential needs. Lack of guidance, or even notable concern, on matters ranging from career choice to social deftness to symptoms of personal dysfunction had left many of my peers, including myself, in a fog that led us down wrong roads. On the day I graduated and went out into the world, I knew more about the Renaissance than I knew about myself.

But as part of me doled out blame, a larger part acknowledged that I wasn't being fair. My own experience wasn't the norm of the place, after all. Not a scholar, not possessed of a passion that provided clear direction in terms of career or avocation, not sure of who I was or what I wanted, I needed from external sources what most of my classmates found within. The urge to blame the college for the pedestrian course my life had taken was to credit it with more magic than it had or could possess. Nevertheless, I couldn't help but wonder how my peers felt about the contours of their lives after the send-off the school provided— whether they saw themselves as predestined champions of a grand design, or, like me, as the illegitimate offspring of a random chance. For the time being, it was enough to acknowledge that the school was a lovely place, whose surfaces made you proud. What lurked behind the heroic stone facades and the sad small smiles of the faculty and staff was far more problematic.

I parked the car and extracted my bag from the trunk and lugged it toward the check-in desk, with Gil leading the way like a tackle leading the fullback on a power sweep, which he had done for me in former times as well. Although most of the faces in the crowd were familiar in the sense the billboards along the freeway are familiar, I had trouble coming up with names to match. Scurrying like a squirrel, I made do with generic gestures of greeting that were reciprocated with equal languor. By the time I was in line for a key to my room, I decided my initial impulse had been apt—attendance was a big mistake that would only be compounded as the festivities began to snowball.

I was already formulating a retreat when Seth Hartman

materialized at my side, looking miraculously identical to the day we'd met and immediately become fast friends, which was the second day of freshman orientation when we noticed we were each reading *Goodbye, Columbus* as we waited to be photographed for the zoo book. In a reversal of mood of an amplitude that had been endemic in my student days, I was glad to be where I was again.

"Hey, Marsh," Seth said, his grin at once crooked and timid and genuine.

I grinned a ton and shook his hand. "Whatever you're taking will make you a fortune if you can sell it through the mail."

His blue eyes sparked with pleasure. "If you're referring to my eternally youthful aspect, I ascribe it to a purity of heart and mind plus a jigger of Jack Daniel's of an evening, to ward off the chill."

"I didn't think it got below ninety in Charleston."

The grin made way for an aphorism. "Chills aren't exclusively external. As I believe you know."

I looked to see if there was a message in there someplace, but the result was inconclusive. To all intents and purposes, Seth Hartman seemed unstruck by the sniper fire of time. His body was as lithe and fluid as ever, his hair still clipped to prep-school perfection, albeit with an edge of gray. His jaw was defined and strong, his skin taut and Southern-fried, his attire a peerless blend of light linens and soft leathers. As I watched him accept the fellowship of others and dispense his easy and gracious responses, it was obvious that Seth remained fashionable and funny and bright and self-effacing, a star in spite of himself as he had been in the days when I'd basked unabashedly in his glory, which had been grounded not in what he had done but simply in who he was. It was not an exaggeration to say that my friendship with Seth Hartman was the most auspicious achievement of those four young years of my life.

"It's great to see you, Marsh," Seth was saying.

"You, too."

"I almost called when this reunion thing geared up. Got your number from Directory Assistance and everything, but couldn't bring myself to dial the phone."

"I know what you mean," I said, because I did. Seth and I had been pivotal to each other once, a reciprocal support system that boosted one and then the other over the bumps and thumps of maturation. I think one of the reasons we'd stayed apart ever since was the sense that whatever we became to each other now would only undermine that bond.

"You're still in San Francisco, right?"

"Right."

"And still a . . . whatever you call it? Private eye seems so *film noir*."

"Well, that's me. *Noir* to the core."

"We'll have to talk about that sometime, how you got from lawyering to sleuthing."

"After we talk about why you traded New England for South Carolina. I'm no expert, but your accent sounds straight off the plantation. I'll bet you named your firstborn Rhett."

A switch momentarily shut down the mechanics of his face—the light went out of his eyes, and his smile grew stiff with effort. But a second later the social systems were on-line again, and he bowed from the waist extravagantly. "I'm a Son of the South all right. You should see me stroll down Tradd Street of an evening in my white suit and walking stick."

Oddly enough, I could see it quite easily.

"I'm in the next room, by the way," Seth was saying as he looked at his watch. "Just in case you have nightmares."

"A minute ago I'd decided this whole *weekend* was going to be a nightmare."

Seth laughed. "Too soon to tell, I think, but I know what you mean. And if I know you, you've already got your escape mapped out—motel in town, then off to the airport Sunday morning without saying good-bye to anyone. Am I right?"

I felt myself redden. "Something like that."

"Stick around for at least one night. Promise?"

I shrugged. "Sure."

As Seth slapped me on the shoulder, I found myself pleased that he had read my mind, that even after all this time our instincts traced parallel planes.

"So what's on tap?" I asked, eyeing the agenda again, this time without comprehending it.

"Now?" Seth looked at his notes. "Reception at the president's house, then a panel discussion entitled 'Where We've Been and Where We're Going and How to Be Sure We Get There.' Gil's one of the facilitators, which may give you an idea of how complex the discussion is going to get. Then a concert by the class pianist and a reading by the class poet and a film by the class filmmaker. Then dinner, then free time, then a sock hop in the gym."

"You forgot the A. A. meeting."

"Right." Seth squinted and looked at me. "That of particular interest to you?"

"Not yet. You?"

He shook his head. "Booze is the least of my problems." Solemn for just a moment, Seth's look quickly turned mischievous. "I forgot the most important item."

"Which one?"

"Faculty open house—five o'clock at the library. Be sure to get there early, so you can exchange affectionate recollections with some of your favorite profs."

I swore. "There isn't a member of this faculty who has ever known my name. Maybe we should sneak off to . . . what was the name of that place?"

"The Jabberwock. So soon you forget your home away from home."

"Actually I always hated that joint. Smelled like kerosene or something."

"I think it was mostly the stench from gouging starving students." Seth looked at his watch again. "I've got to make some calls. If I don't see you at dinner, meet me here at nine? Maybe we can get away from the hubbub and chat for a time. Catch up and all that."

"Sure."

"And maybe just you? For an hour or so? If he wants to join us, tell Gil we'll see him at the Jabb at ten."

"Okay."

"Good. See you later."

"Right."

Seth started to walk away, then paused and looked back, not quite meeting my eyes. "I've missed you, Marsh. I wish I'd done something about it a long time ago."

"Me, too."

"We'll have to make up for it from here on out."

"Right."

"Right. Well. See you later."

"Yeah. See you."

As he hurried off to make his calls, I wondered what was going on, not with the concert or the open house or the panel discussion, but with my friend Seth Hartman.

THREE

Suddenly I was alone, deep in the midst of people I'd once envied and avoided, admired and feared, coveted and shunned. It was hard to remember why it had all been so complicated.

I lugged my bag to my room, decided I'd been in jail cells more inviting, then returned to the common area. As I made my way through the crowd, I was bent on a cup of coffee and an easy exit; luckily, only etiquette prevented me from either.

Styrofoam in hand, I opted for a stroll among the buildings and through the groves and gates and gardens, to wallow in such memories as bestirred themselves. My route was random and unfocused, a fit with both my current mood and my academic career. The day was partly cloudy, which was a mutual match as well.

The battered lounge in the student union where I'd wasted eons playing Hearts, the Gothic dorm in which I'd lolled away my senior year, the Bauhaus library where I'd spent too many evenings in resentful deference to the inclinations of the institution, the antique appointments of the Tea Room where we'd flaunted the latest flowering of our brilliance after the library shooed us off—over the next hour I revisited those and other venues, including the chapel I'd haunted the winter of my sophomore year in the grip of a variety of religious experience I hadn't approximated since.

It was pleasant enough on an aesthetic level, and the recollections that came and went were not entirely repugnant. The good times had mostly been adventures—forays to other dorms or other schools in search of harmless booty, parties where something poignant or preposterous had occurred, performances where timeless marvels were revealed to my unenlightened mind. The bad times were more memorable because they seemed more searing—goals unachieved, friendships squandered, romances severed, caves of knowledge overlooked or, once explored, forgotten.

If asked as a freshman, I would have said my goals were simple—I wanted to become witty and intelligent, sophisticated and erudite, philosophical and comical, articulate and ironic. I wanted to know something about everything and everything about something. I wanted to be liked, and I wanted to be loved. Then four years slipped past, and when I said good-bye to all that, I wasn't any of those things. I didn't know why.

Despite the rush of memory, the expectancy that spurred my walk, the hope that I would be informed or even altered by the journey, went unrequited. I was visited only by the realization that the life I'd aspired to and the one I was living had only trivial points of congruence, and were in many ways polar opposites. In contrast to the world of reason and restraint toward which my education had directed me, the world in which I lived and worked was marbled with violence and cruelty, jealousy and greed, outrage and addiction, pain and degradation. Which raised the possibility that, at least for me, the time spent on this campus, acquiring a host of misperceptions I still labored to be rid of, was less a blessing than a curse.

The rose garden was my last stop, the only *mise en scène* I'd scripted, the only site that needed special notice. I entered the arboretum with reverence, made my way along cool pathways toward its center, then saw that I was not alone.

As though we were featured players in the sequel to a classic film, with cameras rolling to the rear and grips and gaffers in the underbrush, Libby Grissom stood beside a hybrid tea, at the spot where I'd first dared to voice my feelings for her. Then as now, the moment toyed with time, created fusion and fission simultaneously, compressed the present like a concertina, then stretched it thin like taffy. Short of breath and tingling with uncertainty, I waited for something to happen without knowing what I wanted that something to be.

Locked in a time dance of her own, her hands flighty at her sides, her eyes fixed on a perfect yellow bloom, Libby didn't notice me at first. From the expression on her face, the accompaniment to her trance was more a dirge than a minuet. I had no doubt that I was the source of the song.

She seemed taller than before, perhaps because she was as trim as a rake. Her once-blond hair was now a golden brown; the once-lush locks were chopped to a wedge above her ears and neck. Her clothes were sporty and simple: the running shoes well worn, the shorts tanned just lighter than her slim and muscled legs, her top imprinted with a sassy slogan. Her hands were without adornment other than the dollops of pigment that age deposits; her eyes seemed wayward and unplugged.

Once again, my impulse was to turn and go, to postpone an encounter until I was armed with quips and counter-punches, until I had reprised our past sufficiently to know where the equities lay and whence the apologies should flow. But a bird flew off, a tree branch trembled, a leaf fell lazily to earth, and Libby's spell was broken.

When she turned my way, she trapped me; I was as atremble as a rabbit. "Marsh." A hand went to her throat. Her eyes were as astonished as the bird's, then leery as my own. "My God."

I waved inanely. "Ms. Grissom."

"I didn't . . . they told me you weren't coming."

"I didn't think I was."

She shifted left and right, like me in the grip of an urge to flee. "Well. I'm glad you did."

"So am I. You look great, Libby."

Her laugh was terse and deprecating. "After I decided to come, I doubled my aerobic schedule and lost ten pounds. If I'd known *this* was going to happen, I'd have lost five more."

I was flattered but didn't know what to do about it. "So how are you?" I mumbled, shifting about so avidly I pricked my elbow on a thorn. "I mean, you know, has life been gentle with you and all that?"

She frowned and looked away, toward the chapel lordly on the hill above us. "It's not *supposed* to be, is it? 'Do not go gentle into that good night,' remember?"

"You always were too literary for your own good. All I meant was, are you happy?"

A brow lifted as she regarded me the way she had regarded the yellow rose. "Now?" She shrugged. "Not particularly. But I have been, on and off. And I hope to be again."

"Is it something you want to talk about?"

"With you? Here? Now? I don't think so." Her smile turned firm, then crumpled. "About a year ago I wanted to talk to you so much it became an obsession. I was hysterical about it for some reason—I got out all the yearbooks and looked at the pictures and dug out all the letters we exchanged the summer before senior year, and, well, it was crazy. Monomania or something. One night I downed three shots of bourbon, then looked up your number and dialed it, then hung up the second you answered. I did it four times in a row before I got control of myself. You must have thought I was the CIA."

"I wish you'd persevered."

She met my eye. "Then why didn't you call me?"

"You're married. Or were."

"That didn't matter."

"Yes, it did."

The exchange revived the taste of our final weeks, when conversation inevitably rose to confrontation, when our views of everything were disparate, when we'd seemed compelled to hurt each other. At the time, I hadn't understood why we'd suddenly become so alienated, but in retrospect the cause seems simple—we were afraid of what was coming next, and each blamed the other for that fright.

As I was remembering how hurtful our qualms had made us, Libby tried to lift the mood. "It's a moot point anyway," she said airily. "My second divorce was final a month ago."

"I'm sorry."

"Don't be; I'm the one who filed. It's what I wanted; what I needed, even. It's just that I still seem to be . . . 'reeling' would be a good way to put it."

"Divorce is never easy."

She frowned. "I didn't think you'd married."

"I haven't. But I'm around it a lot. In my work, I mean."

Her smile slid toward a sneer, or maybe I was just projecting. "Keyhole peeping."

Since I've had a lot of practice, I didn't take offense. "Not quite. But too close for comfort, sometimes." I scrambled for another subject. "I don't even know where you live," I said finally.

"Baltimore."

"Like it?"

"It has its good points. How about you? Still in San Francisco?"

"Yep."

"Like it?"

"Less and less."

"That's pretty much true of everywhere, don't you think? I mean that nowhere is as nice as it used to be?"

"I suppose not."

"Though actually Baltimore has gotten better in a lot of ways."

"That's what I hear."

Irritated at our turn toward irrelevance, Libby took a breath, looked at the rose or maybe at the thorns, then shook her head as though to derail her train of thought. "God. I spent lots of nights hoping this would happen and lots of days praying it wouldn't. Now here you are, and I don't know what to say to you."

"Me, either."

"Maybe we should retire and consider the options."

"Maybe so."

"And convene later and report our conclusions."

"Sounds a lot like independent study."

For the first time, her smile was an expression I'd seen before, an expression I'd once cherished. "Right," she said. "A term paper. 'Love Later On,' we could call it. Libby and Marsh, thirty years thereafter."

"Twenty-five."

"Twenty-nine, actually. We met the first week of freshman year."

"Barely."

"Barely for you, maybe; I've thought about you every day since I drew your name for the sack race during orientation." She made a face at her hyperbole. "That's a lie, but the truth's not far from it." She shook her head and sighed. "I hope they've gotten rid of that *sack* business. It was very demeaning to women."

I wasn't in the mood for feminism. "When do you want to meet?"

She shrugged. "Tonight? There's a dance or something, isn't there?"

"Sock hop. Gym."

"You don't seem enthusiastic. But then you never were."

"Not about dancing, at any rate."

"Not about much of anything, as I remember."

"Enthusiasm gets tempered by good sense on occasion," I rebelled. "How about if we meet by the stadium? The ticket booth."

Libby stuck out her tongue. "I know what used to go on in *that* place, don't think I don't. The bleachers by the tennis courts?"

"Fine."

"What time?"

"I have to see Seth at nine, so . . . ten-thirty?"

She nodded. "Ten-thirty's fine. I'll take a nap."

"Great. See you then."

"How's Seth, by the way?"

"He seems to have something on his mind."

"What?"

"I don't know; I'll probably know more when I see you."

"So will I," Libby said simply, then waved good-bye and disappeared behind a hedge, leaving me with a bleeding elbow and an ochre rose and a host of reckless emotions about a woman I hadn't laid eyes on during the most recent half of my lifetime.

FOUR

I wandered back toward my room, my brain stuffed with tufts of memory, my inclination still to abdicate the enterprise so that at least this portion of my past would remain where it had lain for a quarter-century, in a shallow grave from which it could do no further harm. But the past is never truly buried or even truly dead, and part of me still wanted to war with it some more, to make it explain itself more fully so it could in turn explain the present. Since I wasn't making progress on my own, I detoured to the lounge and found people who held their collegiate experience in sufficient esteem to want to talk about it.

And so it went for the remainder of the afternoon and early evening. In the garden of his stately home, the president made a subtle but pointed plea for funds. On a more elevated plane, the pianist was worthy of his hire, the poet didn't show for reasons unexplained but rumored to involve cocaine, the film was blessedly brief, and the futures panel was commandeered into a debate on the Thomas/Hill confrontation and Gil Hayward was hooted from the room.

The ad hoc ethic of the occasion found me talking volubly to people I'd barely known in the early days, while struggling to chitchat with people I'd once considered friends. Along the way I made small talk with an heir to an oil fortune, a self-styled schizophrenic and a similarly branded genius, a playboy who plied his trade from Buenos Aires, and a woman who'd forsaken pediatrics to farm herbs and spices up in Oregon. Inquiries concerning my own vocation were easily finessed—I think most people thought I was joking when I told them what I did. At one point, I decided I was the only person in the room who didn't own a house.

For the most part, discussion was oddly guarded and carefully circumspect, as though we had such glittering reputations to protect that candor was out of the question. Although bubbles of humor and pathos and even profundity surfaced along the way, after eight hours of conviviality the results were mostly disappointing. What I was looking for was perspective, a sense of what people felt about their world and their lives and themselves, but despite the buzz of easy patter and an occasional spike of introspection, I couldn't get a reading—the more direct the inquiry, the more slippery the evasion. In general, the women seemed happier or at least more open than the men; the men seemed numbed and somewhat cowed, by the occasion or by their lives, it was hard to tell which. Maybe those were simply the types I was drawn to, for reasons of self-defense.

My basic impression was that twenty-five years hadn't changed anybody very much, and the evolutionary stasis made me sad—if a good education and twenty-five years of putting it to use had no effect on philosophy or psyche, what was the point of it? What I guess I hoped was that someone would confront me with proof that contrary to the evidence I regularly accumulate in my work, life is both benign and consequential. But if such proof were to be had at the reunion, I hadn't found it by the end of the evening even though I fancy myself a good detective.

By the time the dinner speeches were over, I needed a drink more potent than pilsner. Luckily Seth was waiting in his room when I got there. It took five minutes to realize the dorm wasn't conducive to communication, so we headed for the local bar.

When our drinks had come, we toasted each other. "It's been a long time," Seth said.

"Too long."

"Why'd we let it get away like that?"

"Because we live three thousand miles apart, for one thing. Because we're cowards, for another."

"What are we afraid of?"

"Amending memories," I suggested, then wondered if Seth regarded our friendship as nearly as hallowed as I did.

"We should step up the pace," he was saying. "Schedule a rendezvous from time to time."

I recalled my recent humiliation at the bank. "My budget may not have a rendezvous in it for a while."

"I could cover your expenses, no problem."

"It would be a problem for me."

Seth laughed. "Still the noble savage."

"More the latter than the former, but I work on it."

We drank.

"So how's your life, Marsh?" Seth asked, as earnestly as I had inquired the same of Libby. "I mean basically."

"Basically it's good. Not great, but good."

"Why not great?"

"Too lonely, too selfish, too ordinary to be great. But good is good enough. Most days. How about you?"

"I've had my ups and downs." He quickly reversed the focus. "What's the best part?"

"Of my life?" I shrugged. "The fact that I get people out of trouble once in a while, I guess. That I do what I want to do the way I want to do it and make enough money to qualify for Social Security but not so much that I'm tempted to vote Republican."

Seth laughed. "I know what you mean—back home I'm considered a traitor to my race and class. I may be the only

Caucasian Democrat in town. Me and the mayor," he amended. "Speaking of which, why don't you come South with me?"

"When?"

"Sunday. Fly back with me from here."

I looked at his white cotton sweater and his pale yellow slacks. "I don't have the wardrobe for it."

"I'm serious, Marsh. Life's too short not to go on a toot once in a while. We're sneaking up on fifty, you know."

"I know that better than I know my bookie's phone number, but I've already got my ticket home. The airlines don't like you to improvise."

"I know a doctor. He'll tell them it was a medical emergency requiring a physic of red beans and rice."

I offered a considered evasion. "I would like to see Charleston someday; I've never been to the Deep South before. Maybe next winter."

When Seth spoke again, the words came laden with insistence. "It would help if you could come now."

Seth's blue eyes quickened with the intensity he used to display before an exam, the electric surge that would carry him through a night of cramming and the stress of the test and the partying of the next evening as well, all without the overload of exhaustion that turned the rest of us to stone.

"That sounds like more than a casual invitation," I said.

Seth's eyes darkened toward the color of good grapes. "That's the only reason I came back for this," he said. "To recruit you to help me out."

I didn't know what to say, so I said, "I'm flattered."

Seth looked away uneasily. "But I don't want to ruin your weekend. There's no need to discuss the situation if there isn't a chance you can come down and get into it. If you'll agree to come, we can leave it where it is till we get home. If you can't, just forget I said anything."

He looked at the neon beer sign blinking in the window,

then beyond it into the depthless threat of night. "You can't get a sense of what's happening to me unless you come to Charleston, anyway," he mused quietly. "Like most things in the South, it's more a matter of feel than fact."

"What *is* happening, Seth?"

He looked around the bar. What he saw didn't cheer him. When he spoke, the words were as dry as the dust on the floor. "Someone's trying to destroy me."

"You're serious."

He nodded. "Remember the summer of '66? When I went South to do voter registration work for SNCC?"

"Sure I do. I've never forgotten your stories about being chased around the countryside by pickups full of rednecks and shotguns and coonhounds."

In the echo of the final word, Seth looked away again, this time toward the knot of people at the next table. "It got dicey a few times. For a lot of us."

"But what does that have to do with now?"

"I'm not sure, but the thing that's happening seems related to those times, somehow. Or at least to those issues."

"I guess I still don't get it."

Moving as slow as Sunday, Seth took out his wallet and extracted a paper that had been folded and refolded and stuck in with the currency. After he spread open the square of cheap bond, he examined it for several seconds before he handed it to me the way he would hand me a rodent:

NOTICE OF RACIAL JUDGMENT
NOTICE IS HEREBY GIVEN that the
ALLIANCE FOR SOUTHERN PRIDE has
identified SETH HARTMAN as an ENEMY of
the SOUTHERN WAY OF LIFE.
Your advocacy and agitation on behalf of
the DEGENERATE, WHOREMONGERING,
RACE POLLUTING, ALIEN, ANTI-WHITE

AND ANTI-CHRISTIAN forces that have been
and remain dedicated to the DESTRUCTION of
the SOUTHERN WAY OF LIFE make you,
SETH HARTMAN, a TRAITOR to the SOUTH
and a BETRAYER of the GREAT WHITE
RACE.
THEREFORE, BE ADVISED OF THE
FOLLOWING JUDGMENT:
YOUR SENTENCE: DEATH
YOUR EXECUTIONER: The
PURIFICATION BRIGADE of the ALLIANCE
for SOUTHERN PRIDE
YOUR SOLE SALVATION: REMOVAL of
your PERSON from the LANDS of the NEW
CONFEDERACY
Sentence is suspended for 60 days to allow
you to depart the jurisdiction. But BE IT DULY
NOTED that failure to remove yourself within
the allotted time will result in your RACIAL
SENTENCE being duly executed FORTHWITH.
FIELD ORDER #7
THE ALLIANCE FOR SOUTHERN PRIDE

SOUTHERN PRIDE = WHITE POWER
SAVE THE SOUTH

"This is serious, isn't it?" I said as I handed the paper
back to Seth, my mind awash in images of white sheets and
burning crosses and the men who made use of such symbols.

He nodded. "I think so."

"What's behind it, do you think?"

Seth rubbed his eyes and shook his head. "That's the
problem—I don't know. But I don't want to go into it now,
Marsh; I just need to know whether you can help me get to

the bottom of it." His voice broke at the end of the entreaty; I had never seen him so abject.

"I don't know, Seth. I've got clients and—"

He gathered himself with effort and managed a crooked smile. "Since the Notice of Judgment didn't do the trick, maybe this will convince you."

Seth dug in his wallet again and handed me a news clipping that described a local fund-raising event:

> The main drawing card is the opportunity to watch a cow defecate on a high school football field. Not only do the parents, students, and supporters have a once-in-a-lifetime opportunity to witness this display firsthand, they are also afforded the chance to place bets on where this historic event will occur: The field has been subdivided into numbered squares for ease of wagering.

When I'd finished, I looked at him and grinned. "Carolina, here I come."

FIVE

Seth didn't realize it, but his efforts to get me to Charleston had touched a nerve more likely than any other to recruit me to his cause. The nerve was guilt, and the root was civil rights—the defining social and political movement of my youth, the heroic wrenching of the nation out of the pit of apartheid onto the road to racial justice. That the racial wound still festered, and was more septic today than only a few years earlier, diminished neither the nobility of the quest nor the courage of those, like Seth, who once pursued it at their peril.

Seth had asked me several times to go down with him and work for SNCC that summer. I'd given it much thought, but ultimately demurred. I had to earn money for school, I needed to spend time with my family, I wasn't good at canvassing or recruiting or any other organizational skills. True but insufficient: I should have done my part but hadn't.

Why I hadn't done more to advance a cause I fervently believed in is a question I'd thrown at myself more often than was healthy over the years, because the answer invariably included elements of sloth and cowardice. But that was then and this was now. That Seth's death sentence from the Alliance for Southern Pride constituted a belated opportunity to redeem myself was a myth I eagerly embraced.

Gil showed up at the Jabberwock just as I was leaving.

Without being told, both he and Seth knew where I was going when I bid them a brief good-bye, and they teased me as I hurried toward my rendezvous.

As I drove toward the campus, thoughts of Seth and the South began to fade, and Libby Grissom—not the current Libby but the one I'd loved and lost—materialized in their place. When I began the hike down the slippery slope toward the tennis courts—a dimly lit oasis of Hopperesque geometry in the spring-crisp shroud of night—blood was thick in my veins and my breaths were high in my chest. By the time I reached the bleachers, my brow was iced with sweat.

But she wasn't there. More disappointed than I expected to be, I stood by the bleachers and warred with a persistent squadron of mosquitoes as I watched a succession of far-off silhouettes stroll toward the wooded arboretum on secret trysts of their own. That the only privacy the school afforded lovers was the same it afforded field mice was one of its supposed charms.

In less than a minute, I'd decided Libby's decision was a wise one: Nothing good could come of this. Whatever attraction we might have had for each other if we had met this week as strangers, our past made us forever estranged in some sense that was both minute and ineradicable.

"Sorry I'm late."

The voice was small within the cloak of night, crimped with cold and nerves.

"I decided you'd decided not to come."

"Were you disappointed?"

I opted for candor. "Yes."

She lingered in the shadows, her most visible aspect the orange trim around her shoes. "I did decide that," she said softly. "And then I decided that standing you up would be petulant and immature. And then I decided that meeting you would be more . . . provocative than I ought to be. And *then* I decided, what the hell. But Linda Barnard wanted to tell me about her photo safari to Kenya, and Gladys Sandstrom wanted to talk about estrogen therapy—I had no idea there was so much controversy about . . . Anyway, better late than never. I hope. Sorry to keep you waiting.''

"It's all right; I'm pretty good at it, as it happens."

"Because of your work, you mean."

"My work. My life. Whatever."

Her lips went prim with irritation. "You've gotten stoic in your old age. I'm not sure it suits you."

"Sorry about that," I said, irritated in return at both her attitude and her accuracy.

"I would like to hear more about it sometime, though. Your work, I mean."

"Why?"

She shrugged. "It seems romantic. And dangerous. And . . . inevitable, somehow."

"I'm not sure you're right about any of that, but we can go into it if you want."

"Maybe later."

During the preliminary skirmishing, Libby seemed to reach a decision. With the boost of fresh resolve, she walked to my side and planted a kiss on my cheek, dry and cool and casual, the dutiful buss of former lovers. "Hi." Above her snow-white sneakers, she wore jeans and a POWDERMILK BIS-CUIT sweatshirt and a hat that would have fit a fishing trip.

"Hi."

"So what have you been doing since dinner?" She sniffed. "I think I smell beer."

"The Jabb."

"Bonding with the boys?"

"Seth, mostly."

"Did you find out what was on his mind?"

"What was on his mind was convincing me to go to Charleston with him when the reunion's over."

"Well? Did he?"

"I think so."

"How?"

I shrugged. "I've blamed the South for a lot over the years; it's time to make sure I was right."

"What if you weren't?"

"Then I guess I'll have to apologize."

She laughed. "To whom?"

"Maybe that's why I voted for Jimmy Carter."

Libby put her hands on my chest and shoved. "You're as weird as you ever were," she charged, then tugged me to the bleachers and sat me down. "Anything else of interest happen?"

"Not much. How about you?"

"Memories, mostly."

"Me, too. When you got here, I was thinking about the night we broke up."

She slid down the bench, a further foot away from me. "I've replayed that tape a couple of times myself this evening." She sighed. "I've been divorced twice, and watched my father die of cancer, and nursed my kids through some rough spots, too, but that's as miserable as I've ever been."

"We were pretty vulnerable right then. Senior year; another transition coming up; both of us about to be thrust into the cold, cruel world from the fuzzy womb of this place."

Libby nodded thoughtfully. "You're right about that part. I was in absolute panic, I remember, because I didn't know what to do with my life. I thought I was supposed to have a plan that covered the next forty years, and I didn't have one that covered the next three days."

"Plus, going with you was the first time I envisioned myself with a spouse and a child and a mortgage and the rest of it. Then we broke up, which suggested emotional life was going to be even more complicated than academic life had been."

Libby nodded. "The night before the breakup, I stayed

up all night talking to Marcia Wells about marriage, and careers, and my needs and obligations as a woman. One thing I decided was that having a man in my life would keep me from fulfilling my destiny.'' Her smile warped. ''At this point, it seems arrogant to have assumed I even *had* a destiny.''

''Maybe you were right—maybe I would have held you back.''

''Or maybe having you in my life was more my destiny than anything.'' The rue in her laugh made me sad. ''But probably not—I don't seem to have been cut out for eternal bliss.''

''Me, either.''

''I blame the school, a little. For my troubles with men, I mean.''

''Why?''

''Because of how they isolated us. Talk about segregation—boys on one side of campus, girls on the other. Now the sexes share the same floor, even the same *bathrooms* if the rumors are true. Back then, we weren't able to get to know each other, to learn how the other sex thinks and feels and reacts. I think it was harder on the men than the women.''

''Why?''

''Because so many men our age really don't seem to *get* it. What women are about, I mean. It might have been different if there were a tribe of us living down the hall for four years.''

I agreed and told her so.

Beyond the tree line, someone squealed with pleasure. Libby looked toward the sound as though it had been offered in a foreign tongue. ''Are you in a relationship now?''

I thought about my friend Betty; I looked at Libby in the moonlight; I lied a little. ''Not really.''

She laughed. "That's what someone on the make would say."

As I reddened, I hoped it was too dark for her to notice. "If what you're asking is whether I still find you attractive, the answer is yes."

"It wasn't, I don't think, but thank you." She raised a foot and examined her ankle. "My legs should have come in plain brown wrappers, you told me once. I think it was the first night you saw me naked."

We found things to look at other than each other.

"What did you come back for, Marsh?" Libby asked after the moment had cooled.

"To see what made the difference, I think."

"Between what?"

"Success and failure, I guess. For want of better terms."

"I'm not sure what you mean."

"We had such grand plans in those days—Richard Williams had a strategy for getting himself appointed to the Supreme Court, I remember. And some people actually achieved them—Bill Grayson is on the cutting edge of biotech; Jason Stevens made a mint in real estate, then started a foundation to build low-income housing; Lana Maxwell is a congresswoman."

"And Sally Lincoln is a grandmother."

"And I'm a private eye, with emphasis on private. I'm not in any clubs, I don't have any employees, I don't even have a family. So what happened? Why haven't I made a dent in the world? What's the difference between guys like me and guys like Grayson? Talent? Luck? Genetics?"

"A little of all of those, I imagine."

"I'm not sure. Some of it has to do with motivation, and some with energy, but a lot of it has to do with maturity, I think. Basically what I do for a living is play hide-and-seek. I feel like a kid a lot, the one outside the candy store with his nose pressed against the glass, wishing he was inside with the grown-ups but not knowing how to get there.''

Libby nodded. ''I feel that way, too, sometimes. As though everyone else has found the answer, but I'm still asking the questions. It's like there's a book out there that everyone's read but me, some required reading that I haven't heard about and keep failing the exam because of it. I have dreams like that, sometimes—everyone knows about the test but me, and by the time I find out, it's too late to do anything but flunk.''

She felt for my hand and took it. ''You don't really consider yourself a failure, do you, Marsh?''

''I don't know. Maybe that's why I'm here.''

I squeezed her hand and pulled it to my lap. After a cozy moment, Libby extracted her fingers and walked to the fence that defined the courts, then turned and leaned against it. ''I'm not sure this . . . recapitulation . . . is good for us. The examined life can take its toll.''

When I didn't say anything, she looked toward the distant bulge of the arboretum and the high hulk of the nearest dormitory. ''Well, here we are—free, white, and twenty-one, as we used to say. What do you want to do about it?''

''You used to ask me that a dozen times a night—what did I want to do.''

She met my eye. ''And the answer was usually sex.''

''Hey. I seem to remember a joint venture.''

''Oh, I wanted to, too. Most of the time. It made me feel fallen as hell, but I was in heat as well; of course I was. Maybe that was the problem—we paid too much attention to our bodies and not enough to our minds.''

''The body's signals tend to be more audible at that age.''

''Easier to accommodate, at least.''

''As long as we climaxed by curfew.''

She walked to me and wiped something off my cheek. "Curfew," she repeated. "No wonder we never grew up."

She took my arm and tugged me toward the hill that climbed to the central campus. "So how come you never called me?" she asked along the way.

"I suppose because I thought it might complicate your life."

"If you'd called in the eighties, I wouldn't have even noticed—my life couldn't have been more complicated if I'd been running for president."

"Like what?"

"Complications? A drug problem with my son. A health problem with my daughter. A fidelity problem with my husbands. And a career problem with me."

"I don't even know what you do."

"What I *wanted* to do was interior design. What I *do* do is be a surrogate wife to a bunch of Baltimore business-women."

"Which means?"

"I'm a caterer. Hors d'oeuvres for the lady vice presidents who have the sales force in for cocktails before the awards banquet at the Marriott."

"You seem a tad less enthusiastic than the Galloping Gourmet."

"If I see another canapé, I'll scream."

"So why don't you do something else?"

"I don't know if you've heard, but there *aren't* any jobs out there these days. None. For anyone."

She was right. Times were tough and getting tougher, and the recession would last till the end of the century.

"So," she went on. "Like I said. What do we do now?"

I was too tired for more analysis, of us or of anything. "We could go to the dance."

"You hate dancing."

"One good thing about middle age is, you don't mind making a fool of yourself once in a while, at least for a good cause."

She clutched my arm and snuggled against my side. "That's what I always wanted to be—a good cause. How are you at geography, by the way?"

"B-minus, as I recall. Why?"

"I wondered if you knew that Baltimore isn't all that far from Charleston."

Six

On Saturday, the reunion turned earnest with a vengeance. Immediately after breakfast, the crowd subdivided like so many metastatic cells and launched discussions ranging from the prospect for peace in the Middle East to the danger inherent in the collapse of the Soviet Union to the roots of the palsy that laid claim to the economy. The group I joined, or rather was engulfed by, took off in pursuit of the election.

All but two of us were Democrats, it turned out, the exceptions venerating Bush because he was the anointed apostle of the Holiest of Holies—Ronald Reagan. Most of the rest were pining for Cuomo—more because of his debating skills than his policies or his personality—while pulling for Clinton and fearing Perot, although there was one unreconstructed Tsongasite and two who were eloquent for Brown. Many of us were passionate, even illogical, on this issue or that; all of us saw the election as the last chance in a generation to constitute a compassionate government that was run for the benefit of the common man rather than big business, yet none of us had donated our time to a cause we felt was vital.

At some point, somebody mentioned Rodney King.

"What a travesty."

"The verdict or the riot?"

"The verdict, of course."

"Did you see the tape? The *whole* tape?"

"I saw a man being pulverized, if that's what you mean."

"Only when he resisted. Whenever he assumed the position, they stopped hitting him. The cops were only doing their job."

"Was it their *job* to spout racist filth over the police radio? Was it their *job* to keep pounding him when it was five against one?"

"That wasn't a trial, that was a metaphor."

"For what? Black irresponsibility?"

"That's such bullshit. The black man has been oppressed in this country for two hundred years. This was just an official reminder that they should keep their place, in case anyone forgot."

"That's liberal pap. The black man has been looking for an *excuse* for two hundred years. Now he's blaming Koreans, for God's sake."

"It's true that lots of people are pissed at being called racist, and not just conservatives, either. They think blacks had their chance and blew it."

"They think blacks just want to have babies out of wedlock and mug whites to buy drugs."

"Statistics say they're right."

"That's not true. Most blacks in America are *middle* class, not *underclass*. And most people on welfare are white."

"The *problem* is, fucking and doing drugs are the only thing this racist society *lets* them do. Every time the black man starts to rise, the power structure knocks him down."

"How can a society that created Michael Jordan and Bill Cosby be called racist?"

"Gladiators. Jesters. Fools. Oppressors have always made allowances for their amusements."

"What about Jesse Jackson?"

"Another entertainer."

"What's sad to me is that so many blacks—"

"You mean African-Americans."

"—African-*Americans,* including black intellectuals, think their problems result from a conspiracy to destroy their race. Like drugs, for example."

"And AIDS."

"What *I* can't believe is that some people actually *want* those young studs to impregnate as many women as they can."

"'Babies having babies' is what Jesse calls it."

"You realize that if Jesse had run *this* time, he would have gotten the nomination."

"Why do you think they didn't let him run?"

"Blacks will never get anywhere until their leadership stops looking for scapegoats. What's wrong with black people is black people—conspiracies are the refuge of tiny minds."

"Conspiracies are what's left after the government holds hearings to find out what happened."

"*JFK.* Right. Great film. I think it was the CIA, myself."

And so it went. Although the debate was typically dry and distant, it strengthened my resolve to go to Charleston with Seth, to finally involve myself, no matter how tardily and tangentially, in the cause of racial peace some twenty-five years after I should have first stepped forward.

Nothing occurred on a more engaging level until Gil and I were next to each other in the lunch line. After he'd filled his plate, he tapped my shoulder. "This is where it happened, right?"

"What?"

"The crime spree."

"Oh. Yeah." I pointed. "That window over there."

I'd forgotten about it, incredibly enough, but what Gil was referring to was a burst of criminality I'd engaged in during the winter of my junior year. Seth and I had become so addicted to a certain chocolate cookie the dining hall served from time to time that we decided to steal as many as we could get our hands on. After planning our caper down to the last detail, we snuck down to the kitchen at 3:00 A.M. the night before the cookie usually appeared on the menu, broke a window, climbed in, found several trays of the tasty morsels, appropriated as many as we could carry, then scrambled back to our room and feasted for forty-eight hours.

A week later, the dean of men suspended me for ten days and confined Seth to his room during evening hours for a month.

As I was recalling the tongue-lashing I'd endured from Dean Antley, Gil was laughing at me. "I hope you're better at solving crimes than committing them," he said. "How much they nail you for, by the way?"

"For the cookies?"

He shook his head. "The class gift."

"Oh. Uh . . . five."

"Thousand?"

"Hundred. How about you?"

"Twenty-five."

"Hundred?"

"Thousand."

"Oh."

At the cocktail hour, a dentist who owned a half-interest in a winery graced us with a taste of his first crush. At dinner, some former thespians staged a parody of *Laugh-In* that lampooned some of the more notorious professors. Only the professors found it funny, further proof that academic egotism is boundless. At the awards ceremony, a historian, a performance artist, a newspaper columnist, and Gil received achievement awards—afterward, the consensus seemed to be that this was the first time the artist had been seen on campus. And suddenly we were in line for the final gathering of the weekend but for breakfast Sunday morning and an A.A. meeting for the road.

I was sorry to see it end, surprisingly. I'd met people who had been important to me back then and was pleased to see they were doing well. I'd also heard sad stories about classmates who hadn't put in an appearance, raising questions about fate and predestiny and similar credos we used to discuss *ad nauseam* in the days before we had to get jobs and life itself became philosophy. Best of all, I'd heard several self-effacing narratives from some true heroes of our time—teachers in inner-city schools, social workers in Appalachia, cancer researchers in teaching hospitals. And pastors and physical therapists and day-care workers, too, a sturdy parade of people who were doing good in the world out of sight and mind of all but the objects of their bounty. From time to time I try to believe I am part of the parade myself, but I seldom get the job done.

Seth had avoided me all day, presumably because he was afraid I had decided to turn him down. When I had a chance, I told him I'd changed my reservation and had an open ticket on the morning flight to Charleston. He smiled and whispered, "Thanks."

And then I was left with Libby.

Eighteen hours earlier, we'd parted after a single dance, surrendering to the demands of fatigue and mixed messages. By unvoiced consent, we'd pursued separate agendas all day, but the end of the evening found us face-to-face.

We maneuvered to an unoccupied corner of the hall and sat side by side on a tufted couch. "Do you ever get back East?" Libby asked after a minute.

"Haven't for years. Do you ever come West?"

"Haven't yet."

People looked at us, and grinned and whispered. "We're causing talk," I said.

"We always did. People thought we were extremely mismatched. Do you think we'd have survived if we'd stayed together, Marsh?"

"I doubt it."

"Why not?"

"Because most people don't. And because we each had some problems to work out."

"I still have most of them."

"Me, too."

Her smile was wan. "I thought we were supposed to have it figured out by now."

"I don't think that's part of the cosmic scheme—when you solve one riddle, another has to take its place. The indestructibility of angst, I think it's called."

We people-watched for a time, taking stock of our fellows, whose moods seemed to range from the ecstatic to the miserable. After a while, Libby leaned my way and whispered. "Here we are, at a cross-roads of life, with all kinds of momentous things to discuss, and I can't stop thinking about sex." She wriggled her fingers as though they hurt, then placed them on my thigh. "But it would be wrong, don't you think?"

"Why?"

"There are standards, Marsh. Principles. It's why we went to *school*, for God's sake."

"Nothing we learned in school governs what you and I should do in the next hour." I put my hand on hers. "But if you think making love would be immoral, you shouldn't do it."

"Then I guess I won't."

"Fine."

A moment later, she pinched my bicep. "You're not even going to *debate* the issue?"

"Nope."

"You never were very assertive."

I laughed.

"But not being assertive is what I always liked about you, come to think of it."

"It's what I always liked about me, too. Tell me about your children."

Libby's face softened, and she looked closer to thirty than fifty. "As a matter of fact, they're pretty neat. They had problems early on, big ones, but they've come out in good shape. I'd like you to meet them sometime." She reached in her purse and pulled out some pictures of kids that looked like all kids.

After I'd said the right things and handed them back, Libby bit her lip. "What did you think of *Thelma and Louise*?"

"Good B movie."

"Not a mirror of the times?"

"Not even close."

"Who did you believe, Hill or Thomas?"

"Hill."

"Are you pro-choice?"

"Secondarily. Primarily I'm anticonception."

"Have you read *Backlash*?"

"No. What is this, a litmus test?"

"I think this is foreplay."

"You used to be better at it." I grabbed her hand and pulled her to her feet. "Your place or mine?"

"Whichever's warmer," she said.

SEVEN

The next morning I made do with a vending-machine meal—coffee and a Baby Ruth—in lieu of the Mother of All Breakfasts, which was the fulsome offering in the dining hall. By 8:00 A.M., I'd managed to load my bags in my rented Taurus and corral Seth and his stuff as well. Moments later I was on the freeway pointed north, relieved at having avoided anything resembling an awkward good-bye, including one with Libby.

My leave-taking wasn't as craven as it seemed. Over the course of the previous evening, Libby and I had said everything we could bring ourselves to say to each other and done everything it occurred to us to do. Initially tentative and even fearful, our lovemaking became increasingly comprehensive as we exchanged the awkwardness of uncertainty for the finesse of the familiar. Sex became not a source of shame but solace, was no longer ambiguous but essential. With far more gratitude than lust, we allowed ourselves to revel in it—energy was summoned and spent, again and again, our only pause a moment's test to confirm the condom had survived the storm. On the brink of aerobic breakdown, wet with sweat and laboring for air to fuel our frenzy, we entwined in a consuming clutch for succor, as if we were each other's only haven. By the time we climbed toward climax, it was both easy and imperative to believe we were bound together once again, our fates mutual and interdependent, our journeys joint and endless, as they had seemed so long ago. But in the postcoital gloom of my excessively monastic room, we knew we were mistaken now as then, that the truth we had tried to manufacture would only last the weekend. Whence came ensuing melancholy.

But not for long. When we had bathed and dried and were alternately sipping Pepsi from a single can as we lay naked and knotted in the moonlight, we joked and laughed and poked and kidded, told silly deprecations on ourselves and also bragged a little, voiced reasonable hopes and immoderate fears, remembering why we'd loved each other. At some point, I put a slip of paper in my wallet with Libby's phone number scrawled on it, and she took a similar souvenir of me, along with my pledge that I would call before I headed home from Charleston and consider a detour to Maryland. I've made such promises before, always without keeping them; I wondered what I would do this time.

At my side, Seth was quiet for several miles, until it became unnerving. "If you had a good time," I said finally, "you're good at keeping it secret. Must be those years in the Drama Club."

"Since none of *my* old girlfriends showed up, the festivities seemed pretty bland."

"Speaking of which, where was Miranda?"

He shrugged. "Somewhere in Europe, I heard. Not that I'd have done anything if she'd showed up," he added sleepily.

"Why not?"

"I'm spoken for."

"Unless you and your wife exchanged some off-brand vows, that doesn't forestall conversation."

"I'm not married anymore."

"Since when?"

"Three years ago."

"If you're spoken for, who's doing the speaking?"

"Fiancée. Jane Jean Hendersen. A belle to her bustle—greatgranddad fell at Chickamauga. We first met when I went down to work for SNCC—in some sense I've loved her ever since." Seth's look turned lewd. "I hope you're not telling me all you did with Libby was converse."

"No comment."

"Comment's not necessary—it sounded like rugby in there."

Seth smiled at my good fortune, then closed his eyes. I knew why I was tired—Libby and I had played till three—but I wasn't sure why Seth was. "You found the encounter with your beloved classmates less than marvelous, I take it," I offered after a few more miles.

He shrugged. "For one thing, the wrong people were there. Most of the interesting ones didn't put in an appearance. Remember Boskitts? The rock climber who stole the statue of Voltaire from the library and hauled it up the bell tower and hung it in effigy to protest the war? They don't even know where he is; last seen in Nepal, someone said."

"Probably underneath a glacier."

"And Castle. Remember him? SDS and all that? They say he's in Peru with the Shining Path. A real live revolutionary."

"So you didn't find any kindred spirits. What else is bothering you?"

Seth sighed and shook his head. "Nothing to do with the reunion."

"Which leaves the Alliance for Southern Pride."

He nodded. "I think it would be better if we pretend to be strangers, by the way. We can arrange to share a cab from the airport like we're businessmen trying to make a buck on the per diem. When we get to town, I've got a place to stash you till we get a chance to talk. Is that a problem?"

"Fine with me, but why the cloak-and-dagger?"

"You might be more effective working incognito. Safer, also." Seth closed his eyes so I wouldn't ask more questions. "I know a woman in Charleston you'll like," he murmured after a few more miles. "She thinks the best thing about the South is its degeneracy."

I laughed. "I spend the prime of my life duplicating the sex life of the Dalai Lama, then I tiptoe up on fifty and all of a sudden I'm hip-deep in women."

"Is that good or bad?"

The response seemed to carry a subtext, but I was too tired to pursue it.

"The South is an interesting place," Seth went on after a minute. "I became obsessed with it the summer I spent with the voter drive. Those times have been on my mind a lot lately, what with the ASP business, and the reunion, and some guy going around town asking questions for a book he's doing on the SNCC days. All the *hassles* we had to go through so black people could do a simple thing like vote. The blacks were so amazingly brave and the whites so amazingly *frightened.* I thought for a while they were afraid of empowering black people for fear they'd turn the tables, and for the up-country whites that pretty much was it. But for the upper classes, I think what they were most afraid of was facing up to what they'd done."

"You mean slavery."

"No. Slavery wasn't the worst of it, in my opinion—there were historic and economic reasons for slavery, after all. It was Jim Crow that was unmitigated evil, the systematic dehumanization of the black population instituted after Reconstruction. Nothing up North was *nearly* as wounding to the black psyche as the sanctioned stigma constructed down here in the name of God and segregation. *That's* what the South can't face about itself—that so many good people ignored it for so long, or pretended it didn't matter. A guy I know claims Southerners romanticize their past for the same reason Hilter revived the *Nibelungenlied*—to mitigate a holocaust. Anyway, it was that kind of schizophrenia that made me want to go back one day and help them get beyond it.''

"Speaking of romantic," I suggested.

"Of course. You remember those days—we thought we could change everything. I decided the best way for *me* to go about it was to become a trial lawyer. Daddy had some clout in Washington, and when there was a spot with the U.S. attorney in Charleston, I crossed the Mason-Dixon Line with my bride of six months and my J.D. from Yale, and ended up within spitting distance of Fort Sumter. Callie couldn't stand it, then or since, but I pretty much got to love the place.''

"How come Callie didn't like it?''

"Because the thing about Charleston is, the blue bloods may smile and say 'How y'all doin'?' when they see you on the street, and sweet-talk you in support of their charities, but no matter how friendly they seem or how long you've known them, you'll never be more than an interloper and you'll never set foot inside their front door. Which suits me just fine, to tell you the truth, but it didn't fit Callie's sense of her place in the universe. Callie's a Brahmin—she wasn't an outsider till she married me.''

"Is she back in Boston now?''

"Nope. Moved down to Kiawah with a guy who's an inch above a mobster. Since every other film out of Hollywood seems to be a biography of one of his peers, he's become quite a celebrity; Callie's coming back with a vengeance.''

"How long were you with the U.S. attorney?''

"Three years. Drug stuff, mostly. We're only a few miles off I-95—the Miami-to-New York connection—plus we've got hundreds of miles of open shoreline, so there was plenty of contraband to keep us busy. Drugs made me my first million.''

"How so?"

"After I left the government and hung out my shingle, defending drug cases was my specialty, and I got damned good at it. Could have made more, but when my kids started school, I decided I didn't want to be part of that life, even indirectly. Now I represent respectable criminals."

"Could one of your disgruntled clients be behind this Alliance outfit?"

He shrugged. "If I knew who was behind ASP, I wouldn't have gone north to lasso you."

"Are you the only Jew in town?" I asked after a minute, both because I was interested and because bigotry seemed to be at the core of his trouble.

"Not nearly. Jews came here at the end of the seventeenth century. The oldest Reform synagogue in the world is in Charleston—the Nazis took care of the other contenders, of course. One of the most illustrious Charleston Jews lost his fortune during the Civil War. After he made a second one, he paid to have the South Carolina boys who fell at Gettysburg brought back to the state for burial, even though he'd been strongly opposed to secession. Charleston has plenty of stories like that."

"I'm sure it does."

Something in my tone made him laugh. "Keep an open mind, Marsh. Yankees are conditioned to see Southerners as reprehensible—ignorant, racist, inbred, brutal."

"You're saying it's not true?"

"I'm saying it's no more true here than a lot of places; the South just isn't good at hiding it. But don't blow out a brain circuit trying to figure us out. Better minds than yours have gone mad trying to explain the place."

"What about the New South I hear so much about?"

"I guess I'm one of those who suspects the New South is just the Old South with some big banks and a Voting Rights Act. Don't think for a minute the Bubbas wouldn't prefer things the way they were back before Rosa Parks got uppity." He chuckled dryly. "The proponents of the New South have a hard time explaining why the Confederate battle flag still flies from the state capitol and why Strom Thurmond is still our elected representative."

"You're kidding. About the flag, I mean."

"Nope. A popular history of Charleston calls the residents 'unrepentant,' and I think that about covers it."

"You're telling me nothing's changed down there since Reconstruction?"

"On the contrary. The shanties are gone from the roadsides, and the White and Colored signs have come down from the rest rooms, and everything from public accommodations to the political process is open to everyone—Charleston's mayor has done wonders with race relations in the city. Hell, Charleston even has a black police chief. A black *Jewish* police chief, if you can believe it. But a racial subtext is out there—David Duke would have gotten a lot of votes in South Carolina if Buchanan hadn't stolen his thunder."

"Duke was a subject of some discussion at the reunion. There was a variety of opinion about what was behind his popularity."

"Hard times make hard attitudes, North *and* South. Basically bigotry is fear. Jews are feared for their prowess with money; Asians are feared for their intelligence; Mexicans are feared because they'll work for next to nothing; and blacks are feared for the most primal reason of all."

"White men are afraid black men are going to beat them up and rape their women."

"That's the prosaic part. The poetic part is that we're afraid the women are going to *like* it. The musk of black sexuality is still overwhelming—it's why Emmett Till was slaughtered and why after the yoke of slavery was lifted after the Civil War, the chains of Jim Crow were clamped on.

And why the young black male remains the most imperiled component of the population to this day, North *and* South.''

Seth paused to catch his breath. The intensity of his exegesis seemed to make him tired. ''The South has problems, Marsh. Lots of them. But I can tell you this—if you're white and have a job, Charleston's a pretty nice place to live.''

I found the encomium odd. ''That flyer you showed me didn't make it seem so nice. I thought the business with ASP had to do with the Southern stuff.''

Seth's face clouded to match the sky outside the window. ''In South Carolina, *everything* has to do with the Southern stuff.''

EIGHT

Seth and I didn't have adjoining seats on the plane, so I spent the leg to Chicago thinking about Libby Grissom, trying to decide what to do about her. I finally decided that for the moment I didn't need to do anything, which was my most common conclusion regardless of the object of the exercise.

In keeping with our guise as strangers, Seth continued to avoid me when we changed planes at O'Hare. So studious was his disengagement that I began to entertain the possibility that I'd been lured into a web of intrigue, that the chilling judgment handed down by the Alliance for Southern Pride had its origins in the oily enmity of the Middle East or the reemergent Nazism in the bowels of the greater Germany.

Although I tried my best to quell it, the sense of the surreal enlarged when we reached the Charleston airport. Filled with soldiers coming and going in fuzzy hair and be-medaled greens, its distant runways lined with gross black airships whose drooping wings and snarling snouts made them seem eager to flatten any city in the world at a moment's notice, the place was a petri dish for paranoia. As I took it in, then tried to discount it, Seth continued the ruse that had at its core the impression that he and I had never laid eyes on each other before.

The cab ride to town took twenty minutes. Seth and I

made small talk—Seth told me the rivers we'd flown over were the Ashley and the Cooper, which came together at the tip of the Charleston peninsula to form a harbor at a place called the Battery, and that an English ship named the *Carolina* had deposited the first settlers on the banks of the Ashley back in 1670. Then he told me that what I'd thought from the air was funny Southern scrub brush were in reality the jagged stubs of the thousands of trees that had been snapped in two by Hurricane Hugo back in 1989.

For my part, I cheerfully proclaimed that this was my first visit to the area and I was looking forward to it, that I was in town to look at some prime retirement real estate on behalf of an investment syndicate in Ohio and was considering an option on a parcel south of the city. We maintained our pose all the way to town although it seemed wholly unnecessary—the cabbie wasn't paying attention to the road, much less to our charade.

We fell off the freeway at King Street and descended into a cluster of denuded and decaying wood houses interspersed with a jumble of churches and taverns and featureless storefronts that seemed equally infirm. The people on the street were mostly black and the goods in the store windows had been put on display back when the voters still liked Ike. After passing what looked like a medieval fortress but was in reality some municipal office space, we entered the Charleston that people bragged about.

As befit its age in this section of the city, the road turned narrow and bumpy, an anachronism from two centuries before Henry Ford altered the functional size of streets. The buildings on our flanks were too close to traffic and off-kilter with age, but the establishments within them were far from anachronistic—chic boutiques and jewelry stores and a clutch of antique shops whose seams seemed to swell with silver trays and walnut occasional tables. There was even a store for blazer buttons.

As we passed an S.S. Kresge, Seth told me it had been the scene of one of the first lunch-counter sit-ins in the sixties, and had continued to serve its clientele up until a year ago. When we passed a building labeled the Library Society, he told me it was the oldest private library in the nation.

As the cab waited at a spotlight beside the post office, Seth pointed to his right. "South of here—South of Broad, they call it—is the core of antebellum Charleston. Several of the historic families still live there. Some have lost everything they own but the roof over their heads and their surnames, but they're still venerated for who they are, or rather for who their forebears were." Seth's smile turned sly. "I like to take a stroll through there of an evening, just to remind them where some of their money went."

A block later Seth told the cab to stop. When I looked out the window, I saw a large, ungainly building, its jaundiced facade crumbling with age, its decor an inelegant mix of neoclassic motifs that didn't quite make sense. The legend "Ruined by the Earthquake 1886. Restored by the People of the Union 1887" was chiseled in the architrave. A weather-beaten sign beside the wooden door was headed by the label THE CONFEDERATE HOME.

"You're kidding," was all I could think of to say.

"Nope," Seth answered, pleased at my astonishment. "Your Home away from home."

We got out of the cab and pulled my luggage from the trunk and set it on the sidewalk. After we'd finished, Seth pointed to the sign, and I read it: "This handsome building, c. 1800, was constructed by Gilbert Chalmers. From 1810 to 1825 it was the home of Gov. John Geddes, who married the builder's daughter. During Gov. Geddes' term of office, Pres. James Monroe visited here. In 1867 Mary Amarinthia Yates Snowden and her sister, Isabella Yates Snowden, established a home here for Confederate widows and orphans and subsequently opened a college on the premises. It is still known as the Confederate Home.''

When I'd finished my homework, I looked back at Seth. "I hope you named your daughter Amarinthia.''

He grinned. "No. But I was tempted.''

"So I'm going to stay in this place?''

He nodded. "Nowadays it's divided into studios for writers and artists and creative folks like that. I keep a room for a hideaway from when things get frantic at the office. It's not luxurious, but there's a bed and a chair and a TV, plus a shower down the hall. All the comforts, plus some interesting people roaming around at odd hours. I thought you'd prefer it to a hotel, but if you don't feel like roughing it, I can book you into the Mills House, no problem. It's up the street a few blocks.''

I looked around. "This is fine. I've always had a secret desire to be Jubal Early anyway.''

"I'm not sure Jubal ever spent the night in Charleston, but feel free to conjure up an intensely tragic tale and put yourself at the core of it—it's what the South does best, pretty much.'' Seth looked up and down the block, as though my presence were a felony. "Why don't you settle in and I'll come by around nine and fill you in on my situation. In the meantime, take a look around—there's a guidebook up in the room. We're at the corner of Church and Broad; lots of history any way you turn, plus a decent restaurant in the next block.''

"Sounds great.''

"And, Marsh?'' Seth put a hand on my arm. "Thanks again for coming. If you don't like the feel of things after I tell you what's been happening, you can back out anytime.''

"Agreed.''

We slapped each other on the shoulder, then Seth glanced at the cabbie, who was behind the wheel and out of earshot. "I guess I shouldn't show you to your room.''

"I guess not."

"It's room two-ten." He fished in his pocket. "Here's the key." He slipped it to me surreptitiously. "Welcome to South Carolina, y'all."

"Pleased as punch to be here, Colonel."

Seth climbed back in the cab, and I shouldered my way through the heavy door that opened onto the inner courtyard that flanked the three-storied brick structure. As I lugged my bags up the exterior steel staircase toward the veranda that paralleled the second floor, I imagined the host of defeated heroes whose families had preceded me to the premises. By the time I got where I was going, I was on the alert for spooks.

My room opened directly off the porch, whose floor joists creaked as I disturbed them. Both the transom above the door and the thin window beside it were curtained in white muslin. As I fumbled for my key, the place seemed quiet as a crypt—apparently the writers and artists were out gathering material and the disembodied spirit of the widow of Johnny Reb was taking her afternoon nap. I freed the stubborn lock and dragged my bags inside.

Although decorated with style and a masculine touch, the room was dark and dank, its atmosphere heavy with moisture. The ceilings were high, but the walls were predictive of claustrophobia. The smells of mildew and dry rot weren't quite absorbed by the fragrances off the bouquet in the basket beside the door and the jar of potpourri on the edge of the desk. The window looked across the courtyard to an adjacent park; the fan in the ceiling was motionless. In homage to Jubal Early, I stowed my bags and inspected my quarters.

Desk, easy chair, coffee table; wardrobe, daybed, TV; bookcase, refrigerator, stereo. That was pretty much it, except for the art on the walls and the carpet on the floor, both of which were sumptuous and ornamental, but faded a tad with age. I turned on the radio in time to hear a voice announce that it was broadcasting from the Pri Fly of the *Yorktown* in Charleston Harbor. I knew the Southern penchant for keeping politicians in office until they were well established in seniority and senility meant there was a major military presence in the Charleston area, but an aircraft carrier for a public radio station? Lordy.

I threw some things on the bed, hung some stuff in the wardrobe, then changed my shirt and cleaned myself up. After thumbing through the guidebook and noting points of interest, I tucked a map in my pocket and retreated to the street. More than a little amazed at where I was, I took my first stroll about the fabled South, the latest in a long line of carpetbaggers to invade the place, yet another Yankee come down to teach it a lesson.

NINE

The first thing that struck me was the sidewalk. Made from stone that had been cut into heavy squares and irregularly laid out, it was so dislodged by time that the upturned edges reached for my feet and tripped me every few steps until I learned to lift my stride above my normal shuffle. It must have been a horror to old folks—maybe that's why there were so few of them around.

A second oddity was the cars—every one I saw was new and expensive. I was about to brand Charleston the most prosperous city in the land when I remembered the hurricane—the cars were no doubt courtesy of the casualty companies, replacements for those destroyed in the storm. Given the general state of the economy, the car dealers must have been praying for another one.

A more interesting surprise was the speech patterns. Although I eavesdropped to the best of my ability, only a handful of people seemed to sport the drawl of song and legend, the slippery Southern slur that can be so alluring or forbidding, depending on its message. The majority of people I encountered, particularly the younger ones, didn't have much of an accent at all. Conceivably they were transplanted Yankees, like Seth, but I suspected another culprit—television has usurped both family and friends as the prime source of sound in our lives, and we are colorless because of it.

But such observations were footnotes—the overwhelming sense of the place was history. As Seth and the guidebook had advertised, the past was all around me, omnipresent and inescapable, proclaimed in the names on the monuments and the plaques on the buildings and the books in the stores and, most musically and humorously, in the polished narratives that issued from the drivers of the ubiquitous horse-drawn carriages that toted tourists through the streets while pert young guides offered up their carefully edited versions of Charleston's naughty history. The guides wore Confederate caps; the horses wore diapers; the tourists wore plaid.

Energized by atmosphere, I peered and peeked and poked and pried, and took a trip through time. In the dozen square blocks that surrounded my digs in the Confederate Home, there were at least a dozen churches, each older and more magnificent than the last. Several marked the first meeting place of the denomination in this nation. One tolled the time at every quarter-hour. Another was round. A third sported columns on its portico larger than those at the White House. A fourth included in its graveyard the remains of John C. Calhoun, the man who had taken the floor of the Senate to proclaim slavery "a positive good." True to its plantation heritage and its legacy as the first state to secede from the Union, South Carolina was proud of him as well.

Most of the structures were built of stone and brick— on Broad Street every other one seemed to house a lawyer or a real estate agent—but they were not nearly as old as the city. From eavesdropping on a carriage driver, I learned that in addition to the destruction wrought by the siege of Charleston during the Civil War, a series of more organic calamities—five fires, ten hurricanes, two earthquakes—had destroyed the city time and again as well, the most devastating being the earthquake of 1868. Most structures in the city dated from that year rather than from the period after the Civil War or the time of original settlement, which still made them older and more fascinating than most of the architecture of the city in which I lived.

Thanks in part to the most recent hurricane and even more to the coins of the tourists who now flocked to the city in droves, most of the old section had been refurbished. The paint on the homes was bright, the piazzas looked cool and comfortable, the gardens were lush and bubbling with blossoms. Indeed, the restoration was so slick that an air of unreality polished the place—it was hard to believe people had ever really lived like this, regardless of their station.

On every corner, historic markers on the long, grand houses sported names that dripped with history—Calhoun, Rutledge, Pinckney, Beauregard. Each step brought me next to something new: One building had once been a powder magazine and another advertised itself as fireproof; the Slave Mart Museum was a block from the provost dungeon, which was behind the Exchange Building, which was next to the spot where the slaves had been bought and sold. At the time of the Civil War, more people in Charleston had owned slaves than in any other city in America, although true to its complex origins, three thousand free blacks resided in the city then as well. Illustrative of the diverse origins of the city's founding families, the headquarters of the German Friendly Society was near the more elaborate gathering places of the Hibernians and the Huguenots.

The past as present, history as religion, the future as a continuum of myth and ancestor worship—I had never been in a place that celebrated its past so passionately. I was not from a family that kept track of who and what it was—I don't know what my great-grandfather did for a living, for example, or even where he was born—so it was difficult to understand the nostalgic vapor that occupied the city like an army. This was particularly true because for some of us, the history the South so raptly worshiped sported one distinction that made all others trivial in comparison.

Fairly or not, for people of my age and inclination, the South remains the symbol of America's greatest shame, the stain left unremoved, the virus that debilitates us more than any other. Despite the accomplishments of the civil-rights movement, and the deaths of its martyrs and the statutes and court decisions that it spawned, racism remains an aneurism, as the Rodney King debacle demonstrated. Its dimensions are increasingly denied, and its elimination is increasingly problematic. Whites stubbornly refuse to acknowledge their bigotry and blame the victim instead of the victimizer; blacks find racism an excuse for everything, including self-destruction. And in an age of sound-bite journalism and political correctness, the issues can't be meaningfully discussed.

The most crippling legacy is the way race still perverts our politics. Whites flee one party in droves because the other is perceived as too solicitous of blacks. To court additional defectors, Republicans brandish cries of "No more taxes" and "No more quotas," which are interpreted by some as race-based slogans that promise further alienation by implying the government will no longer seek to redress the deprivations imposed on people of color throughout our twisted history. The swing vote that elects our politicians is increasingly made up of those who support the candidate most likely to keep minorities on the rung below them and begrudge all federal expenditures on persons other than themselves.

Although, unlike Seth, I hadn't been a player in the racial drama, I had always been fascinated by the subject, had searched the books for explanations and for answers, sought evidence in signs and symbols, and been shamed by the manifestations of my own store of racial fears and stereotypes. Which was why my attentions soon turned from Charleston's heroic monuments and pristine buildings and focused on its peoples.

If not as dominant as they'd seemed on the way in from

the airport, blacks were nonetheless plentiful in the more exclusive part of town. Most seemed to be running errands, some were performing menial tasks, several were carrying mail, and a few looked to be professionals, serious and businesslike, dressed for the state they aspired to. Unfailingly, when one black person would meet another on the sidewalk, a greeting, not negligent but heartfelt, would be exchanged. The whites were not as friendly, even with each other. On the whole, the mood among black people seemed less of oppression than endurance, less of resistance than accommodation, less of hostility than circumspection, less of hope than resignation.

In the midst of such musings, I began to laugh. Despite Seth's explicit warning, after only an hour in this most Southern of Southern cities I was already trying to decipher its racial coding. Whatever the truth might be, and whatever the likelihood that I was capable of unearthing it, I had to admit that in Charleston, South Carolina, on a sunny Sunday in a middle day of June, James Baldwin's fires of racial Armageddon seemed an unlikely prospect. An invisible lubricant seemed to smooth the social engine, to create an easy intercourse both among and between the races that was in clear contrast to the scraping confrontations that grate in Northern cities, where the sense of imminent antagonism creates a pall that all but mugs you.

A similar tension had to exist down here, didn't it? This was where it started, after all, the state whose need and greed had caused the problem in the first place.

So why wasn't it repulsive?

TEN

Seth tapped on the door at nine sharp, came in without a word, looked around to make sure I had settled in, then stood behind the desk, diffident and uneasy, uncertain where to begin. There was a briefcase in his hand and a crease across his forehead.

"Comfortable?" he asked finally.

"Yep."

"Have everything you need? Towels? Toothpaste? Trashy novels?"

"I'm fine."

"Have a chance to look around a little?"

"Yep."

"What'd you think?"

"Nice place."

He raised a brow. "That's it?"

I smiled. "I'm reserving judgment."

"Until?"

"Until you tell me what the hell's going on with you and this ASP outfit."

Seth surveyed the room, slowly and critically, as though he had expected it to prompt more enthusiasm than I was demonstrating and was upset that it had let him down. "We can still move you to the Mills House," he repeated absently. "Shall I call and tell them we're coming over?"

I shook my head. "If it's okay with you, I'd just as soon stay here. I'm pretending I'm a cavalry major just back from Appomattox. Ten horses were shot out from under me. I have a limp, a goatee, and a swagger stick. And a pocketful of worthless money."

Seth's grin was halfhearted. "How's your repatriation coming along?"

"Slowly. Sherman burned the farmhouse to the ground, and I can't seem to find my slaves."

"Sherman sacked Savannah and set fire to Columbia, but he left Charleston to the devices of the navy. And the slaves aren't slaves anymore."

"How inconvenient."

"Depends on how you look at it, they tell me."

Our farce fell into a fragile silence. I sat down on the daybed and leaned against the hard, cool wall and waited for Seth to take us where he wanted us to go.

After a long look out the window, he put his briefcase on the desk, examined the contents long enough to make me wonder what they were, then extracted an object that was flat, rectangular, and plastic. He sat in the desk chair, swiveled, fit the object into the cassette deck on the credenza behind him, then pressed a button.

"This is going to be unpleasant," he said. When I started to respond, he raised his hand after the first word. "Just listen a minute."

A buzz and a hum and then a voice—accented, officious, fat with self-importance but bearing far less sophistication than it tried to project—began reading from what sounded like a prepared text, muffing several pronunciations along the way:

"*This is Supplement Number One to Directive Seven from the Office of the First Field Marshal of the Alliance for Southern Pride:*

"*The Alliance has determined, after consultation at the*

*highest councils of its staff and field units, that a prepon-
derance of the evidence proves that Seth Hartman—attorney-
at-law, Yankee, Jew, whoremonger, Antichrist—is and has
been since at least 1966, an enemy of the Great White Race.
The Alliance has further determined that Seth Hartman has
been and continues to be engaged in plots and actions which
constitute a clear and present danger to the Southern Way
of Life.*

*"Evidence accumulated by the Purification Brigade es-
tablishes beyond doubt that Seth Hartman is and has been
for many years intent upon destroying the most honorable
and Christian institutions in the city of Charleston and the
state of South Carolina, and has been and is now acting as
a paid agent of the international conspiracy of the forces of
Zion, in cooperation with allied mud peoples. Hartman has
proven ties to the Trilateral Commission and to the heirs of
the Illuminati, and is an active agent of the Zionist Occupation Government.*

*"Unless foreclosed immediately, Hartman and those
acting in concert with him intend to bring about a Second
Reconstruction of the social and political life of the Low
Country, in accordance with the perverted and alien ideas
of Northern liberals and their regional co-conspirators, who
continue to have as their mission the destruction of our
Christian heritage and the Southern Way of Life.*

*"Hartman's conduct constitutes a sufficient threat to
Christian values, to Saxon Israel and the Great White Race,
and to the purity of the young white minds of the Carolina
Low Country, that the Charleston Field Office of ASP has
declared him a traitor to the South and has further declared
the elimination of Seth Hartman to be the chief priority of
its purification campaign.*

*"In keeping with ASP policy, means and methods will
not be disclosed. But be assured that ASP will deal appropriately with this menace: Seth Hartman will fall before the*

year is out. The Alliance for Southern Pride must, and swears on the texts of the True Scriptures that it shall, wage unrelenting war against the forces of darkness until it liberates the Holy City from the alien ideas and degenerate behavior of Seth Hartman and his ilk.

"Southern pride is white power.

"White power is Christian patriotism.

"ASP—over and out."

The tape hissed like an imperiled reptile till Seth pressed another button and achieved a blessed silence. My heart was pounding; my stomach burned—I felt as if I'd been poisoned. "Jesus," I managed.

Seth couldn't meet my eyes. "Indeed."

"They're serious, I suppose."

"I think we have to assume so."

Without intending to, I did what I usually do when I'm upset, which is try to make light of it. "Are you really a whoremonger?"

Seth's smile was infirm; his shrug was infinitesimal.

"Maybe that's all this amounts to," I hurried on. "A jealous husband rearing his ugly head."

Seth looked at me. "You don't really think it's that simple, do you?"

Chastened, I shook my head. "Do you think it has to do with you being Jewish?"

"I don't know, but I assume there must be more to it than that. I'm hardly active in temple; I'm not even sure many people know I *am* Jewish." He managed a small smile. "Among other things I've done since receiving that tape is talk to a rabbi about receiving instruction in the Torah."

I finally had enough of my wits about me to begin to practice my profession. "How long have you had that thing?"

"The tape? Less than a month."

"Does anyone else know about it?"

He shook his head. "Not from me."

"Did anything come with it?"

"The first thing they sent was the Notice of Racial Judgment I showed you at the reunion. Then came the tape. Then a phone call later on."

"From whom?"

"From the First Field Marshal himself, supposedly."

"Ever heard of this ASP outfit before?"

He shook his head. "But I don't pay much attention to that crap. The Klan marches through town every other year or so, but there's usually five cops for every Kleagle along the route, so it doesn't amount to much but bad burlesque. The Klan people look so pathetic it's hard to take them seriously."

"The media's thrall with David Duke seemed to give the hate crowd new life."

"That's probably all it is—some Klan spin-off flexing its muscles." Seth's words were deliberately offhand, as though we were discussing abstractions. In a way, we were, I suppose, but the inner winds that had iced my flesh since the venom had spewed from the tape indicated I was already convinced that ASP and its fulminations were more than theoretical.

"It would be nice to know for sure if this judgment against you was real," I said.

Seth smiled. "Why do you think you're here?"

I expected him to provide more evidence on the issue, one way or another, but instead he leaned over and opened a drawer. "Drink?"

"Double."

He got two glasses and a bottle of Ballantine from the desk and poured us both a healthy shot. "To better days," I said.

"And restful nights."

I took two quick sips. "Any idea why they're doing this?"

"To coerce me into doing something I don't want to do, I presume."

"Like what?"

"I don't know yet. So far they mostly seem to want me to leave town."

"That was the gist of the phone call?"

He nodded.

I thought things over, looking for a lead I could use. When I didn't find an obvious one, I asked Seth to start at the beginning.

He took a deep breath, exhaled heavily, then walked to the door, opened it, and looked up and down the hall. Certain that no one was lurking, he closed the door and returned to the desk.

"The tape arrived three weeks ago—marked 'Personal and Private.' Local postmark; no note; no markings on the cassette. When I saw what it was, I put it aside—I've represented some musicians over the years, so I thought it was something from one of them, a demo tape someone wanted me to send to Clint Black's manager or something. I only got around to listening to it a couple of days later."

"What did you think when you heard it?"

"That it was some rednecked nut who had bought into the Jewish Conspiracy nonsense. Or maybe a client who'd been convicted for drunk driving and blamed me because he had to serve time. But when I listened to it a second time, it seemed too . . . skilled to be that."

"What happened next?"

Seth drained his drink and poured another. "Two days before I left for the reunion, a man called the office and asked if I'd received the tape. I told him I had. He asked if I'd listened to it. I told him I had. Then he asked what I thought.

I told him I wasn't in the habit of devoting much thought to racist lunacy.''

"What did he say to that?''

"He laughed. And told me I'd hear from him soon regarding how I could keep the brigade from executing its judgment. I told him I was going out of town for a week. He told me I'd hear from him when I got back. I told him if he harmed my family or friends in any way, or made any attempt to communicate with my clients, I'd make sure he was prosecuted for extortion and assault and every other offense I could think of. He told me I was the one committing the crimes. Then he advised me to consult the Bible to learn the error of my ways. Then he hung up.''

"No idea who it was?''

"None.''

"Educated?''

"Yes. Somewhat.''

"Southern?''

"Yes.''

"White?''

"I think so.''

"Same voice as the one on the tape?''

"No. Older.''

"The Field Marshal.''

"So he claimed.''

"So what's your best guess?''

"About who's behind it?'' Seth stood up and walked around the room, as though its nooks and crannies might hold an answer.

"As I said, I'm an outsider in this town,'' he began after a minute. "The Alliance is right: I'm Jewish and I'm a Yankee, so in many ways I *am* an alien—always have been; always will be. The upside is I don't have to curry favor with the establishment—I don't depend on them for either my livelihood or my self-esteem. But I'm smart. And

I make a lot of money. So I'm not a pariah, either. What I am is a house nigger, as folks used to say—better off than most of my peers, but a nigger all the same.''

"You've lived down here too long, Hartman," I said softly. "That sounds like something out of another century."

He met my glance. "Charleston lives most of its life in another century."

I walked to the window to stretch my legs. The birds in the trees in the park were the ugliest creatures I'd ever seen. The people lounging on the benches below them didn't seem to mind: Maybe the South was more tolerant of birds than people.

"This is getting pretty Gothic," I said, just to be saying something.

Seth didn't seem to hear me. "What I've become is the champion of causes the Sons of the Confederacy won't touch," he continued grimly, the essay as much for himself as for me. "I've inspired a lot of umbrage over the years, exposing sores the gentry would have liked to keep hidden."

"In other words, you've pissed people off."

"Practically the whole town, at one time or another."

"Give me a sampler. Of some current stuff you're involved with."

Seth reached for the Rolodex on the desk and gave it a spin even though he didn't seem to be reading it. "A digest of my most incendiary files." He spun the wheel a second time. "We're not talking run-of-the-mill, like divorce or a criminal thing, I don't think. They can explode on you, too, of course, but they usually come at you more directly."

"Like how?"

Seth met my eye. "You can't call yourself an effective advocate in this part of the country unless someone's taken a shot at you at some time or other. But this thing with the Alliance seems different."

"Political, maybe?"

He shrugged. "Maybe."

I looked at the legal pad on the corner of the desk. "I think I'd better write this down."

Seth shoved the pad toward me and dug a pen out of a drawer. "The most controversial case I've got right now involves the Palisade," he said when I was ready.

"The military school?"

He nodded. "Steeped in tradition. Fired the first shots in the Civil War; its grads in positions of influence all over the state; its more unsavory aspects supposedly laid bare in Pat Conroy's novel *The Lords of Discipline*. And, of significance for my purposes, exclusively male, and funded by the state of South Carolina."

"Wasn't there something in the news recently about a football player who quit school because of hazing?"

Seth nodded. "It gets rough up there sometimes. The Fourth Class System, they call it—verbal *and* physical harassment, the product of a century of sadism that goes by the name of tradition. A recent variation was to fill various bodily orifices with Cheez Whiz—one knob almost choked to death on the stuff." Seth shook his head with disgust. "The alumni say hazing builds good soldiers, of course—hardship and perseverance breed coolness under fire and all that. Hardly a day goes by that there isn't a letter to the editor to that effect. But other people are looking into the sadism problem—the case *I've* got is a nineteen-year-old black girl who wants to be a Palisade cadet."

"You're kidding."

"Nope. She figures they've got women at West Point and Annapolis, why shouldn't there be some down here?"

"Sounds like she's got a point."

"Of course she does, and it's of constitutional dimensions. And most people with half a brain know it, and it's driving them crazy—I've got a stack of hate mail a foot high on that one alone. But none of it from ASP."

Seth leaned back in his chair and closed his eyes, as if the imbroglio he'd just described was acting as a sedative. "I also represent a Vietnam vet who was denied membership in an American Legion Post because of his race. And some black Cub Scouts who were barred from going with the rest of their pack to a picnic at a private lake on the same basis. Then there's the guy who claims the Federal Disaster Assistance folks gave preference to whites over minorities in compensating for hurricane damage. And a woman trying to stop development down on Hilton Head Island on environmental grounds—wetlands and water quality and all that. You know Hilton Head, right? God's gift to golfers?"

"I've seen it on TV."

"Next to the Palisade thing, I suppose my most controversial case involves the state legislator who got netted in a sting operation for allegedly selling his vote to support a bill to allow gambling on Seabrook Island—FBI claims they've got a video of the guy pocketing some cash on a yacht up by Myrtle Beach. 'A business doing pleasure with you,' was how the undercover agent put it." Seth laughed dryly. "More than twenty state officials got nailed in the thing—Operation Broken Promise, they called it. Only guy besides mine who's going to trial instead of copping a plea is defending on the ground that there was no criminal intent because he was too dumb to know he was being bribed."

I laughed. "No wonder so many novels get written about this place."

Seth's nod was slow and weary. "Last but not least, I've got some animal-rights people busted on a charge of hunter harassment for driving the game out of a private preserve up by Conway and a black cop who thinks the local custom of calling a saloon a private club so they can screen out undesirables, which is to say minorities, is an illegal evasion of the Fourteenth Amendment. Not to mention assorted thieves, prostitutes, burglars, and misdemeanants. Think that's enough to keep you busy?''

"I'm a little surprised you're still alive."

"Yeah, well, if this thing with ASP is for real, I may *not* be for long. You spend much time down here, one thing you learn is to take the crackers seriously.''

Seth fell silent. His expression was fixed and forbidding, as though he were girding himself for battle; I began to be afraid for him.

"So what do you think we should do?" he asked after a minute.

"Who do you know that has a line on the Klan-type groups around here?''

"The best source is probably Kounter-Klan up in Greenville. They're an offshoot of the Klan-Watch project out of the Southern Poverty Law Center in Birmingham. Kounter-Klan keeps track of hate groups in the Carolinas.''

"I'll give them a call."

"Better let me blaze a trail for you. Normally they won't talk until they run a background check. Lots of paranoia on each side of this race stuff.''

"Touch base with your clients to see if any of them have had a message from ASP. Same with your Jewish friends."

"Will do."

"That might indicate whether this is a vendetta against you specifically or whether you're just one name on a long list of someone's enemies.''

He met my look with hooded eyes. "I think they're mostly after me.''

"Why?"

Seth looked more distressed than he had since we'd been busted for stealing cookies. "The voice on the tape?" he said.

"What about it?"

"I think it belongs to my son."

ELEVEN

Despite my prompting, Seth was reluctant to tell me any more about his son—why he might be mixed up with a group like ASP, how I could get in touch with him, why he might have lent himself to a bizarre vendetta against his father. All I got was his name, Colin, and the fact that he and Seth had been estranged over the three years since the divorce. I was still pumping for information when Seth stood up, gave me a desultory wave, and left the room. As he closed the door behind him, he was as dispirited as I'd ever seen him.

Thanks to the tape, I wasn't in a great mood myself. Naked brutality is bad enough, but the blend of ersatz philosophy with boundless savagery is somehow worse, perhaps because it suggests how easily intelligence can be perverted, that reason remains a fragile flower. I decided the best thing to do was to try to get a good night's sleep and worry about the rest of it tomorrow.

I dialed in the aircraft carrier, listened as the church bells chimed ten times, looked out into the deserted courtyard of the Confederate Home, and marveled at the quiet in the center of the lovely city. I pulled out one of the novels Seth had piled beside my bed—*Rich in Love,* by Josephine Humphreys, a Charlestonian herself, the flap copy informed me—then propped some pillows behind my head and began to read, hoping it would tilt me toward sleep.

But the novel was far too good—its voice and language captured me from the first page. And even the excellence of Ms. Humphreys's prose couldn't ward off the demons loosed by the taped invective out of the mouth of Seth Hartman's only son.

Awful in the absolute, the diatribe was made even more chilling by the place where it had found me. Racism is rampant in California, admittedly, and always has been. California refused to ratify the Fourteenth Amendment and barred intermarriage. Indians were treated abominably—driven from their lands, sold into slavery or prostitution, deprived of treaty rights for years. Neither blacks nor Chinese were allowed to give evidence against white people. In 1912, an Alien Land Act prohibited Japanese immigrants from owning property; in 1929, a study by a San Francisco civic club declared Filipinos "unfit for American society." In the schools, Mexican-American children were segregated because of "matters of personal hygiene." And racially restrictive convenants ruled real estate for generations.

A variety of hate groups has found fallow ground in the Golden State over the years—the White Aryan Resistance still spreads its bile from there, as do similar tribes. But still and all, racism and its adherents do not seem a part of California to the degree that the Klan and its ilk seem interwoven with the South: Men in white sheets and pointed hats, flaming crosses lighting a mottled sky beyond a chorus of savage slurs, black bodies hung from trees. But awful as the past has been, the present seems equally depressing.

Three decades ago, racial hatred as a mainstream message was relegated to a fringe insanity by the airing of its evils and a collective urge toward change, and even reparation. But it has been invited back in recent years, by politicians who court its proponents regardless of the stain to the social fabric and demagogues who profit from its traffic. The sociologists would probably say the issue was more compli-

cated than I realized, more laced with nuance and meliora-
tion. But how could any definition of racism's real dynamic
make the words of Colin Hartman less despicable?

I was still warring with such rhetoric when I heard a
knock on my door. Given the hour, it was easy to find a
reason not to answer it, but the cage my thoughts had put
me in made me needful of diversion.

"I brought you a wedge of Key lime pie. If there's a
swallow or three of gin left from last time, we can—" That
was as far as she got before she realized I wasn't who she
thought I was.

The words had been headlong and singsong, flirtatious
and fun, the prelude to a party. The woman who spoke them
was blond and blue-eyed, petite and perky, abubble with
mirth and, from the cast in her eye and the lift in her lip,
potentially even mischief. Her Levi's were chopped off and
rolled high on her thighs, and her feet were as bare and
brown as her arms, which emerged from a shirt with the
words STOP STARING across the chest. One hand was holding
a covered plastic plate and the other was canted above her
eyes in a semblance of a salute, as if to improve her view.

She squinted in the dim light of the porch, backed away
a step to look at the number above the door and confirm it
was the one she wanted, then regarded me with more than a
dollop of wariness—it was the first sign I'd come across that
Charleston might be plagued by the urban uncertainties the
rest of us must deal with.

"Who *are* you?" she demanded archly.

"My name's Tanner. A friend of Seth's. From San
Francisco."

She tried to look beyond me. "Is he here?"

I shook my head. "Just left."

"And you're . . . ?"

"Spending the night. Seth promised it would provide

more color than a hotel, but he didn't say it included room service."

As synchronized as swimmers, we glanced at the pie plate, then as quickly back at each other. In the space of a blink, she made a decision.

"Pie and people spoil real fast down here, Mr. Tanner; don't let it go to waste." She thrust the alm against my chest. "Welcome to Charleston, friend-of-Seth. If you need a utensil, I've got one up at my place." She glanced at the ceiling overhead.

I took the plate from a hand that was graced with a silver thumb ring and a diamond solitaire. "Thanks very much, Mrs. . . . ?"

"Raveneau. As opposed to Ravenel, which you have no doubt seen plastered on half the doors in town. That's *eau* as in snow. Huguenot. *Very* antebellum. But to y'all it's Scar. Short for Scarlett, which tells you as much about my mama as you need to know. The ring is no longer symbolic, by the way; it's more like a souvenir." She broke off her essay and laughed. "I seem to be babbling. Enjoy the pie. But don't let it sit out, or the roaches will haul it home and party with it."

"Roaches?"

Her eyes doubled to the size of walnuts. "No one told you about our roaches? Honey, they're our pride and joy. They say the Yankees *complain* about them up in New York City, but down here we think highly of the critters. If I get hungry of an evening, I just toss a saddle on the next one that happens by and ride him to the Piggly Wiggly. They got a corral out back and everything; handy as all get out." She looked over my shoulder and pointed. "There's a nice one now."

What I saw crawling across the floor toward the credenza was big enough to put the pie in his pocket. I began to have doubts about how restful the night would be.

For the second time in a minute, Scar put a hand on my arm—like many friendly women, Scar was a toucher. "He won't bite; probably won't even climb in bed unless you take the pie in with you. It's been a grin, Mr. Tanner. Have a nice night."

"I'd be happy to hunt up that gin if you give me a hint where to start," I offered quickly.

When she had absorbed what I was asking, her countenance contracted. To buy some time, she crossed her arms and tapped a foot. "How do you know Seth?"

"College. We were just up North at our reunion."

"He told me something about that. So how was it?"

"Don't know yet."

She raised a brow. "That bad?"

"Depends on what it does to me."

She wrinkled her nose. "Sounds too psychological to me; I dropped out of high school to run off with the quarterback."

"How'd it work out?"

"About how you'd expect—turned out what he wanted was a football he could fuck." She brushed bangs from her forehead and looked up and down the veranda. "It is a tad thirsty out tonight. And I seem to remember there's some Tanqueray in the credenza and tonic in the fridge that's wedged beneath the desk."

"Gin and tonic, coming up," I said, and backed into the room and let her join me. She walked straight to the chair and sat down—Scar had been there before. I guessed she was the rebel Seth had mentioned, the one enamored of the South's degeneracy.

"Do you live in the building?" I asked as I was rounding up the fixings.

She shook her head. "Got a condo the size of an outhouse over by the medical college. World's smallest kitchen; world's largest electric bill.''

''So what brings you to the Home?''

''Home?'' She frowned. ''Oh. The Confederate thing. I have a studio here.''

''Studio for what?''

She shrugged. ''Art, I guess.''

''What kind of art?''

''Watercolors.''

''Of what?''

''Why, Charleston, of course. A framed and matted watercolor of one of our precious historical sights is just about the most wonderful gift you can *give* a person, next to a white leather Bible with their name embossed on it.''

I tried not to smile because I wasn't sure I was supposed to, but her next statement gave me some direction. ''It's real fortunate that when God made tourists, He gave them a lot more money than good taste.''

''Do you exhibit in a gallery?''

''Fence around St. Philip's graveyard. It's the only place I can afford, me and a couple hundred like me.''

''Are you successful?''

''I earn more than I spend, if that's what you mean.''

''That's the only definition I know.''

I presented her with a gin and tonic. The ice had given up its half-life by the time she raised it to her lips.

''Tell me about Seth,'' I said after a minute.

''I thought he was your friend.''

''He is, but I haven't seen him in twenty-five years. I've got some catching up to do.''

She took time to assemble her response. ''Seth's a sweetie,'' she offered finally.

''How'd you meet?''

''He got me my restraining order. And my divorce. And

my share of the assets Luke had stashed in a deposit box in Charlotte. Seth's a hellion in court.''

"He's had some matrimonial troubles himself, he tells me.''

Scar grinned cryptically. ''Callie. Talk about a fish out of water. She thought we were dumb as posts and raunchy as rabbits.'' Scar threw me a wink. ''Problem was, she was only half right.''

"Does she carry a grudge? Over the divorce and all?''

She raised a brow. ''Why should she? Neither of them was working on fidelity hard enough to be good at it, and the guy she's with now worships the ground she walks on and is rich enough to plant it in platinum. What's she got to complain about?''

"Nothing, obviously.''

Scar scowled. ''If you believe that, you'll believe that bug over there can whistle.'' She pointed at another impressive specimen of roach, this one climbing the wall about an inch behind my head.

"How about Seth's kids?'' I asked as a shudder rippled down my chest.

"What about them?''

"How'd they turn out?''

"Too soon to tell, 'specially with the boy.''

"Colin.''

"That's the one,'' she said without affect.

"What's his problem?''

"The divorce, probably. Kids get mad when their folks give up on each other—*my* daughter didn't speak to me for six months. I didn't notice for four, of course, which *really* pissed her off.''

"What does Colin do?''

"Over at the college, last I heard.''

"What college is that?''

"College of Charleston, on George Street. Got a late

while but couldn't sing a lick, then had a major involvement with drugs if the rumors were true, which they always are in Charleston. Haven't seen him for a while; hope he's stayed straight.''

"He ever been in trouble?''

"Like jail or something?''

"Whatever.''

"Not that I know of. Why?''

"Just wondering. How about the girl?''

"Chantrelle? She's a real estate lady. Making a mint selling swampland to Canucks, is what I hear. Looks like she is, anyway—I could live for a year on her wardrobe budget.''

"Married?''

"Not that I've heard and I would have. One of those women who enjoy money more than sex, seems like. Got a sour side to her like her mother.''

"Seth tells me he's generated some controversy over the years.''

Scar shrugged. "He's a boil on the rebels' ass, that's for sure.''

"Rebels?''

"That's what I call the folks still fighting the war. Which is pretty much everyone south of Broad and west of Goose Creek.''

"This is the *Civil* War you're speaking of.''

Her eyes twinkled in the night light. "We call it the War of Northern Aggression, and far as we're concerned, that's the only war there was. Rest were just skirmishes.''

"So the North-South thing is still happening down here.''

"One fifth of the male population of South Carolina was killed in that war; it's not something folks forget, even after a century.''

"Even so, it's hard to understand why it's still so important."

She shrugged. "Slight problem of communication. Northerners think we're incestuous and retarded and intent on lynching every black buck with a cock over two inches long; we know for a fact that Yankees are hypocrites and Communists and perverts—every Yankee man I know is, more concerned whether his wife is wearing her underwear than whether she's losing her mind." Scar looked at me and softened. "But maybe you're the exception that proves the rule. Or should I go put on some panties?"

Without a conscious prompt, my gaze dropped to her lap. By the time I'd retrieved it, Scar Raveneau was laughing at me.

We finished our drinks in a hush that had somehow become a comfort. "So what's *your* story, Miss Raveneau?" I said when she seemed ready to leave. "As turbulent as your namesake's?"

She shrugged. "Lucky at cards, unlucky at love."

"That's hard to believe. You're an attractive woman."

For some reason, the cliché made her angry. "Guess you misheard me. I didn't say I was unlucky at fornication— I can walk to that window and spit on a dozen lawyers who've spent at least one evening trying to make me their hobby. You know what a hobby is, don't you?—something to fool with when you don't have anything better to do. Fucking adulterous bastards."

The epithet betrayed wounds inflicted far more recently than the Civil War. "Sounds like you've been burned a few times," I said.

"My heart's as black as barbecue, Mr. Tanner. And it's still dangling over the pit."

"Is Seth Hartman one of the fires?"

Her next breath sizzled. "None of your goddamned business. Doesn't matter anyway—he's got someone."

"Jane Jean."

She nodded. "He tell you about her?"

"Not much."

"Maybe they hit a rough patch. Now wouldn't *that* be a shame?"

I decided not to plumb her jealousy just yet. "Know anyone around town who's got a serious bone to pick with Seth?"

It didn't seem to strike a chord. "He's made a pack of enemies, but then so has the mayor. I don't know of anyone settin' snares for him, if that's what you mean. What makes you think there is?"

I shrugged. "I don't, necessarily. But he seems worried about something."

"Probably whether Poogan's is going to run out of crab cakes before he gets his ration—the man has a *serious* fit for food. Speaking of which." She lifted her glass.

"More gin, Miss Raveneau?"

"Since you're twisting my arm. And fix one for yourself, Mr. Tanner. Then maybe we'll slip off our shoes and do some *serious* communicating. Did you know *Porgy and Bess* was written about Charleston? Catfish Row is just down the street from here."

TWELVE

Seth called before I was out of bed the next morning. I tried to pretend I'd been up for hours, but he saw through me immediately, probably because I was having trouble forming phrases.

"Sounds like a rough night," he said as a chuckle rumbled through his voice. "Hope it wasn't the bed."

"More like the neighbors."

"Oh?"

"Your friend Ms. Raveneau paid a call."

"Ah. The lovely Scar. Let me guess—you tried to match her drink for drink."

"Something like that."

"What you should know is that Scar's immune to gin. It's like lemonade to her—she's left a lot of fallen soldiers in her wake, including yours truly more than once. I assume I should replace my stock."

"A case ought to get us through the week."

"Unless she decides to throw a party; she's been known to invade with friends in tow."

A particularly effective blow percussed the base of my skull. I winced, then took a tack. "Scar seems fond of you."

"The feeling is welcome and reciprocated."

"Which means?"

Seth paused. "Just what I said. When my marriage

started going bad, Scar and I had some good times for a year or so.''

"I guess what I'm wondering is if it would be a problem for you if Scar and I got . . . friendly.''

Seth's laugh was warm and quick, without an agenda as far as I could tell. "It would pleasure me no end. But I warn you, she's also hard to best in contests with weapons more erogenous than juniper berries.''

"Sometimes those games are more fun to lose than win. She seems to think I'd be entranced by the significant other in *your* life, by the way.''

"I know you would be. I've been trying to set us up for lunch, but Jane Jean's even busier than I am.''

"Doing what?''

"Practicing law with her daddy on Church Street.''

"I always wondered how it would feel to love a lawyer.''

"A bit like loving a porcupine—stimulating as hell, but you've got to watch your step.''

I grinned at an image of Seth impaled on a thicket of sharp spines. "Maybe we can double-date; I'd enjoy watching you watch your step.''

"I don't know if that's a good idea.''

"Why not?''

"Scar and Jane Jean are a lot alike.''

"Which means?''

"They hate each other's guts.'' Seth laughed long enough for me to regret the years we'd gone without such banter.

When he spoke again, it was with far less levity. "I talked to the head of Kounter-Klan this morning.''

"And?''

"He said he'd be happy to speak with you.''

"I'll call him right away.''

"I didn't mention ASP, because at this point I don't

want him to know I'm being targeted personally. But give him an hour before you call—while I was talking to him, someone on the other line called in a bomb scare.''

"Bombs. Racist garbage. I feel like I'm back in the sixties,'' I said.

"More like the thirties, Marsh. Times are hard and people are scared and blacks are back to what they've always been—scapegoats for problems that seem out of control. I'm sure Rick Last leads the state in death threats.''

"Last is the name of your friend?''

"Yep.'' Seth gave me his number. "He'll be there till noon.''

Seth hung up, and I went out for breakfast. After coffee and a croissant at the French place down the street, it occurred to me that what was most likely to happen to me in Charleston was a big bump in my weight.

I called Rick Last when I got back. While I was waiting for him to come on the line, a series of thumps and bumps jarred the ceiling overhead: Scar must have been doing aerobics. I decided it would be nice to be watching her sweat.

"Last.'' The voice was brusque and captious and impressively nerveless given the recent scare at his office.

"My name's Marsh Tanner. I'm a friend of Seth Hartman's. I'm calling from—''

"He told me. What is it you need?''

I noted the absence of pleasantry. "I need to know if you have anything in your files on an organization called the Alliance for Southern Pride. Have you heard of them?''

"Some.'' The word was measured and grudging. "What do they have to do with you?''

"They've been harassing someone down here. A friend of Seth's. He thought if I knew who they were, maybe I could convince them to stop.''

"Why would he think that?''

"Because that's my business, on occasion.''

"Meaning what?"

"I'm a private investigator."

"In Charleston?"

"San Francisco. I'm just visiting."

Last thought it over the way a cop thinks over your cover story whenever you invade his turf. "Let me offer some Southern hospitality, Mr. Tanner," Last continued, suddenly sunny and obliging. "Outfits like ASP can ruin a vacation real quick. You'd be wise to watch yourself if you go looking for them, and even wiser to let someone find them who's more . . . familiar with our ways."

"More Southern, you mean."

"Close enough."

"I'll keep your advice in mind. In the meantime, I'd appreciate knowing what you know."

Last sighed. As it reached me through the phone, the sound was dreary and disappointed, the drone of a true cynic. "What form has this so-called harassment taken? Has ASP done anything criminal that can be traced to them?"

"As far as I know, so far they've made do with threats," I said. "Delivered by telephone and on tape."

"Audio or video?"

"Audio."

"Threats to do what?"

"Unspecified as yet."

"What's the quid pro quo?"

I hesitated. "That's going to have to remain confidential for now."

"Really."

"Afraid so. I'm not a free agent in this. There are things to consider I don't even know about."

Last's laugh was dry and piqued. "That goes without saying, Mr. Tanner. Even when you *think* you know, you won't."

His condescension rankled. "You Southern guys like to see yourselves as pretty Byzantine, don't you?"

His response was curt and uninvolved. "At the very least, Mr. Tanner."

"I hate to break it to you, but I don't think you're all that complicated. Freud would get a fix on you guys in a minute."

"Maybe. But our women would drive him crazy."

We laughed, then checked ourselves for wounds, then decided to let our contretemps evaporate. "So," I went on finally. "Is it that you don't know anything about ASP, or are you just not telling?"

Last took time to organize his essay. "We know some, but not much. ASP is new to the scene, first sighted maybe a year ago. They've only surfaced in and around Charleston so far, though there are signs they're branching out. They seem to have come up with some seed money."

"Where?"

"Don't know. Could be anyone from a rich patron to a similar group passing on a dividend. Bank robberies out West by members of the order a few years back financed a dozen other hate groups for a long time."

"There's no money trail to ASP at all?"

"There's a P.O. box listed on the pamphlets—where to send donations. We checked it out, of course—just a mail drop. There's no DBA statement on file, either."

"What is it they're after, basically?" I asked.

"I don't see a definite agenda out of them yet—they're less clear about their aims than their principles."

"Which are?"

"Racist, nationalist, and fundamentalist. They're ultra-patriotic, ultra-Christian, and ultraconservative."

I couldn't resist—"The Southern Way of Life."

"A perversion of it, Mr. Tanner. I imagine you would

regard the gang culture of places like Compton and South Chicago as a similar perversion of your own values.''

"Touché, Mr. Last.''

"Noted, Mr. Tanner.'' He paused to say something to someone else, then came back on the line.

"What's unusual is to find this type of activity cropping up in Charleston,'' Last continued. "There's been plenty of racist activity in South Carolina over the years, of course—seventy-three lynchings between 1882 and 1900 alone, if you like numbers—but most of it's been up-country. Our legendary race-baiting politicians, Pitchfork Ben Tillman and Cotton Ed Smith, regarded Charleston as the enemy camp—called Charlestonians 'self-idolatrous,' which isn't a bad description even today.'' Last's laugh was low and mordant.

"You're saying there's no hate-group activity in Charleston except for ASP?''

"The only visible Klan activity in this state in the past year or so happened over by Pelion and Swansea. But the Klan has been on the rise in the region in general ever since the Greensboro Massacre in '79—the Klan refers to it as their Fifth Era. Most of the activity lately has been in North Carolina—Glenn Miller's White Patriot Party and groups like that. But racism is like a rash—you never know where it's going to break out—so it's not surprising it finally found its way to Charleston.''

I took time to digest what he'd told me. "What else do you have on ASP? Anything that could point me to the leadership?''

"The front man is a guy named Bedford. Calls himself the Field Marshal. He may or may not be the real honcho.''

"Tell me about him.''

"He's about thirty. Headed the Young Republicans at the College of Charleston, then founded the White Student Union when party politics got too tame for him. Moved on to the National Association for the Advancement of White

People while Duke was in charge, then got religion. Spent a month with the CSA in Arkansas, then—''

"CSA?" I interrupted.

"Covenant, Sword and Arm of the Lord—a little nugget of fanaticism over in the Ozarks. Then he went up to Idaho and got schooled in Christian Identity for a time—that's Aryan Nation stuff. Came back to Charleston a couple of years ago but wasn't visible till recently, probably studying his Bible. Then all of a sudden he pops up with this ASP organization. The Purification Brigade and all that.''

"Do you know where he lives?"

"No. He's careful to keep it secret. Paranoid to the gills.''

"What's his favorite tactic? Cross-burnings, parades, hate mail, what?''

"Nothing that dramatic so far. They've written letters to the newspapers opposing affirmative action and abortion and slipped pamphlets under windshield wipers advocating compulsory sterilization of welfare recipients and resegregation of the schools. They've made some phone calls to this office, too, ordering us to cease and desist our maiming of the great white race, as they put it, but that's pretty much par for the course around here. As far as I know, they haven't staged a public protest yet, though rumor has it one may be right around the corner.''

"Can you send me one of the pamphlets they've put out?''

"We don't like to let that material out of our hands. But if you go by the high schools or the college down there, and look on phone poles and billboards, you'll probably come up with something—they like to go after the throwaway kids who don't have a personal support system and don't know enough history to see the hate-mongers for what they are.''

"Which is what?''

"Devils, Mr. Tanner."

I decided I didn't need him to elaborate. "So what's the bottom line, Mr. Last? What do these guys want to see happen in this country?"

"It depends on who you talk to and when you talk to them. If you're in a public forum, with media around, a guy like Duke will rail against abortion and welfare and foreign aid and attendant evils such as that."

"The Republican platform, in other words."

Last didn't take the bait. "If it's a public forum but no press, they'll start talking conspiracy—the Trilateral Commission is a dupe of the Communists, and the Rothschilds are in control of the banking system, for example. They might bring up their plan for a forced separation of the races as well—restricting Jews to Long Island, blacks to Alabama and Mississippi, Hispanics to Texas, Asians to Hawaii, and so forth. They're also partial to jailing homosexuals, closing the borders to immigrants, and abolishing the IRS and the Federal Reserve System."

"What's wrong with the Federal Reserve?"

"Obviously you haven't heard that FERNS—Federal Reserve Notes—are a tool of the international conspiracy to destroy the white race by strangling it with usurious debt. The Bible comes down hard on usury, you know."

"If that's what they say in public, what do they talk about when they meet in secret?"

Last was silent so long I thought he'd hung up. "Do you really want to know?" he asked finally.

"I think I'd better."

"Then read a book called *The Turner Diaries*. It was written in 1978 by a guy named William Pierce, a former physics professor at Oregon State. What it describes is an all-out uprising by whites against the nonwhites in this country, a racist pogrom if you will, as part of God's plan to introduce a higher species of man on earth. It's an entrancing document if you're sadistically inclined, and terrifying if you're not. The *Diaries* are particularly vivid about the fate of those who collaborate with the lower races, such as white women who keep company with black men and lawyers who advance their civil rights.''

''What happens to them?''

''On what Pierce calls the Day of the Rope, they get hanged from trees with signs around their necks saying, 'I betrayed my race.' As encouragement to others to maintain racial purity.''

''Sounds delightful.''

''It's at least as awful as it sounds. But you would be foolish if you didn't understand that a lot of people see just that sort of Armageddon as their only salvation, and even as God's will. America is the most religious country on earth, after all—forty percent of the population considers itself Born Again.''

It took time to get the *Diaries* out of my head. ''You don't have any idea if Bedford's the real power behind the ASP business?''

''No, but whoever it is, he's not stupid. The pamphlets are literate and rhetorically effective—among the better examples of the genre.''

''The ASP people seem determined to keep their identity secret. I thought Klan-type guys were more public than that.''

''In some places they are, but over the years racism hasn't been good business in Charleston. We'll smoke them out eventually, but it will take time.'' Last paused, then spoke in a gentler tone. ''Sorry I got testy back there—when people don't understand the dimensions of the problem, they can do more harm than good.''

''I'm not out to change the world, Mr. Last; I'm just here to help a friend.''

''I can't quarrel with that. But here's a word to the

wise—the generals in these hate outfits may be educated and sophisticated, albeit sociopathic, but the troops tend to be as low on the pole as it goes.''

"Which means?"

"It's like the song says, Mr. California Investigator—they've got nothing left to lose.''

THIRTEEN

When I tried to call Seth to report my conversation with Rick Last and talk about why Seth's son would have said the words and thought the thoughts I'd heard him voice on the tape, his secretary told me Seth was still in court. When I went upstairs to thank Scar Raveneau for the pie and communication, the sign on her studio directed me not to disturb. Blocked at every turn, I checked the map, finished my carryout coffee, abandoned my Confederate Home, and set out on foot for the college.

The air was soupy with heat and moisture. The natives were walking briskly toward their offices; the tourists were grouped attentively around their hired guides, who narrated the history of where they were by means of humorous anecdotes and harmless jokes. Before I'd walked three blocks, I had rolled up my sleeves and loosened my collar and considered donning short pants in public for the first time in twenty years.

The people around me seemed less smitten by the heat than I was; one elderly black woman greeted another with an expression of thanks that the heat spell had broken. I marveled at that as I marveled once more at the city Seth Hartman had lured me to—it was scrubbed and painted and elegant and aloof, perfectly apposite to the Southern belle. Although I had tried to establish otherwise, as far as I could

tell, it was entirely lacking in the ominous ether and dis-
carded detritus of cities I was more familiar with. Seth had
told me that until quite recently, the crime rate in Charleston
was what it had been back in 1958. In the world that gave
me my living, that qualified as a miracle.

My route took me up Church Street, where I'd walked
the night before, then over to Meeting Street past the Omni
Hotel and the Confederate Museum. The latter seemed closed
for repairs, which I took as a positive sign. Up close, the
stores were even more exclusive than I'd supposed, worthy
handmaidens to privilege and wealth and style. Charleston
wasn't New York or even San Francisco, but it wasn't Ak-
ron, either.

The map suggested I take a left on George Street, and
two blocks later I was on the campus of the College of
Charleston. It was a small institution, Seth had told me, with
a long but undistinguished history, only recently aspiring to
be much more than a finishing school. Over its formative
years, the citizens of Charleston had, reportedly, been far
more interested in debauchery than debate.

Although the buildings were a skillful blend of regional
and neoclassic styles, done up in earthy and pastel hues, the
dominant architecture was not by man but Nature. Dozens
of live oaks, ancient and majestic, draped the campus with a
canopy that produced a shade that I welcomed with relish
even though, according to the woman on the street, we were
in the midst of a cold snap. After taking my bearings, I
strolled through an ornamental arch and took a seat on a
bench beneath a particularly leafy branch.

Overhead, a giant C-141 transport rumbled by, military
in makeup like those I'd seen lurking in the nether reaches
of the airport, its passage so ponderous it seemed arrogant
that it remained aloft. On the ground, several students filed
past my resting place, not in the coarse and frenetic mobs of
a Berkeley or San Francisco State, but in decorous clans of

frivolity and fashion. The men looked chipper and oblivious, the women crisp and anachronistic in their sky-white dresses and ornamental hair. Their words were clever and carefree, doubtless a match for their lives. If there were darker personalities afoot—punks or stoners or even Democrats—I couldn't see them from where I sat.

When my shirt stopped sticking to my back, I got to my feet and began to roam. My effort not to look out of place endured only until I glanced at a reflecting window—in my scruffy brown hair and thick dark clothes and heavy leather shoes, I might have been off the boat from Minsk.

I was looking for signs of ASP, but the more I saw of the campus and its inhabitants, the less likely it seemed that anything that impolitic could rear its head within these confines. For close to half an hour, I trod bricked and landscaped walkways, peeked into the dusky halls of silent buildings, smiled at students who seemed undisturbed and even flattered by my presence, and listened to the chirp and chatter of summertime, but saw nothing more sinister than come-ons for class rings and billboards for frat functions.

At one point, I came across a gravestone, wedged between the library and a smaller wooden building, bearing a homespun message:

NEAR THIS SPOT IS BURIED ELIZABETH JACKSON, MOTHER OF PRESIDENT ANDREW JACKSON. SHE GAVE HER LIFE CHEERFULLY FOR THE INDEPENDENCE OF HER COUNTRY, ON AN UNRECORDED DATE IN NOV. 1781, AND TO HER SON ANDY THIS ADVICE: "ANDY, NEVER TELL A LIE, NOR TAKE WHAT IS NOT YOUR OWN, NOR SUE FOR SLANDER. SETTLE THOSE CASES YOURSELF."

I smiled and moved along, wondering if the slanders that had marred Liz Jackson's life had been any more searing than the televised smears that soil our own.

As I passed the entrance to the library, I got an idea. Inside, the air was almost frigid. I enjoyed it for as long as I could without rousing suspicion, then asked at the reference desk if they had a collection of the school's yearbooks. The woman behind the counter directed me to the second floor and to catalog number LD 891.

The index to *The Comet* contained a single entry for Colin Hartman. On page 68, above the Debate Team and beside the Young Republicans, Colin and four of his peers lounged side by side in insolent black-and-white above a caption that referred to them as "Patriots." There was no description of the club's activities, no prop to suggest their passion. In this day and age, it could encompass anything from fascism to football.

Colin himself looked contrived and convoluted, far too haggard for his age, entirely lacking his father's svelte handsomeness and easy charm, capable of fronting for ASP and worse. I had hoped Seth was wrong, that whatever ASP was up to didn't have its roots in his offspring, but I left the library more depressed than when I'd entered it.

My mind on families and fanatics and the strains between fathers and sons, I was strolling down one of the shaded walkways when I noticed a sizable bulletin board that was tacked across the front of the Physicians Memorial Auditorium. On the board were notices of everything from work-study jobs to rock bands in need of drummers to rides to Columbia and Chapel Hill. As I was sidling to a place from which to read the postings more clearly, I noticed that among the idle onlookers was a young man with a more pointed purpose, a young man whose picture I'd seen in the yearbook only moments earlier, with his arm draped across the shoulders of Colin Hartman.

He was short and stocky, overly muscled to the point that steroids came to mind, with hair shaved to his scalp and ears pierced with silver studs that were bent in the shape of swastikas. The tattoo of an iron cross was etched on the bulge of each swelled shoulder, and below that the word ARYAN. Rather than the rolled blue jeans and ungainly Doc Maartens favored by the West Coast skinhead sect, the Carolina model was wearing baggy surf shorts and well-worn topsiders and a shirt chopped off at his belly. Even allowing for his bald head and Metallica T-shirt, he still looked more attuned to volleyball than venom until I read the tattoo across his abdomen: THANK GOD I'M WHITE.

When he had finished his work at the board, he backed away to admire it, then belatedly realized his efforts might not be met with universal acclaim and looked left and right to make sure no one was about to object. Satisfied his handiwork would last, he set off down the walk with the simian gait of an undersized athlete, pleased with his performance.

After a closer glance at his leavings to make sure my sense of its message was right, I gave him some lead time, then set out in hot pursuit. A block later we were clear of the congestion of the campus, and I was as conspicuous as kelp on white sand.

When he reached a corner across from a row of frat houses that were Victorian in structure and vulgar in decoration, my quarry glanced back the way he'd come and saw me. His smug features quickly bunched into a blend of defiance and panic, and he took off running, with easy speed and electric desperation. By the time I reached the corner, he was nowhere to be seen.

When I got back to the bulletin board, someone had edited it. On the ground beneath the board, ripped into a dozen pieces, were the remnants of the poster the young man had been detailed to distribute. When I thought I could manage it in secret, I scooped up as many fragments as I could, then repaired to a secluded spot and fit them back together:

A MESSAGE TO THE COLLEGE
COMMUNITY
from the ALLIANCE FOR SOUTHERN PRIDE:

WHITE POWER!

STUDY THE WORLDWIDE DESTRUCTION
of the
GREAT WHITE RACE
DISCOVER the PLOT to deliver AMERICA
to KIKES and COONS and SLOPES

LEARN the TRUE and ONLY PATH to
RESTORATION of the
SOUTHERN WAY OF LIFE

JOIN THE
ALLIANCE FOR SOUTHERN PRIDE

ASP

=

WHITE POWER

=

CHRISTIAN PATRIOTISM
555-2244

JOIN US!

I jotted the number in my notebook, then stuck the pieces of poster in my pocket and left the tranquil campus, feeling soiled and sad and very far from home.

FOURTEEN

I ducked into the first phone booth I came to and dialed the number printed on the bottom of the poster. What answered was a recorded recital by someone speaking in a deep, well-modulated voice, transmitting a message that was chillingly calm and casually evil:

"*You have reached the Charleston field headquarters of ASP—the Alliance for Southern Pride. To receive additional information about the war to save White America and preserve the Southern Way of Life, as well as instruction on how you can join hundreds of other white minds and bodies and become a warrior in the Purification Brigade, state your name and telephone number at the end of this recording, and ASP will contact you within the week.*

"*As evidence of your commitment to the Southern Way of Life, we urge you to join hundreds of Purification warriors in a public protest to express our disgust at the maiming of white America through the plague of welfare immorality fostered by the Zionist Occupation Government as a means of crippling the white race and destroying Christian values. Our public proclamation of Southern pride will take place at Hampton Park on Tuesday next at six P.M.*

"*Defensive uniforms only.*

"*Thank you for your faith in the Alliance for Southern*

Pride, for your devotion to the Southern Way of Life, and for your support of the Purification Brigade.

"*Rejoice in your whiteness—purification is at hand.*

"*Racially yours,*

"*First Field Marshal Bedford.*"

At the end of the spiel, I gave my name and the telephone number of Seth's office at the Home, then made note of the meeting place and time of the protest.

When I called Seth's office a second time, he was still in court. Amazingly, the booth I was using contained a usable directory, so I looked up Seth's daughter in the real estate section. Chantrelle Hartman was listed at an address on East Bay Street. I consulted my map and headed that way.

The firm was called Graves Realty. Its offices were on the second floor of a newish building one block west of the even newer park that lined the east side of the Charleston waterfront, on the site where a bustling string of docks and wharves had once served as the trading terminal for everything from indigo and rice to slaves and whiskey. I climbed to the second floor and entered the realm of realty.

The receptionist was glazing her fingernails a salmon pink as she talked through a headset that freed her hands for manicures and similar delicate operations. The sign on her desk told me her name was Orchid Richards and her job title was Properties Coordinator. When she finally noticed me, her smile suggested she had dyed her nails to match her gums. When she wiggled her fingers, I assumed it constituted a more animated welcome, until I realized she was merely urging the polish to set.

Orchid pointed to an empty chair. I followed instructions, got as comfortable as you can get on Naugahyde in summertime South Carolina, then looked and listened without appearing to do either.

"Did he ask you to dance? . . . Really? . . . Not the *shag.* Don't *tell* me Bubba Snowden did the shag in front of God and everyone. . . . I don't want to *hear* what happened when he took you home. . . . Y'all best be careful, girl. . . . No, I *don't* mean his wife; I mean his *germs.* I'm talking *latex,* Lula. . . . Good. Listen, honey, I got to do business. Talk to you tonight. . . . You, too. 'Baa.''

After her unimprovable imitation of a famished lamb had vanished into the hum of the air conditioner, Orchid took the headset off her pelt of blond hair and smiled at me a second time. ''The shag is like the jitterbug, only sexier? Bubba Snowden weighs three hundred pounds; Lula's lucky she's not maimed. What can we do for you on such a lovely morning, Mr. . . . ?''

''Tanner. Marsh Tanner. And you're the loveliest thing I've seen all day.''

Her smile was as congenital as her drawl—Orchid had heard it all before. ''Why, thank you, kind sir. Such gallantry is unexpected from a Yankee like yourself, though most welcome, I *assure* you. Wherever did you *learn* such manners?''

''California.''

''What part?''

''San Francisco.''

''Well. I'm *sure* y'all are finding Charleston a *much* nicer environment than San Francisco.''

She was sly enough to leave room in her editorial for me to guess whether the advantages were moral or meteorological.

''Are you interested in acquiring property in the Low Country, Mr. Tanner?'' Orchid continued with calibrated nonchalance, as though the subject were as randomly chosen as her hair color.

''It's a possibility. I'm just doing a little prospecting at this point.''

''Of course. I'm sure Mr. Graves would be happy to make an appointment to show you some of our best—''

"I've heard good things about Ms. Hartman," I interrupted. "Would she be available?"

Orchid glanced at her phone console and then at her watch. "Chantrelle is on the telephone at the moment. And she has a luncheon engagement at twelve and has to meet her mama at the Omni bar at two, so it's going to be sticky. But if you're available later this afternoon? I'm *sure* she can free up some time to see you."

"Why don't you squeeze me in *before* lunch? Just for a second or two, so I can get an idea of the texture of the local market. I like Charleston a lot, but I'm still not sure I want to move major money out here."

Suddenly not a brainless decoration but a crafty opportunist, Orchid looked me over from head to toe. "Most people we see from out of town are interested in vacation homes. But you don't strike me as a golfer or a fisherman, Mr. Tanner, if you don't mind my saying so—you seem a trifle . . . *intense* for such diversions. So what kind of recreational activities *are* you interested in?"

"The kind that make money." Although it was badly rusted, I gave her my lawyer's smile.

"So you're interested in investment property."

"Right."

"Improved or unimproved?"

"Either. Both."

"We have a stunning new tract that's just opened on the Isle of Palms. Near Wild Dunes?—I'm sure you're familiar with Wild Dunes. Palmetto Pines, we call it. Here's a brochure that describes the model homes and amenities; I'm sure you'll appreciate its potential right away." She plucked a multicolored pamphlet from a stack on the corner of her desk and slid it my way as slyly as if she were slipping me her phone number.

I let it sit there, becalmed and adrift. "Is Ms. Hartman off the phone yet?"

My boorishness made her nervous—uncouth behavior often arrives with the implication that it has serious clout behind it.

Orchid glanced at her console. "Just a moment, please."

I expected her to redon the headset, but she left her post and trotted down the hall. In her absence, I looked at the photographs of Charleston that lined the walls—there wasn't a dark cloud or a black face in any of them.

The brochure on the desk begged me to partake of its splendors, but I still played hard to get. Orchid was back in a flash. "Miss Hartman can give you five minutes," she said breathlessly. "Then she really must prepare for her meeting."

"Fine," I said, and followed Orchid back the way she'd come.

I wouldn't call Chantrelle Hartman beautiful, but she was much more than handsome, tall and self-assured, eager to do business and accomplished at customer cultivation. Her hair was brown and curled in loops like soggy shavings, her eyes were small and cool and calculating behind the lenses of designer eyeglasses. Her suit was dark blue, imprinted with tiny yellow flowers and cut close around her thighs; her shoes were white and high-heeled. Her legs were her best feature, and she knew it.

It took her less than thirty seconds to have me in a comfortable chair with a view of the park and the palmettos, sipping a cup of good coffee in one moment while I lied through my teeth in the next. I kept at it until Orchid left the room and closed the door.

"I'm sure you're already aware that this is the best time for purchasing property in the Low Country in the last ten years." Chantrelle began her pitch as the door squeezed shut with a burp.

"How do you figure?"

She was happy to flash some expertise. "Interest rates are the lowest they've been in decades, the inflation of the eighties has been squeezed out of price, and the market bottomed two months ago. There are *definite* signs of rebound, both commercial and residential." Her smile was arid and adept. "I congratulate you, Mr. Tanner; you're about to make some money. And I'd be pleased to help you do it."

The pitch had been crisp and professional, with maybe a speck of eroticism thrown in to sweeten the deal, just a hint that if my plunge made a big enough splash, Chantrelle's gratitude might extend beyond knocking a half-point off her commission. I doubted the offer was genuine.

I matched her practiced smile. "I'm afraid I'm not interested in real property, Ms. Hartman."

She frowned. "But Orchid said—"

"Orchid was the victim of a con."

She crossed her arms and leaned against the desk. The movement made her thighs spread and her skirt rise, but she was so mad at me it didn't matter. "Do I know you?" she asked abruptly.

"No."

"Are you sure? Your name rings a bell, somehow."

"I know your father."

"How?"

"College. We were roommates. As well as friends."

She examined me until I grew warmer than the room. "The yearbook—the picture of Daddy half-naked tossing something off a roof. You're the guy with him."

I nodded. "Water balloons. Your dad made a great bombardier."

She shook her head dejectedly, as though I were a teacher bringing news of a wayward child, then went behind her desk and sat in her leather throne. "What can I do for you, Mr. Tanner?" she asked wearily. "Does Daddy know you're in town?"

I nodded. "We got together at the class reunion. He persuaded me to come home with him."

"Are you staying at the house?"

I shook my head. "The Confederate Home."

Her nose wrinkled. "That old thing? Why?"

"I'm a big fan of Jubal Early."

She buttoned a button on her blouse. "So what brings you in here? Checking how well the gene pool made it into the next generation?"

"That's part of it," I acknowledged. "Plus I hoped we could talk a bit about your father."

"Daddy? What would you like me to say about him?"

"Well, to start with, how do you think he's getting along?"

She yawned to establish unconcern. "Professionally? He's making tons. Personally? He's finally keeping company with the woman he's been in love with for more than twenty years."

"How about psychologically?"

She met my look. "I have no idea. Why don't you ask him?"

"I probably will."

She paused and looked perplexed. "I don't get it. You sound like you think something's wrong."

"I'm just concerned about him."

"Why?"

"He seems uneasy. Maybe even frightened."

"Of what?"

"I was hoping you could tell me."

Chantrelle looked at me quizzically, then went to the window and looked at the water that was lapping at the shore in the next block. "Did he send you here?" she asked without looking back. "Is this some kind of trick? A plea for sympathy? An effort to get Daddy and me to reconcile?"

"None of the above," I said.

"Don't tell me he found out about me and . . . but he couldn't have."

"Couldn't have what?"

"Nothing. But why should I believe you when you say you're not up to something?"

"Why shouldn't you?"

"Because you're a friend of his."

"How does that make me a liar?"

It took a while before she answered. When she did, the words were quick with pain. "Daddy lied to me about everything—his feelings for Mama, his feelings for me, his messing around with other women: *everything*. If you're his friend, you're probably lying, too."

"Why would I bother?"

"Men lie to women all the time. They seem to enjoy it."

"Not me," I said. "You can ask anyone. I'm as honest as an Indian. That was a joke," I said, when Chantrelle didn't respond with anything less hostile than a grunt.

When she finally turned and looked at me, her eyes were a match to the sea—green and cloudy and turbulent. "I haven't seen much of Daddy lately."

"Since the divorce."

She nodded.

"You obviously hold it against him."

"Why shouldn't I? He destroyed our family."

"In my experience, the wrecking ball tends to swing both ways."

"Shit." Formerly competent and commanding, Chantrelle had come to resemble a waif. To confirm the transformation, she raised a hand to squash a tear. "Only one side couldn't keep his prick in his pants, Mr. Tanner. I can't forgive him for that."

The pain in her voice and the tears in her eyes made me want to be of comfort, but I doubted my attentions would be welcome. I stayed where I was and watched as she dabbed her eyes and rubbed her nose, then dug a compact from her purse to help repair the damage.

"He was everything to me," she said through hasty ministrations, "but he betrayed that devotion. He told me it was going to be all right, that the problems with Callie could be worked out, that there wasn't another woman. And all the time he was screwing that . . . bitch."

"Jane Jean?"

She nodded. "Have you met her?"

"No."

"Be prepared to swoon."

"Why?"

"She has that effect on men. Why, I don't know, other than the size of her breasts—I hope to hell they're implants and they're leaking like a sieve." Just shy of the boiling point, her anger began to cool.

"Are you involved with someone, Chantrelle?"

She regarded the question as a come-on. "That would be a little incestuous, don't you think?" Her lips bunched like old knuckles.

I smiled. "I wasn't asking for a date, I was wondering whether you had a boyfriend."

"Why would you care?"

"Because I was wondering if he might be such a Southern gentleman it would occur to him that he'd be doing you a favor by making trouble for your father, given the way you feel about him."

She folded her arms and stared at me. "What's good for the goose is good for the gander."

"What does that mean?"

Her smile was thin and smug. "Only that Daddy wouldn't approve of *my* boyfriend, either."

"Why? Who is he?"

"None of your business."

There didn't seem to be anywhere to go with that, so I took another tack. "How has your mother stood up to all this?"

She turned away from me once more, back to the comfort of the harbor. "How do you think? Daddy brought her down to this Gothic dollhouse of a place, then humiliated her in front of the entire town, then left her so broke she had to take up with a . . . *thug* just to put food on the table."

"You sound less than enamored of your stepfather."

"Aldo? He's a mobster. Or used to be. He'd break your legs in a minute if he thought you were a threat to his reputation or had designs on my mother. Do yourself a favor and stay away from Kiawah."

"How about your brother? What's he up to these days?"

"Colin?" She shrugged helplessly. "Colin thinks God wants him to get tattooed and wear army clothes and blame black people because no one will give him a record contract."

"Do you know where he lives?"

Chantrelle shook her head, then looked at her watch and walked to the door and opened it. "I have to go eat johnnycakes and sign closing papers."

I'd gotten all I'd hoped for from her, so I did her bidding without protest. When I was at her side, Chantrelle put a hand on my arm. "I really could make you some money, you know."

"I doubt it," I said.

"Why? Don't you think I'm competent?"

"On the contrary. It's just that lately the only people who seem to be making money are the ones who already have a bunch."

On my way out of the office, I heard her tell Orchid to try to reach her mother and explain that she wouldn't be able to make it to the Omni bar; she had to go out to Snee Farm and show a condo to a chiropractor.

FIFTEEN

Seth's office was nearby, on State Street in the block above Broad, on the ground floor of a tilting brick building that traced its origins to the eighteenth century according to the brass plate tacked to the corner. The reception room was a crowded mix of antique furnishings and abstract art, and the woman who presided over it was the most compelling object in the place—I was beginning to think the ladies of Charleston had all been recruited out of *Vogue*.

As I pushed my way through the door and crossed the polished pine floor and the luxurious Persian carpet, she smiled from behind her desk as though I were bringing her a dozen roses. "*Good* mornin'," she chimed cheerily. "How may we hep you all today?"

"My name is Tanner. I'm a friend of Mr. Hartman's. Is he in?"

"Mr. Tanner! Splendid! Seth was *hopin'* you'd drop by about now."

"Why?" I hadn't provoked that much excitement since the last time my Buick stalled at an intersection.

"He wants you to join him for lunch. At Saracen."

When I didn't react, she elaborated. "It's a restaurant? One of the best in town from what they say, but don't worry about that—Seth always picks up the check. He's real good about that kind of thing." She pointed with a digit that was impossibly long and impressively beringed. "Go out the door and turn right, then right again when you come to a little alleyway? Then right at the next block. You can't miss it."

"Is Seth there now?"

"Should be. He left about ten minutes ago."

"Then I'd better get moving."

"Have fun," she directed musically, doubling the syllables in the final word, then rested her chin on her fist and watched me take my leave. The smile at my exit was exactly as bright as the one provoked by my entrance, which meant it wasn't a smile at all.

After I followed directions, I found myself in front of a large stone structure that looked to be out of *The Arabian Nights* by way of Indiana Jones. A sign on the door said it had been built in the nineteenth century, in the style of Moorish picturesque by way of the English Regency. Its swirls and circles and arches and columns created an atmosphere fit for a caliph; I was disappointed when the hostess wasn't veiled like Salome.

She greeted me with the chummy gush that seemed to come with the territory in Charleston. When I gave her my name and the name of the party I was joining, her joy was exactly as boundless as Seth's receptionist's had been.

She ushered me to a table in a corner that was hidden by a leafy ficus growing out of a big clay pot. Beneath the spindly branches, Seth and the woman with him looked to be entwined in intimate palaver. The woman had her back to me, but when Seth saw me coming, he touched her hand and whispered, then got to his feet and beckoned for me to join them.

"I see you got the message. Great. Marsh, I'd like you to meet Jane Jean Hendersen. Jane Jean, this is Marsh Tanner. I believe I may have mentioned him once or twice or a hundred times."

As the surprisingly artless introduction wound to a

close, the woman turned my way, adjusted the drape of her bodice, brushed a curl away from her eye, and gave me one of those Charleston smiles. But this one was real, real enough to melt my heart and make it trickle through my groin and tickle toward my toes.

"We meet at last, Mr. Tanner," she said through the middle of her grin, and lifted a hand from her lap and offered it as my appetizer. Its wrapping was warm and moist, un-scarred by time or labor; its fingernails were lacquered with what my Crayola box called Burnt Sienna. I was tempted to play Lothario and bend at the waist to kiss it, but I made do with a grasp and a shake. The bracelets on her wrist made light of my timidity.

The face above the hand I held for longer than was necessary was full and large-featured, its color a monochromatic wash of white with a hint of blush at the crest of its cheekbones that matched the auburn tresses that dusted her bare shoulders. The lips were more than munificent and waxed to match the nails; the eyes were outlined and orna-mented from a palette of blue-black. The expression she chose to wear was both eager and intrigued, and maybe a little cautious. If I had seen a more beautiful woman in my long life, her name didn't spring to mind.

"It's a pleasure to make your acquaintance, Ms. Hen-dersen," I said, my voice sounding false and uncouth in the circumstance.

"The pleasure is mine, I assure you. Seth sings your praises lavishly."

"As I remember, Seth generally sings off-key."

Her laugh was brief and throaty. "Quite the contrary—in this case it's a veritable hymn." She gestured toward a chair. "Please join us, won't you?"

A writ wouldn't have kept me away.

I don't know if it was Jane Jean's outsized loveliness, or her equally voluptuous charm, or my own endemic state of need that generated the effect, but I was already full fathom five into the swoon that both Chantrelle Hartman and Scar Raveneau had warned me of. All I knew was that if Ms. Hendersen had asked me to remove my clothes and dance on the tabletop, I'd have been up there doing a naked buck-and-wing before she could lick her lips.

Seth remained standing until I took my seat, then took the chair across from me. "Been enjoying your morning of sight-seeing, Marsh?" he asked when I had reluctantly abandoned my gape.

At least I was still sensible enough to take the hint. "Definitely," I said, adopting my own version of the regional rapture. "This is an amazing city."

"We refer to it as America's best-kept secret," Jane Jean said warmly. "And we like that just fine. If more people knew how special Charleston was, we wouldn't have it to ourselves anymore."

She had a point, and I told her so.

"Have you been up to Market Street yet, Mr. Tanner?" she went on pleasantly. "The baskets the women weave from the local sweetgrasses make the nicest gifts imaginable. I *know* every single one of your lady friends would enjoy such a token of your affection." Her smile teased me till I blushed. "It's a historic craft, brought over with the slaves from Africa. They've put several on display in the Smithsonian Institution." Jane Jean sounded truly proud.

"I haven't made it up there yet," I said. "But I certainly plan to."

"And don't forget the art museum. And the Customs House. And—"

"Now, Jane Jean," Seth interrupted as he touched her hand with clear affection. "Marsh isn't writing a travelogue, after all." He looked my way and grinned. "Not that I know of, at least."

"Speaking of writing, we have *several* famous authors

here in Charleston,'' Jane Jean segued eagerly. ''Josephine Humphreys is divine, of course. And Alexandra Ripley, the woman who wrote the sequel to *Gone with the Wind*, is a Charlestonian, too. And there's a young man over at the college by the name of Lott who—''

''Jane Jean gets a commission from the chamber of commerce,'' Seth interrupted with fondness.

''The book reps, too, it sounds like.''

Jane Jean made a face. ''We're very proud of our people and our heritage, Mr. Tanner. I'm sure you understand.''

Since I come from a place where civic pride has reached jingoistic if not xenophobic proportions, I assured her that I did. When we exchanged small smiles of confederacy, I got the better deal.

''Let's order, shall we?'' Jane Jean said suddenly.

''What do you recommend?'' I asked, as if I were competent to judge anything more evolved than a tuna sandwich.

''The shrimp are always lovely, of course,'' she said, ''but then everything here is divine. I particularly enjoy the pine-nut soup, and the lamb with apricot chutney is excellent. And you *must* try the chocolate soufflé for dessert. Promise me you will,'' she added, so I did.

We ordered the food and drink and made small talk all through the meal without a single throb of controversy. Based on my recollection of the right side of the menu, the tab would run more than a hundred bucks. Neither of my companions seemed to care, which is what family money and an expense account will do for you.

''I understand you're a lawyer, Ms. Hendersen,'' I said as we were finishing up.

''Guilty as charged,'' she admitted. ''And I insist that you call me Jane Jean.''

''What's your specialty?''

Seth laughed. ''Guess.''

Which gave me an excuse to inspect his fiancée frankly

instead of surreptitiously. I suppose she was wearing a thousand dollars' worth of makeup and had silicon stuffed under half the surfaces of her body, but God she was lovely—Elizabeth Taylor in *Father of the Bride* lovely.

I inhaled to quell my lust. "Taxation," I said, just to be saying something.

"Criminal," Seth corrected.

I blinked and looked again. "You're a criminal lawyer?"

She cocked her head and pursed her lips. "Why do you find that so amusing, Mr. Tanner?"

"I don't. I just find it . . . incongruous."

"Jane Jean's a chip off the old block," Seth said by way of explanation. "Her father's a legend hereabouts; handled some of the most notorious criminal trials in the state. I first met him when I came down during college to work for SNCC. R. Montgomery Hendersen is one of the main reasons I decided to practice law; back in the sixties, he was one of the few white lawyers down here who helped during the voter drive."

I looked at Jane Jean again. "I'll bet you've never lost a case."

"What makes you *think* such a thing?" The twinkle had returned to her eye—I could have toasted a marshmallow on it.

"I can't imagine a juror who would want to disappoint you," was the fatuity I came up with. Seth and Jane Jean shared a wink and a laugh; under the cover of a blush, I resolved to keep my mouth shut. When a shadow fell across the table, I was relieved at the interruption.

The man blotting out the light from the chandelier was verging on titanic, with a florid face and bulbous nose and turbid eyes and a suit that last fit him ten years ago. His expression demanded deference, and his hands slid down Jane Jean's bare back in a way that made me jealous.

"Daddy!" Jane Jean exclaimed when she twisted to see who had fondled her. "I thought you had a meeting with Crossley."

"Hog's been gutted, sugar," the man said smugly. "Time to feed the furnace." He looked left. "Seth."

"Monty."

"Daddy, this is Mr. Tanner. From San Francisco. He was in college with Seth up North. Mr. Tanner, this is my daddy, R. Montgomery Hendersen."

Daddy slapped my shoulder and stuck out a beefy hand. After I stood to take it, he still loomed over me; his stolid stance and massive flesh made him as daunting as an ox.

"Welcome to South Carolina, sir. Are you enjoying your stay in the Holy City?"

"Yes, sir."

"Fine. Just don't tell your neighbors about us. We got plenty of fruitcakes flitting around already; don't we, Seth?"

"If you say so, Monty."

"I most definitely do." Monty's hearty voice lowered to a conspiratorial hiss, and his eyes turned as dark as the stains on his tie as he leaned toward Seth like a giant cobra. "Might interest you to know I just cut a sweet little piece of cheese for Senator Poulson with our friend Crossley—six months at Club Fed; fine in low five figures; public service in the grade schools as penance. If I were you, I'd get in line while Crossley's still got a warm nose."

"My man wants to go to trial, Monty."

"Don't matter what he wants; just matters what he needs. And what he *needs* is to keep his future out of the hands of a jury of people who elected him to do something up in the state capital besides take bribes from federal agents."

Seth's smile was thin and forced. "I keep telling you Monroe's innocent, Monty. The only thing he took on that tape was good bourbon and a handshake. To my knowledge,

they haven't made either of them a crime." Seth grinned to
take the edge off his intensity. "If they do, we'll *both* be
behind bars."

"You don't cut a deal pretty soon, Crossley will decide
to make an example of him, and Monroe'll spend five years
in Lexington. A word to the wise, son."

Finished with his lecture, Monty checked the force field
of the room. When he didn't find anyone worthy of acknowl-
edgement, he looked back at his daughter. "Did we win one
for the cause this morning, sugar?"

"We surely did, Daddy," she said.

"How long were they out?"

"Twenty-three minutes."

R. Montgomery Hendersen positively beamed. "God
bless her, she could walk Christ out the door and make Pon-
tius Pilate call him a cab. Y'all have a nice day, ya hear?"

Monty wheeled away and joined another table. Seth and
I glanced briefly at each other, then watched Jane Jean watch
her father. Her expression was an odd mix of worry and
rapture—I couldn't tell whether she expected him to drop
dead or levitate. But I had a feeling that Seth and I were
both wishing she would look at us that way just once.

SIXTEEN

Jane Jean had to rush back to her office to catch up on the business she'd neglected during the trial. After she kissed Seth on the cheek and gave my hand a farewell squeeze, all eyes in the place went with her out the door. As she disappeared down the block with a wave that blessed each one of us, from the waiter to the busboy to me, the room seemed to emit a collective whistle of applause.

When the drama of her departure had subsided, Seth looked at me and grinned. "She's something, isn't she?"

"She is indeed."

"You seemed taken by her."

"My eyes still work; blood still moves through my veins—how could I *not* be taken by her?" I stuck out my tongue and panted just a bit, to take the edge off my thrall. "Are you going to marry her, or do I still have a chance to beat you out?"

Seth didn't find my antic as funny as he should have. "I want to; she's still not sure."

"Why not?"

"She's had some tough times with men. You'd think she'd have it all her way in that department, looking like she does, but it hasn't worked that way. Her marriage was pretty rough. He was a drinker. And a sadist. She put up with it lots longer than she should have."

The description was sufficiently ominous to bring to mind the reason I was there. "Where's her husband now?"

"Manages a car dealership west of town. Overindulges on weekends and calls her up and begs her to take him back."

"What's his name?"

"Bilbow."

"Does he threaten her?"

Seth shook his head. "Not that I know of."

"Has he ever threatened *you*?"

Seth blinked. "Why would he do that?"

"He may think you're the reason she won't come home to Papa."

Although Seth quickly rejected it, the idea sprinkled sweat across his brow. He shifted after a moment. "Did you talk to Rick Last?"

I nodded. "Unfortunately he doesn't seem to know much about your friends in the Alliance. They're new players on the scene apparently. Except for a guy named Bedford. Know him?"

Seth shook his head. "What else do you have to go on?"

"Only your son," I said.

Seth's response was a grunt of paternal pain, but if I was going to do my job, it was a line I had to pursue.

"I didn't get a chance to ask last night—do you have any idea where he's living?"

Seth shook his head.

"Not even a phone number?"

"Afraid not." His look was stricken. "That's shameful, isn't it?"

"It's not shameful, but it's unfortunate. Do you think your wife knows how to reach him?"

"Callie? Possibly. I think she sends him money."

Seth looked at his watch, then took a sip of water. "Before you start out after Colin, there's someone back at the office you should talk to.''

"Who?"

"Alameda Smallings. The girl who's trying to get into the Palisade. She got a tape, too.''

While I steeled myself for another dose of racist rhetoric, Seth paid the bill, and I didn't make an issue of it. When we got to his office, the receptionist still held down the fort with blithe good nature—nothing had dented her day during the lunch hour.

As Seth hurried toward the waiting room to greet his client, the receptionist and I made eyes at each other. The steamy sensuality that was as present in Charleston as lizards and palm fronds had rendered me as randy as a rabbit. When I asked her name, she said it was Elmira.

"Marsh?" Seth spoke from the couch in the anteroom and put a stop to my foolishness with his staff. "I'd like you to meet Alameda Smallings."

The young woman on the couch rose to her feet with the fluid grace of an athlete; I hurried to shake her hand.

Her grip was firm and brisk, her figure tall and lean; the legs that emerged from her short brown skirt were at least as long as mine. Her face was solemn and imperious, with skin the tint and density of crude oil and eyes that had decided long ago to regard everything within their focal point as suspect. If we were going to get along, the eyes advised, the burden of persuasion was on me.

I told her it was nice to meet her. She tilted her head and asked me why. The candor was jarring—all I could think to say was that she was pursuing a courageous course, and I wished her well with it.

"Maybe it's just a stupid one," she said without inflection. "That's what most folks think.''

"White folks?" I asked.

"White *and* black," she instructed.

Seth suggested we go into his office. I'd never seen his sanctum sanctorum before, and I was as impressed as I'd expected to be.

The floor was a precise parquet, and the ceiling was covered in gray flannel. The lighting was soft and indirect, the desk was big enough to skate on, the chairs and couches were inviting mounds of leather and gray tweed. In his creamy summer suit and dark and dashing look, Seth fit the room the way Cary Grant fit a tux. The effect was so striking I experienced an epiphany—I'd finally encountered a life I'd have been tempted to exchange for my own.

Seth urged us to sit down, asked if we wanted coffee or a soft drink, then took the seat behind his desk when we both declined refreshment. "If you don't mind, Alameda," he began, "I'd like you to tell Mr. Tanner what it is you're trying to do. With your lawsuit and all."

She swiveled in her seat and looked at me. I wanted her to decide I was worthy of her story, but the hooded eyes declared she wasn't ready to make that judgment. "Who is he, anyway?"

"An old friend," Seth answered. "He's a private investigator, from California. He's spending a few days in Charleston to help me with some problems I've got in one of my other cases. I thought maybe he could help you, too."

"I don't need help," she said simply. "Unless he's got a key to the Palisade."

"Why do you want to go there so badly?" I asked.

Her eyes branded me a simpleton. "Because I want a career in the military."

"Why?"

"Because my daddy said black people have a better chance to advance themselves in the army than anywhere else."

"Alameda's father was a master sergeant with the Ninth

Division,'' Seth interjected. "Killed in Vietnam in 1972. Alameda was born six months later. She never met him.''

"Mama saved his letters,'' Alameda explained, her black eyes animated for the first time. "He knew he might not make it back to the world, and he wanted to leave me words to live by in case he couldn't raise me himself.''

"What makes you so sure he was right about the army?'' I asked.

"I haven't been in the army yet, but what I've observed in civilian life is that white people don't want black people to show their talent and rise up. Whereas Daddy says that the army lets you rise as high as you can go. He says the army couldn't run for a day without black people.'' A smile flattened her lips. "Also I want to go in the military 'cause I like telling people what to do. Mama says I'm like Daddy in that. Except *I'm* going to be a general.''

"You're lucky to have your father's letters,'' I said, still trolling for approval.

Alameda nodded soberly. "I hope to have them published one day. People could learn a lot by reading them. Not just black people, either.''

"What made you pick the Palisade over West Point?'' I went on. "They admitted women to the national academies a long time ago.''

"I didn't get a nomination,'' Alameda said sullenly, her lips rolling into a pout. "I was political in high school— demonstrations against apartheid and pollution at the pulp mill and all. Made me controversial.''

Objective or not, Alameda was direct and determined; it was easy to see why Seth had taken her case and also why he was worried about her.

"So you've filed a lawsuit,'' I said. "To make the Palisade admit the first woman in its history.''

She nodded. "Court date's the fifth of next month.

Summary judgment, they call it. After we win that, I'll enroll as a knob in the fall.''

"There's been a ton of press on this down here," Seth said. "VMI—Virginia Military Institute—which is a state-funded academy like the Palisade, was ordered to admit women a couple of years ago. But that ruling got reversed by one of Reagan's federal judges, so the law in the area is uncertain.''

"The *law* isn't the problem," Alameda said. "Those fat-assed *judges* are the problem.''

"I stand corrected," Seth said, then looked at me with what looked like envy of her spunk. "Just so you won't think this is going to be some kind of lark for her, the Confederate Stars and Bars is the Palisade school colors, and the Palisade song is 'Dixie.' ''

I shook my head in wonder. "Are there any black *men* there?''

"Some," Alameda said. "Mostly athletes. They're just being used—one of them got shot a while back.''

"Where?''

"Right on campus. Had his uniform on and everything.''

"Who shot him?''

"No one knows," she sneered. "Supposedly.''

"You're willing to live with that kind of risk?''

She met my eye. "Got to, to get where I'm going.''

"Tell Mr. Tanner what happened last week while I was away," Seth said.

Alameda twisted her chair so she could speak to me directly. "I've been getting dissed ever since I filed my case, mostly from brothers who can't see why I want to be in the white man's army anyway. There's been lots of calls and letters, from black and white both, telling me to give it up and keep my place. But this one was different.''

"How?" I asked.

"For one thing, he was polite. Made it sound like a . . . business proposition, not just a threat; made it seem like giving up my dream was for my own good. Also, he used my name, not some racial shit. Called me Ms. Smallings—formal and all."

"When was this?"

"Last Monday."

"At your home?"

She nodded. "After dinner."

"It was a man?" I asked.

"Yes."

"Black or white?"

"White."

"Educated?"

"Yes."

"How old?"

"Middle, maybe. Hard to say."

"Southern?"

"Yes."

"What exactly did he say?"

"He asked if I was Ms. Smallings. I said I was one of them—there's a bunch on John's Island. He asked if I was the one trying to get in the Palisade. I said I was. He asked if I minded talking about it. I asked if he was a news reporter. He said he was just a patriot. That's what he called himself, a patriot. I told him I was a patriot, too. As my daddy had been before me."

Seth smiled. "What did he say to that?"

"He said he'd heard that was the case. He wasn't insulting or anything; he said he'd heard my daddy was a fine man."

"What next?"

"Then he asked me to think about whether I wanted to be responsible for destroying an institution of historic importance to the state. Then he said it wasn't that I wasn't qualified—said he knew I was intelligent and was obviously a highly motivated individual. But he said the fact is that the Palisade isn't the place for a woman, even a fine representative of my sex such as myself. He said I surely knew that the traditions that made the Palisade what it was wouldn't survive if women were allowed to enroll.''

''What did you say to that?''

''I told him that wasn't the way I saw it, that it was time the place lived up to the law. That was when he started to get nasty.''

''How?''

''Said if I kept on with my case, I'd be despised by all patriotic Americans. I'd be a traitor to the South and deprived of all opportunity for advancement because of what I'd done.''

''What was your response?''

''I said that as far as I could see, I was *already* being shut out of most opportunities around here, and that the best way I could improve myself was to become an officer in the Women's Army Corps. And the best way to do *that* was to go to the Palisade. And I was pretty sure *they* could learn something from *my* traditions, too.''

I suppressed a grin. ''And he said?''

''He said if it was a matter of money, he was sure some arrangement could be made. And if it was a matter of finding a civilian job, he could guarantee that, too. Thirty thousand a year would be no problem, he said. Maybe not in Charleston, but somewhere in the Carolinas. All I had to do was quit.'' She paused. ''If he'd read my daddy's letters, he'd have known he was wasting breath.''

''Anything else in the call?''

''Nothing particular.''

''Was there a next time?''

She closed her eyes; the hands in her lap became twin

lumps of coal. "Next time I got this. Yesterday. But the man talking the trash is someone different."

She reached in her purse and pulled out a tape and handed it to Seth.

"We don't need to hear this, Alameda," Seth said quickly. "I'm sure we've got a good idea of what it says."

Alameda shook her head. "Might be something that will help you find him."

"I doubt it. Really. There's no need for you to put yourself through this."

She was immense with determination. "I brought it for you to *hear*."

Seth hesitated, then sighed, then fit the tape in the deck behind him.

"*This is Field Directive Number Nine from the Purification Brigade of the Alliance for Southern Pride.*

"*We know what you are, nigger bitch. And we know what you want. Like all mud women, your highest goal in life is to copulate with white men, to be impregnated by a strong white seed, to strengthen your inferior racial strain with the mighty fibers of the Great White Race. That is your true purpose, not the phony claims of patriotism you spout to the mindless media.*

"*Listen closely, mud woman—you will not succeed; if necessary, you will be nullified.*

"*The Palisade cadet is the purest product of the racial South, the warrior of the nation, the golden savior of the Southern Way of Life.*

"*He will not have his body corrupted by your degenerate sexual appetites.*

"*He will not have his health destroyed by the alien diseases that you carry.*

"*He will not have his tissue invaded by the worms that inhabit the food you eat.*

"*He will not have his strength sapped by the effeminate notions you espouse.*

"*He will not have his mind disjointed by the jungle music you are slave to.*

"*He will not have his body broken by the narcotic drugs you are addicted to.*

"*He will not have the power of his mighty intellect diluted by your light-brained incapacities.*

"*God will not allow the Great White Race to be stained by the daughters of Lucifer. Pre-Adamics such as yourself must and will be made to stand separate and apart from the Sons of the South, who are the true and only heirs of Adam. Heed the word of First Corinthians: 'Be not deceived: neither fornicators, nor idolaters, nor adulterers, nor sodomites, nor abusers of themselves with mankind, Nor thieves, nor covetous, nor drunkards, nor revilers, nor extortioners, shall inherit the kingdom of God.'*

"*We hear, O Lord. The Alliance for Southern Pride shall obey Thy clear command.*

"*The mud woman will be stopped.*"

The tape hissed to its end. None of us could look at one another, none of us could use the language. Beyond the door, Elmira's voice chirped cheerily at someone on the phone. That and everything else in the world but the woman sitting stalwart and supreme beside me seemed ludicrous and uninformed, given what had just transpired.

When I looked his way, Seth's expression confirmed what I suspected—that the voice on the tape was the same as the one he had played for me the night before, the voice that was owned by his son.

As if in obedience to unseen command, the three of us drifted toward the door. As Alameda turned to take her leave, Seth reached out a hand to stop her. "I'm sorry," he said simply, ache like a burr in his voice.

She touched his arm to comfort him. "No problem, Mr. Hartman. People been trying to keep me from doing what I meant to do ever since I was a child. It doesn't have anything to do with you."

"I wish to God you were right," Seth said.

SEVENTEEN

Half upscale shopping mall, half luxury hotel, the Omni at Charleston Place was a new brick structure that occupied the entire block between Meeting and King streets at the point where Market intersected them. Its appointments declared that it aspired to be the commercial center of the city, and from the foot traffic that moved through the arcade that flanked the lobby, it seemed to be meeting its goal.

After braving a gauntlet of Lauren, Doubleday, The Limited, and yet another store for blazer buttons, I located the hotel desk, which was buried in the center of the building behind such sirens of yuppie commerce. The clerk directed me to the hotel bar with the tip of her index finger and the shine of the standard smile.

Unlabeled and underlit, the bar was secreted in a shadowy nook behind the staircase that led to the mezzanine. Decorated more in the style of a sitting room than a saloon, it featured easy chairs and occasional tables and carpet that clutched at my shoes; there was nary a barstool in sight. I planted myself in a wing chair and began the search for my quarry.

Given the hour, there were limited possibilities. Two of them were middle-aged women sitting alone and embarrassed by it, their eyes fixed on the entrance so they would know the instant their companions showed up. Because the woman I sought had once been the mate of Seth Hartman, I concentrated on the more attractive of the two.

At the moment, she was irritated and didn't care who knew it. Tapping a fingernail on a marble tabletop, wriggling the toe of the spike-heeled foot that was draped invitingly across the other, steadily sipping her wine, fussing with her excessively blonded hair, she was a model of ire and insult—the former Callie Hartman wasn't used to waiting, for her offspring or for anyone.

Above a plaid skirt and white blouse, a blue blazer was draped over her broad shoulders, its lapels drawn discreetly across her heavy breasts. The skirt was slit to expose a foot of silken thigh whenever she crossed her legs—her daughter's genetic legacy on display. Mine weren't the only eyes in the bar that were on her, but mine were the only ones that were going to do anything but gape.

She glanced my way from time to time, though no more frequently than she inspected the others who shared the space and were thus included in the plot to waste her time. I let her stew for a couple of minutes more and ordered a vodka gimlet when the waitress finally swept my way. After placing my order, I asked her to give the lady at the corner table another round of whatever she was drinking. The waitress hesitated, then shrugged, then went to do my bidding—every cocktail waitress in the world has performed that service at some time or other, even in posh places like the Omni. It helped that Callie didn't look like a woman who was averse to male obsequiousness.

After the waitress had brought my gimlet and delivered my gift, the former Mrs. Hartman looked my way, gave the occasion some thought, then raised her goblet in a silent toast. I mimicked the gesture, then did what she expected me to do, which was to stroll to her table with a grin on my face, the gimlet in my fist for company.

"I hope you don't think it forward of me, but you don't

look as if you're enjoying spending this nice afternoon alone." I delivered the pitch without stammering, but barely. "I thought it might ease the pain if I joined you."

"I assure you I'm not in pain, Mr. . . . ?"

"The name is Swenson, Ms. . . . ?"

"Benedetti."

"That's funny; you don't *look* Italian."

Her smile was as cool as the drink in my fist. "My husband does."

"Of the famous Charleston Benedettis?"

"Newark."

"Ah. The *Newark* Benedettis."

We jousted with our grins for an extra second. "Most men start backing off about now," Callie remarked when we were finished. "Congratulations."

I raised a brow. "I guess I don't get it—am I supposed to think your husband is mobbed up or something?"

" 'Connected' is the way they usually put it."

"Well? Is he?"

She raised a brow as black as a bruise. "I wouldn't know."

"That makes two of us."

She laughed again. "You don't look comfortable up there, Mr. Swenson." She gestured toward the chair across from her. "You may sit if you dare."

I sank into the seat and broadened my smile. "It would help if you had a name that was less polysyllabic."

"Callie." She extended her hand.

I leaned forward and took it. "Marshall."

"What brings you to Charleston, Marshall?"

"How do you know I'm not a native?"

"Your clothes; your accent; your complexion. How many more do you need?"

"A sore thumb, is what you're saying."

"Let's call you a welcome relief from the norm."

I shoved my pawn to queen's bishop four. "I'm here to visit my daughter."

She raised a brow. "I expected something more sinister."

"Why?"

"You have that look. In fact, you remind me of the men my husband—" She snapped the sentence like a twig and looked to be sure she hadn't been overheard. "What's your daughter doing in Charleston?" she said, shifting easily.

"Going to school."

"At the college?"

I nodded. "Transferred from Arizona State last fall. Met a boy at some language thing and followed him out here."

"How romantic."

"That's what she thought, till he ditched her a month after she enrolled."

"The course of true love—"

"Usually runs downhill," I improvised.

She didn't take the bait. "But your daughter decided to stay on?"

I nodded. "She loves it here."

Callie made a face. "That doesn't say much for her intellectual horizons, I'm afraid." When she realized she'd insulted me, or at least my fictional offspring, she tried to make amends. "I didn't mean to imply . . . my son is a student here also." She shrugged. "The College of Charleston isn't Princeton. That's all I meant."

I drained my gimlet and motioned to the waitress for another round for both of us. "What's your boy studying?" I asked.

"Military history, last I heard. He seems to change majors every week."

"That's not uncommon."

"Colin's rather wayward, I'm afraid; nothing about him is common. He has some developmental problems."

"You saying he's retarded?"

She shook her head roughly. "Nothing like that. I'm just saying he's immature, psychologically speaking. He lacks sophistication, which means he tends to be easily seduced by those with more direction than he has. Not by women, I don't mean, but by . . . ideas. He spends most of his time with people who do little with their lives but whine."

"Sound like typical teenagers to me," I opined pompously, then pulled out my notebook and wrote in it. "Colin Benedetti. I'll ask Susie if she knows him."

"Colin Hartman. After my first husband."

I made the correction. "My Susie is cute as a cub. Maybe we should get those kids together."

"I don't think—"

"Susie got burned real bad by the guy she trailed back here. I know she's lonesome; she tells me so every time she calls. Be nice if her daddy could fix her up."

"Colin is . . . peculiar. I doubt your Susie would find him attractive."

We paused while the waitress brought the next round. "Let's let her be the judge of that. Susie likes them wild, anyway. Guy she was stuck on before liked to race Jeeps off-road. What's your boy's number?"

"I'm not sure. I don't have my book with me."

"Address, then. He in a dorm or what?"

"Colin has an apartment on Vanderhorst. Six-two-six, I believe it is."

"Susie's in a dorm. When I see her for dinner, I'll get the ball rolling."

Callie started to object again, then shrugged. "Don't say I didn't warn you."

"Who are some of the kids he runs around with? Susie might know them."

She didn't even consider the possibility. "I'm sure she

doesn't. They're just twisted little—'' She broke off the denunciation and sighed. ''Your daughter shouldn't get involved with Colin's friends. Most of them aren't even students.''

I decided not to press. ''Another glass of wine, Mrs. Benedetti?''

She looked at her watch, then looked out the window, then leaned back in her chair and recrossed her lovely legs, allowing me to audit the procedure. Her eyes were more glassy and her speech more slurred than when I'd arrived at the table—she'd had more than a few before I'd got there.

''I appear to have been stood up,'' she concluded glumly. ''My other child—Chantrelle—is obviously too busy wheeling and dealing to talk to her mother for two minutes, my husband's in Atlantic City doing God knows what, so why the hell not? What's the harm, Mr. Swenson? What's the harm in another glass of wine?''

''Not a thing,'' I said, and semaphored the waitress. ''Is Chantrelle married?''

She shook her head. ''For years she's devoted all her time to her business. She's rarely dated, and even those occasions have been more commercial than romantic in nature. But I have a feeling there have been developments on that front. She's been quite elusive of late.''

''What's his name?''

''I don't know. But I'll find out, you can rest assured.'' Callie watched the waitress do her duty at the next table; the hiatus seemed to sober her. ''Why are you so interested in my family, Mr. Swenson?''

I gave her my most disarming smile. ''Just making conversation, Mrs. Benedetti. It's what I do for a living—I'm a salesman, too.''

''What do you sell?''

''Myself.''

The exchange seemed to disturb her. We took generous

samples of our drinks, then appraised each other in light of what was apparently our decision to get drunk together. "Is your husband really a mobster?" I asked, a bit tipsy myself.

"I'm not sure *what* he is. He has several local invest-ments—cars, boats, real estate—but . . . I know very little about him, actually. I married him in a fit."

"Aren't you interested in learning more?"

"Would you be?"

I grinned. "Probably not."

"Then let's talk about something else. Anything but *this* godawful place."

"You don't like Charleston?" I said. "Looks pretty slick to me."

"That's exactly what it is—slick on the outside but rot-ten as a peach underneath. I've been treated like scum for twenty years because I wouldn't become a hypocrite like everyone else in this town."

"I don't get it," I said, trying to keep her talking.

Her face flushed with repressed resentment. "What's a hypocrite? Someone who thinks one thing but says another, right? Well, to get along in Charleston, that's what you have to do—you don't dare speak your mind about anything from God to the hired help."

I wasn't in town to chronicle social conventions, so I decided to change the subject. "What happened between you and your first husband?"

She frowned. "Seth? Why?"

"No reason. But I've just been through a divorce my-self, so I was wondering. It's still messing with my mind, you know? I'm still trying to figure out what happened."

"It'll *keep* messing with your mind, believe me. You won't sleep right or eat right, and you'll do things you shouldn't with people you should never have . . . but what the hell. She dumped you, I take it."

"Yep. You?"

"Welcome to the club."

"What'd he do, sleep around?"

"He *slept* with me. That's about the *only* thing we did together, but fucking, that's something we could always—" She pressed her hand to her lips. "There I go again. Running my Yankee mouth. Let's just say that Seth was fascinated by everything in the South but me."

I looked her over. When she noticed, she dropped her hands to her lap so I could get a better view. "That's hard to believe," I said.

"Familiarity breeds contempt, and we were damned familiar. But I was rough to handle, I'll admit. I hated this place so damned much, I bitched about *everything*." She sighed. "I suppose we're both better off," she concluded, but it didn't look as if she believed it.

"How does husband two feel about husband one?"

"I'm certain he doesn't feel anything. Why?"

"Sometimes there's bad blood in that situation."

"Not in this case—Seth isn't foolish enough to make Aldo jealous, even if he wanted to, which he doesn't. He finally has the woman he's always wanted."

Callie took a lengthy sip of wine. When she lowered the goblet to the table, her body drifted off plumb. "Are you staying at the Omni, Mr. Swenson?"

It took me a while to decide on an answer I could live with. Finally I shook my head. "Mills House."

"They say it's quite nice there now; they redecorated last year. I'd like to see what they've done with the rooms sometime; I'm a bit of a decorator myself."

I looked at my watch. "We could run over there now, except I have to meet my daughter in a while. She's going to show me the campus, then take me to dinner. But if you're free later on, why don't you leave a message at the hotel, and we can—"

Second thoughts swarmed over her face. "I don't live

in Charleston, Mr. Swenson; I live on Kiawah. I couldn't possibly come all the way back to town for . . . I couldn't possibly." She took a breath and tried to salvage something to look forward to. "Maybe if you have time, you could drive down tomorrow evening. I'd be happy to fix a light supper."

"That sounds great, but Susie's probably going to keep me busy. If I can squeeze in some free time, I'll let you know."

"Fine." Her surrender was curt and grudging. She finished her drink in a single swallow. "It would have been fun, Mr. Swenson." She waited until I looked her in the eye. "Wouldn't it?"

It didn't bother me much to admit it.

EIGHTEEN

The address Callie had mentioned was on the street just north of Calhoun, a few blocks west of the campus. The neighborhood looked to be a blend of black and white and young and old, with housing dyed to match. The building itself was a white wooden structure, three stories high, which stretched along most of the block. It was sufficiently large and pedestrian to have served as a boardinghouse or transient hotel at some time or other, but now it seemed primarily devoted to students, its doors and windows festooned with anarchist slogans and nihilistic posters and snatches of saccharine sentiment, the artifacts of modern youth. The local variation on the theme were the Confederate flags that occupied more than one of the windows.

A directory of sorts, handwritten and heavily edited with lineouts and insertions, had been posted above the mailboxes next to the entrance. It said that C. Hartman lived in apartment 26. It also said, opposite the name, in the jagged, blood-red letters of a manifesto, WHITE CHRISTIAN PATRIOT.

I climbed the stairs to the second floor and knocked on the corresponding door. Just below the point where I applied my fist, a hand-painted swastika confronted me with nervy insolence, above the words WHITE POWER. As I waited for someone to respond to my summons, I was increasingly conscious that the heat had become homicidal.

When no one put in an appearance, I stepped to my left and looked in the window. The curtains were sheets of heavy canvas, and the inside of the apartment was dark—not conducive to snooping. The only thing I thought I saw was a flag on the opposite wall that looked more like a souvenir of the Third Reich than of the States of the Confederacy.

I was debating whether to pick the lock and get a closer look at Colin's neofascist nest when a young man came out of the apartment two doors down. He was blond and tubby, with a book under his arm and a blue baseball cap on his head. The art on the cap was a rainbow; the book was *Under Fire*.

The look he gave me seemed more antagonistic than the occasion warranted. "Y'all need somethin'?"

"I'm looking for Colin Hartman."

The name provoked a scowl. "Ain't here."

"Know when he'll be back?"

The young man started to say something rude, then reconsidered. He rubbed his belly as though it were a magic lamp that came complete with genie. "You his daddy?"

"No."

"Cop?"

I shook my head. "I'm with the college. Dean's Office."

"What you want with Hartman?"

"I wish to speak with him about some of his . . . activities."

The young man nodded sagely, as though he had already divined my lie. "It's about time someone clued that sorry sumbitch in—guys like Hartman give school a bad name."

"Are you a student at the college?"

He nodded and stuck out his hand, suddenly the hearty booster. "Furman Hobbins, Junior. From up near Spartanburg."

I managed to hold my own against his grip. "I believe I remember the name. Psychology major, right?"

He shook his head. "Phys. ed."

"Ah, yes." I glanced back at the apartment. "Do you know Colin well?"

"No better than I have to—the dude's a total possum. Him and the rest of those Alliance rejects."

"The Alliance for Southern Pride. Yes. That's the activity I'm concerned about. Colin's political views are somewhat . . . extreme, I'm afraid."

Furman summoned some Southern pride of his own. "He's a fucking Nazi, is what he is."

I gestured toward the swastika. "Does he conduct political activities from this apartment?"

"Used to, till a bunch of us got together and told him if he didn't stop bringing those skinheaded geeks around and playing those fucking marching songs all night, we'd dump him and his flags in Colonial Lake."

"He held meetings here?"

"Meetings; speeches; singsongs—always had their ears laid back about something. The sorry sumbitch even tried to get me and Royal to join up, but me and Royal told him we didn't want none of it." Furman lowered his voice. "I mean, it's not that some of their rap's not legit, you know? Welfare rip-offs; discrimination against white people—it's happening, right? But the Nazi trip ain't the way to levitate the situation. The media made Duke and them look like morons because of that Klan crap, which makes *real* conservatives look bad, too. Take care of business without making a federal case about it, is what I say; look out for your own, but don't advertise it."

Furman's de facto embrace of the Alliance credo had me at a momentary loss. "Were the other ASP people mostly students?" I asked finally. "Or were there older people involved as well?"

Furman looked suspicious at that line of inquiry, so I had to come up with a rationale. "We're trying to nip ASP at the source," I explained. "Find out who's financing the overhead, preparing the literature, that kind of thing. And whether they're linked with established groups like the Klan. What we're particularly interested in is who's responsible for linking ASP to the college. As you say, our reputation is at stake in this matter; we're quite certain Colin Hartman is only a tip of the iceberg."

Furman nodded a tribute to my strategy. "Mostly all I ever saw was kids," he said. "Students and Nazi wannabes. Except once there was a guy in a suit. Old dude; business type. Came around one weekend, went in Colin's pad for a couple minutes, then came out and walked toward town. Don't know if Hartman was there at the time or not." Furman glanced at the parking lot. "I was changing my valve covers, is how I know about it."

"Did you recognize the man?"

He shook his head.

"Ever see him since?"

He shook his head again.

"Would you say Colin Hartman was the leader of the student adherents of ASP, Furman?"

Furman made a face. "Colin? He couldn't lead a drunk to a urinal. Guy named Bedford's the honcho. Forrest Bedford."

"That name's somewhat familiar."

"You're likely thinking of the reb general—Nathan Bedford Forrest? After the war, he was a Grand Dragon in the Klan or some such, he maybe even invented it. The ASP guy borrowed the name from him."

I looked down the corridor. "Forrest Bedford lives in the building?"

"Used to, but no more. He was chief agitator; me and Royal ragged his ass so much he moved out."

"Where'd he go?"

Furman shrugged. "But good riddance, right? The thing is, when I get out of school, I want me a good job, a *damned* good job, maybe with the shipyard or the mill. But if Hartman and that bunch keep on with their Nazi shit, makes the rest of us look like numb nuts, too. What I'm saying, there are ways to help white folks without throwing a keg party on Hitler's birthday, know what I mean? A lot of other students are with me, too. So if you need help getting rid of him, just holler."

"I appreciate your cooperation, Furman. The college won't forget it."

"Great. Well, I got to get to class. Making up an incomplete in psych this summer—got heavy into partying last term, time to suck it up. Good to meet you, sir."

"See you on campus, Furman."

Furman trotted off. I didn't know whether he or the swastika was more depressing.

NINETEEN

On the way back to my apartment, I followed Jane Jean's advice and took a trip down Market Street, which proved to be a true bazaar, a whirlwind of homespun commerce smack in the center of town. A series of covered stalls down the center of the bifurcated street offered everything from seashells to T-shirts to bonsai trees to ready-to-cook packets of red beans and rice. Some of the jewelry looked interesting, but the most compelling items in the array were those Jane Jean had recommended—the baskets woven by local black women out of sweetgrass and pine needles and dried flowers.

I bought one for my friend Betty. The woman who sold it to me was working on a large basket that lay in her lap, half finished, its unbound stays flopping in the breeze like the tongues of large lizards. When I asked how long she'd been making them, she told me she was sixty-three years old and had been making baskets since she was five. I don't know why it bothered me; it didn't seem to bother her.

When I got to the apartment, I called Seth and asked him what was on the agenda for the evening. Hurried and apologetic, he told me I was on my own—he had a dinner meeting of the Restoration Committee of the Preservation Society and couldn't skip it. I told him not to worry, that I could amuse myself just fine; I'd been doing it for thirty years and had almost gotten the hang of it.

At some point, I fell asleep. When I woke, the light in the room had paled several shades, and the shadows had moved ten feet toward the east. It took a while to get my bearings. When I had them, I realized I was hot. And tired. And lonely. I decided to address two of the three and take a shower. I made sure no one was lingering on the porch, then collected my kit and a fresh set of underwear and scampered down the veranda to the bathroom at the end of the building. If anyone saw me, they didn't bring it up.

The coldest water the system could produce cascaded over me for ten minutes, till goose bumps had replaced the glaze of perspiration on my flesh and the fog had lifted off my brain. I dried off, put on the underwear, wrapped a towel around my waist, clutched my clothes in my free hand, and beat a retreat to my room, leaving watery footprints in my wake. I might have heard someone toss a wolf whistle at me from behind a darkened window, but I wasn't sure.

When I got where I was going, someone was there to greet me. "Figured that was you down there," she said, arms crossed, grin as wide as a river across her face, enjoying my attire and my discomfiture. "Not many locals make use of the shower."

"They should; it's a good one. You ought to try it."

She raised a brow. "Now?"

"Why not? I can give you some hands-on instruction in the finer features of the implement."

Scar Raveneau poked me in the ribs. "I think I'll pass, thank you very much. I was wondering about dinner."

"What were you wondering about it?"

"Whether you intend to observe the tradition this evening, for one. And whether you'd like to join me, for another. Or do Seth and Jane Jean have you booked up?"

I shook my head. "Seth has a meeting. Restoration or some such."

"Ah, yes. Rich folks preserving our precious heritage

for future generations. As long as they get a tax break for their trouble."

I shook my head in mock exasperation. "You're far too cynical for a Daughter of the Confederacy, Ms. Raveneau."

"Thank the Lord for small favors, Mr. Tanner." She looked me up and down. "There aren't many places in town that get real enthused about people having dinner in their underwear. I know it's retrograde and all, but . . . Shall I leave the room while you finish your toilette?"

"I can finish my toilette if you look out the window for ten seconds."

I was in my trousers by the time she looked back, which she did in precisely the allotted time because she counted it off out loud.

"Rats," she said when she saw my nether regions were demurely ensconced. "I could have used a cheap thrill."

"In due time, Ms. Raveneau," I said, and put on my socks and shoes. While I combed my hair and put on my shirt and transferred my wallet to the clean trousers, Scar roamed in search of treasure. Although her interest in Seth was certainly more than platonic, its precise dimension didn't seem to be my business.

"Seth has one of my paintings in his den," she said at one point.

"That's a compliment; Seth has good taste."

"I think it's more a trophy than a compliment," she said. "Or maybe it's a welfare grant."

I looked at her. "Is the thing between you and Seth anything you want to talk about?"

She sighed, less with anguish than regret. "Not really. He was with me for a while when he was married but deciding he didn't want to be; then Jane Jean took aim at him, and he dumped me and Callie both. Which I knew going in was what would happen—Seth's been sweet on her for years." Scar shrugged a shoulder to show disinterest. "Met her yet?"

I nodded. "Lunch."

"And?"

"I have to admit, Sophia Loren came to mind at one point."

"Probably when she dropped her spoon to give you a look at her cleavage."

"Now, now."

"So I'm jealous. So shoot me."

Scar pouted for another moment while she returned from wherever the talk of Seth had put her, then looked me up and down. "If you can figure out how to button your fly, you'll be fit to take me out and feed me."

I blushed and made myself suitable. "Where to?" I asked as I locked the door behind us.

"Carolina's," she said, and we set off down the street.

Carolina's turned out to be a gleaming swirl of food and frolic filled with customers coincidentally in pursuit of the selfsame ingredients. The fixtures were art deco; the walls were bright with glass and mirrors; the tablecloths were checkerboards of black and white, though the color scheme of the clientele was far less balanced. For the most part, the crowd was young and happy, well dressed and well behaved, its collective antennae up, and its well-tuned senses on red alert for signs that before it ended, the evening would engender something memorable.

Scar and I were seated against a mirrored wall, cheek by jowl with a couple so smitten with each other there might have been a fence between us. We ordered drinks and an appetizer of she-crab soup. Scar suggested I try the crayfish pasta, so I did, though not without debate. For dessert I ordered a slice of chocolate pound cake that came afloat in a raspberry sauce as thick as STP.

When I had scraped the last of the pound cake off the

plate and overtipped the waiter, we left the restaurant and strolled to the waterfront and meandered through the park, watching the waves eddy through the marsh grass and listening as they licked the muddy shore. The air was warm enough for kids to frolic in the fountains; the humidity had dropped to a percentage that let my shirt stay separate from my skin. Scar took my arm and snuggled to my side. She was comfortable and cute; I felt as though I could walk to Atlanta. A host of locals seemed to have the same idea—the ambience was relaxed and friendly, the racial mix more equitable than in the trendy restaurant, probably because this alfresco fare came free.

We left the park and stopped for a drink at the Moultrie Tavern, which was trying to be of historic note but wasn't quite getting the job done. As we lingered over a B&B, we began to talk more seriously, about our lives and loves, our wins and losses. Scar was interested in why I'd stopped being a lawyer and why I'd never married. I told her as much as I knew about each phenomenon, but my answers were subdued because they weren't definitive—among the fallout from the reunion was my sense that the responses I'd assumed for so long to be adequate were more evasions than explanations.

I expressed interest in her work, then wondered why she seemed to disparage it. I finally got her to agree to show me her studio, but only after I promised to tell her about my more notorious adventures while plying my trade. For the most part, we dodged the painful stuff, though on occasion we gave off hints of where the potholes were. By the time we decided to walk some more, we each had a pretty good idea of where the other's life had foundered and where it had soared free.

We left the tavern about nine and headed for the Battery. The warm breeze that washed across the elevated flagstone walkway billowed Scar's skirt and scrambled my hair.

Out in the harbor, the lights of Fort Sumter glowed dimly in the distance, beyond the nearer lights of shrimpers. Scar suggested I take a tour to the fort in the morning. I told her I thought I'd pass. It didn't seem to make a difference.

West of the walkway a bevy of handsome mansions sat on sites where the rice planters and slave merchants had lived until the Union put the city under siege and began the bombardment that lasted through the war and forced the planters to move up the peninsula. I tried again to imagine why those days remained so current in Charleston's hearts and minds, to understand how such a viral nostalgia could be a wholesome thing. All I knew for sure was that this was a different world from the one I inhabited, a society that nourished itself on myth and romance, artifice and charm; a world that seemed to thrive on such a diet.

I also knew that despite the blot of ASP and its attendant musk of evil, I was beginning to like Charleston a lot—I wondered if it could use a good detective. Since romance is often a cloak of its opposite, and myth a mask on immorality, I decided it probably could.

TWENTY

We got back to the Confederate Home about ten. Scar lingered at the door, humming a Cole Porter tune that had to do with moonlight, then looked at her watch in the enfeebled glow of the street lamp. The mood between us was scattered and fragile, in need of a catalyst. "I suppose I should go home," she said softly.

"Don't."

For a moment, I wasn't sure she'd heard me. A car drove past and she watched until it disappeared. Across the street, a man curbed his dog and she waited until they finished.

"Why not?" she said softly, the words indistinct and directionless, moths circling in the brittle night.

"You promised to show me your studio."

"We can do that tomorrow."

"It would be nicer now."

She held my eyes on hers. When I didn't seek a different perch, she looked to the church spire at the end of the block, symbolic across a spectrum of both spiritual and sexual longing. "I'm warning you—it's not the Louvre up there."

"That's all right—I've seen the Louvre." It was a lie, but a good one.

We climbed toward the third floor in silence and indecision. In front and above me, Scar's body moved in easy exercise, hips oscillating in unintended provocation, sandals slapping at her heels. I started to pinch her but stopped myself. Whatever we were up to, it wasn't high jinks.

When we reached the room above mine, Scar unlocked the door, flipped on a bright light, and led me inside. "Don't drown," she said, and stepped aside to let me look.

Even for an artist, the place was a mess. A forest of easels; a cascade of canvas; a collection of set pieces prepared as inspiration. Paint jars had clustered here and there like oddly mutated floribunda; the brushes stuffed into coffee cans created tufts of some strange shrub. Bottles and vases and fruits and flowers lounged around like extras, waiting for cues to go on.

To get a better look, I walked through the studio the way I walk through a prison, hyperaware of geography, leery of making a misstep, careful not to disturb anything. My objective was a store of completed work, matted and framed, propped in a far corner ready for insertion into a carefully crafted set of slotted racks that stood empty on the floor beside them.

When I reached the batch of paintings, I flipped through them quickly. Primarily they constituted a series of swift and pastel renderings of various scenes around town, several of which, like the college and Omni and the market, I'd observed that very morning. The style was more impressionistic than architectural, the hues sunny and suggestive of gaiety, with no trace of the blacker moods of the artist who'd contrived them.

"See?" Scar said roughly at my back. "I told you it was dreck."

"It's not and you know it. It's perfectly fine for what it is."

"For what it is. Right. What it is, is dreck."

"And this is fine in any category," I said.

What I was looking at was an oil rather than a water-color, the only one in the studio as far as I could tell. The canvas was larger than the rest, leaning against a wall in arrogant isolation, its image only partially completed but identifiable nonetheless as a portrait, almost life-size, of a naked woman, seated with one knee up and the other bent under her, her arm resting atop the upraised joint, left draped casually in her lap.

The model looked straight ahead, unsmiling and un-ashamed, confronting the viewer with what seemed like bel-ligerence, as though daring me to find pleasure in her nakedness, as though willing me to look away. I returned her stare as candidly as I could, letting both pleasure and ad-miration rage, till I proved my point and won the war.

Next to the painting was a mirror of the same dimension as the canvas, but I didn't need a clue to know I was looking at a self-portrait of the artist. Stark, severe, determinedly un-glamorized, Scar Raveneau was more naked on that canvas than she could ever be in bed.

"Shit," she said behind me. "I forgot that thing was out. It probably violates some kind of ordinance." She plucked a drop cloth off the floor and draped it over the painting. "There. Eyesore eliminated."

"It's very good," I said. "And you're artist enough to know it."

"It's just practice. An exercise. An indulgence."

"It's probably therapy, too. But it's also art."

She wrinkled her nose. "Yeah, well, that and a dollar will get me a cup of coffee in any joint in town."

"Money doesn't have anything to do with it."

"It does if you like eating." She looked at her watch. "I should go. I'm doing one whole side of Colonial Lake tomorrow. That's a lot of geography in one sitting."

"Don't," I said again.

She crossed her arms and leaned against the doorjamb, eyes lazy and lidded. "Why not?"

"I want you to spend the night with me."

"Why? Because all this heat has made you horny?"

"Because I like you. Because we've had a good time this evening, and it would be nice to end it making love."

"What makes you think I do things like that?"

"Like what? Enjoy yourself?"

"Sex is always more than fun. Even Yankees know that much."

"Even assuming you're right, you know tonight was special, you know we're attracted to each other, and you know the reasons not to do it aren't nearly as good as their opposites."

She looked away from me and out the window, at the silent streets of the ancient city that had heard a million ploys like mine. When she looked back, her expression was equivocal. "You'd make a good Southerner," she said simply.

"I'm not going to beg you, Scar. Or use some verbal voodoo. I just know one thing."

"What's that?"

"One of the main purposes of life is making memories. Doing things you want to do so you can remember them when you need to and feel good about what you did instead of regretting what you let slip away."

"Memories, huh? Is that all it would be?"

"No, that's the least it would be?"

"You must have made a mint as a lawyer," she said, then looked around the studio as though I had asked her to forsake it. "The couch isn't very comfortable," she mused absently, the criticism directed at a sagging sofa that was skulking in a corner.

"The daybed downstairs makes out into a double."

"I know." She looked at me until she was sure I had absorbed her message, then grinned at me like a scamp. "I have to admit it heats me up a bit to think of screwing some-one else down there." She glowered in mock chastisement. "And you know it, don't you, you bastard?"

I muttered a pro forma disclaimer, then took her by the hand and led her down the stairs.

As we plowed through the preliminaries—washing up, bed expanded, clothes removed, condom readied, bedside claimed—I realized that the past week had been a watershed. I'd made love with Betty Fontaine the night before I left for the reunion, with Libby Grissom the night before I flew to Charleston, and, lo and behold, I was on the brink again: My cup runneth over; my libido had known no better days.

Or had it? Each sex act may diminish those that went before, each new partner may devalue partners past. The equation is the basis of a big branch of Western morality, after all—the crux of the sacrament of marriage and monog-amy, the wellspring of the rejection of contraception and di-vorce. Although I don't think I believed it, deep down, and certainly didn't intend to live my life according to such spec-ulations, enough of the doctrine lay unsullied in my psyche that a part of me felt diabolical.

But part of me definitely didn't. A smorgasbord of sex, who could possibly complain? Unless, as Scar had suggested, sex is always more than fun.

Good and evil; right and wrong; fidelity and faithless-ness. A bed was the worst place to debate such polarities, an orgasm an inappropriate resolution of any issue. But if not noble or untroubled, neither was I lonely. Crouched above my chest, breasts brushing at my belly, teeth nibbling at my neck, Scar Raveneau wreaked a quick revenge on my friend Seth Hartman, and made me her amanuensis.

TWENTY-ONE

Scar was up and out before I woke; the only thing she left behind was a note in my shoe—*Good morning from the Belle of the Ball. I had a nice night, so have a nice day, hear?* In the bathroom, I found a second message, this one scrawled inside the shower stall in what looked like pink lipstick—*Holler if you need me to scrub your back. Love, S.* I was smiling as I washed it off.

When I was dressed, I called Seth and took him up on the offer to lend me his car. When he asked where I was going, I told him I was going shopping.

I was halfway out the door when the phone rang. I was about to ignore it, assuming it was someone for Seth, until I remembered who might have been trying to reach me.

"Mr. Tanner?"

"Speaking."

"This is the First Field Marshal of the Alliance for Southern Pride. I understand you're interested in joining our movement."

"Yes, I am."

The voice was brisk and commanding, not the fractious boy on the tapes sent to Seth and Alameda, more a match to the man who had phoned to follow up. I came up with a ploy, then waited for a chance to use it.

"How did you learn about us?" he continued.

"The posters at the college, primarily."

"Are you connected with the school? You don't sound like a student."

"I'm not. Is that a requirement?"

"Not at all. But I was wondering what form your support of ASP might take. Some of our activities tend to be rather . . . strenuous."

"I was thinking more in terms of financial than physiological participation. Is that allowed?"

"Affirmative. May I tell you where to send your check?"

"Not so fast. I'd like a meeting first. With you and the headman."

He paused. "For what purpose?"

"My knowledge of ASP is pretty sketchy; I'd like to know what I'm buying. In the past, I've wasted a lot of money on groups that talked a good game but didn't follow through when opportunities arose. Time is of the essence in these matters; the nation is imperiled. I don't want to join forces with anyone who's not ready to pay the price to make a difference. Plus, I want to be sure my contribution will remain . . . anonymous."

The Field Marshal flashed his best bravado. "You can count on ASP to do whatever it takes to prevail against the forces of darkness, Mr. Tanner. What level of support are we talking about?"

"Let's say in the neighborhood of ten thousand."

"That would be most welcome."

"I've never had anyone turn me down, Mr. . . . ?"

"Bedford. Forrest Bedford. First Field Marshal of ASP; Commandant of the Purification Brigade. You don't sound like a Southerner, Mr. Tanner."

"Is that important?"

"I'm only wondering why an organization devoted to

restoring the Southern Way of Life would be of interest to a Yankee?''

I dredged some data from my memory. ''I recently moved here from Denver, Mr. Bedford, where I was a significant supporter of the resurgent Klan activities in that area. Moral and racial issues transcend regionalism, as I hope you know. Do you know the Denver leadership, by any chance?''

''Only by reputation.''

''There's a young man there who will go a long way on the national scene—he's David Duke without the baggage. From what I hear, you may have similar skills. Well? When do I meet the Chief of Staff, Mr. Bedford? Or shall I send my funds to Denver?''

Bedford hesitated. ''We have a march at Hampton Park this evening. Unless things get out of hand, which of course we would welcome, we should be finished by eight. There's a baseball stadium nearby. I could meet you at the entrance after our demonstration, and we can go somewhere and satisfy your curiosity. Somewhere secure,'' he added heavily.

''Fine.''

''Eight o'clock.'' When he spoke again, it was to issue a warning. ''We are pledged to assassinate any and all agents of the Zionist Occupation Government who attempt to infiltrate us, Mr. Tanner. Just in case you aren't what you seem to be.''

The phone went dead. I replaced the receiver with a hand as wet as soup.

I picked up Seth's car in the lot behind his office, then drove west on Calhoun to the bridge across the Ashley. On the west side of the river, the contrast with the historic district was stark. The usual mix of suburban commerce defiled the roadside, the K Marts and Burger Kings and Jiffy Lubes that convince us they make life convenient when in reality they just make it dreary.

After a couple of miles of blight, conglomeration

yielded to uniformity—the highway became an Auto Row. Every make of car imaginable was on display, from cheaply made Korean clunkers to outrageously expensive Italian roadsters. One dealership flew the largest flag I've ever seen, looming like a supple spacecraft over the Chevys and Geos and BMWs that were a melting pot of metal in the lot below. At the far end of the row, in the last gasp of consumptive civilization before the road turned rural and plunged through marshland as it headed for Savannah, I found the store I wanted.

Seth's car was a new Thunderbird, which is why, I suppose, no one hurried to greet me before I'd shut the engine down—I didn't seem likely to spin off a commission. I got out of the car, browsed the sales lot long enough to establish some bona fides, then went inside the showroom.

The only person in sight was the receptionist. She smiled like a sunflower at high noon, searched in vain for a salesman, then blinked and said good morning. Her dress was billowy in the bodice and low cut; the flesh above her breasts was freckled. The sign on the counter said her name was LaWanda.

"Howdy," I answered cheerfully, then surveyed the empty showroom. "Guess the staff must be on coffee break."

"Bubba Martin's the only agent that's checked in so far—we don't get customers before noon much anymore—but he's out on a test drive. Should be back any minute, though. Were you interested in new or previously owned?"

I looked back at the showroom again. "I'm kind of partial to that convertible over there."

Her eyes ignited. "Isn't that the sexiest thing you ever *saw*? I'd *love* to have an EX-four-hundred."

I leaned forward and worked with her enthusiasm. "Now tell the truth, LaWanda. Is this outfit prepared to deal a little?"

She nodded briskly. "Bubba's *great* at building a deal you're comfortable with. This is a good time to buy, too—financing's the lowest it's been since, like, forever."

"I'm told the man who signs off on 'em is Bilbow."

"Beau?"

"Is there more than one?"

"No."

"Then Beau's the one I mean."

Our brief excerpt from Pirandello put LaWanda off balance for a moment, but true to her heritage, her smile couldn't stay submerged. "Mr. Bilbow is the general manager; I know he'd be happy to discuss our entire line with you. It's the best we've ever had; all the publications say so." She reached for a shelf behind her. "I've got this copy of *Motor Trend*? December issue? It says—"

"He here?" I interrupted.

"Mr. Bilbow? I expect him any time."

"Like when?"

"I'm not sure. He had an appointment at the bank, so . . ." She shrugged helplessly, to let me know how banks were behaving these days, then fussed with her hairdo. "I'm not very good at this, am I? I guess that's why I'm still on phones."

As if on cue, one of them started to ring. "If you want to wait," she said as she reached for her instrument, "there's coffee down that hall."

She pointed to her right, then turned her smile into its verbal equivalent and blessed the caller with a greeting. I debated what to do and decided it wouldn't hurt to take a look at the EX-400 in case I won the lottery and my Buick took early retirement.

I strolled over to the convertible. The sticker price was twenty-one-five. EPA estimates were seventeen and twenty-two. The paint looked as deep as the Ashley. I walked around it a couple of times, then opened the door and climbed in.

The feel and smell were as they should have been—plush as a palace and pungent as mint. The buttons and gauges made me feel like a pilot; the steering wheel made me feel like a Petty; the sticker made me feel like a pauper.

I was headed for the Thunderbird when another car whizzed into the lot and stopped on a dime in front of the door. It was a clone of the convertible in the showroom—top down, windows up, the man behind the wheel handsome but harried, running late and maybe scared as well.

He was tall and thin in the legs and chest, but there was a bulge at his belt the size of a melon and a sag to his lips and chin that made him look petulant. He wore a white shirt and a red tie and pants too short in the seam. His hair was combed back in an oily compress that clung to his skull like paste—he must have thought it looked suave, but what it made him look was feral.

Without acknowledging my presence, he hurried to LaWanda and asked for his messages. She gave him several slips of paper, then said something I couldn't hear. The man glanced my way, then beyond me toward the sales lot, then said something else to LaWanda and headed toward the coffee.

When he'd gone, I returned to LaWanda's desk. "That Bilbow?"

She nodded. "I told him you were waiting on him. He said he'd just be a minute."

"Looks a little haggard—bank must have given him a hard time."

"Business hasn't been that great what with the recession and all, so he's had to lay people off. He's been working harder than he's used to."

It was an interesting way to put it—not exactly a tribute to Beau Bilbow's industriousness, but not exactly a slur. "Who owns the dealership?" I asked.

LaWanda seemed befuddled. "I don't know for sure. Folks from up North, I think."

"Ever hear of a group called the Alliance for Southern Pride, LaWanda?"

She frowned and shook her head. "What is it, kind of a historical-type group or something?"

"Something like that. I thought I saw Bilbow at a meeting one time. I just wondered if he ever talked about it."

"Not to me." She gestured toward the convertible. "Looks great, huh?"

"A little steep in the sticker for a second car, though."

"If it's the down payment you're worried about, we've got a lease program that—"

I put a plug in her spiel. "I'm running late, sweetheart; better save it for the next guy." I started down the hall, toward the coffee and Bilbow both.

He was lugging a Styrofoam cup into his office when I caught up to him. He didn't like it that I had followed him into his private lair, and he liked it even less when I plopped into a chair without being asked.

He stirred his coffee and loosened his tie and rearranged the papers on his desk, debating what to do with me. "You must want a car real bad," he began with a humorless chuckle. "If I told you I could put you in that convertible out front for nineteen even, would you do it?"

I smiled. "No."

"Tough bargainer, huh?"

"I don't bargain. I name a price; you say yes or no. If it's yes, I write a check. If it's no, I take a hike."

A drop of sweat leaked down his temple. "That's not the way we do business."

"That's not the way I hear it."

He scratched his nose. "From who?"

"Let's just say I'm a close personal friend of a close personal friend of a former member of your family."

"Who the fuck are you talking about?"

"Your ex-wife."

He frowned and squirmed and sweated even more. "Seth send you out here?"

"Why would he?"

"He don't like me much."

That would have been my guess. "Why not?"

"Thinks I've still got the hots for his woman."

"Is he right?"

"Shit. I got better things to do with my dick than stick it down a dry hole." Beau's grin tried to turn lascivious, but it was more moronic than erotic. When I tried to mate him with Jane Jean, I couldn't come close.

Still discomfited, Bilbow looked at a picture on the wall, a color photograph of the intercoastal waterway with a big yacht gliding through it—I assumed it served him as a security blanket. Next to the picture was a diploma from the Palisade, which was next to a framed photo of Bilbow wearing the high-necked gray tunic and white dress hat of a cadet, which was next to a pair of ceremonial sabers crossed beneath a bright blue sash.

"So what are you," Bilbow blurted nervously, "one of her boyfriends from back in her nigger-lovin' days? Hey, it don't make no never mind to me; they crawl out of the swamp ever' other week, seems like."

Bilbow started to say something else, but LaWanda peeked in the door. "Can Bubba see you a minute, Beau? Needs you to authorize a write-down."

Bilbow glanced at me. "We done?"

"Not yet."

He started to object, then shrugged. "Be right back."

He left the office, and I looked around. The only thing of interest other than the Palisade mementos was his Rolodex. I gave it a spin, then inspected it more purposefully. Except for Jane Jean and Seth and her daddy, only one person I'd heard of was in there: There were three numbers listed for Aldo Benedetti, of the Newark Benedettis, each with a different area code.

I wrote the numbers in my notebook and was minding my business by the time Bilbow came back, far more composed than when he'd left. "Know anything about the Alliance for Southern Pride?" I asked as he sat down.

Nothing registered on his face; the shift of subject didn't faze him. "What is it, one of those old-maid societies?"

I shook my head. "Patriotic group."

He shrugged convincingly. "Never heard of 'em." He clasped his hands behind his head and smiled. "What did you say your name was?"

"Tanner."

"Did you say you wanted to buy a car?"

"No."

"Then why don't you get the fuck out of here?"

I couldn't come up with a reason.

TWENTY-TWO

On the way back to Seth's office, I drove by his son's apartment and tried again to connect with him, but no one answered my knock and no one emerged to challenge me the way Furman had during my first visit. When I looked through the window to make sure there were still signs of life in the place, the only thing I saw that was different from my first visit was a weapon leaning against the wall beneath the Nazi flag, surrounded by a nest of ammunition clips. It looked like a MAC-10 or similar engine of rapid-fire destruction, which meant it looked at once terrifying and childish.

On my way to the car, I checked the directory for Forrest Bedford's name but didn't find a listing. What I found five minutes later was a booth with a phone book in it at a gas station on Calhoun, but when I looked for Bedford in the listings, I came up with the same result. Empty all around, I parked the Thunderbird in the lot from which I'd claimed it and took the key back to the office.

Elmira was precisely as glad to see me as she had been three hours earlier. "He in?" I asked her.

She glanced at her console. "Phone."

"I'd like to see him when he's free."

She consulted her book. "He's got a client coming in at noon."

Everyone in Charleston except me was booked to capacity. "I'll be brief," I promised.

I started to repair to the waiting room but fired a shot in the dark instead. "You don't happen to know Seth's son, do you?"

"Colin?" For the first time ever, the smile fell off her face. "Sure, I know him. Or used to. We were in the same class at Bishop England. He took me to the summer formal." I thought she suppressed a shudder. "He totally trashed my dress; Mama could have killed him."

"What's this England place?"

"A school."

"Private?"

"Yes."

"Rich kids?"

She stiffened. "It's not like up North—lots of kids go to private schools down here, even black kids. Bishop England has all *kinds* of people on scholarship."

"When's the last time you saw Colin?"

She shrugged. "Months. I talk to him once in a while. On the phone, I mean."

"What about?"

"His daddy. How his cases are coming along, things like that. I *think* Colin wants to be a lawyer. Fat chance," she added meanly.

"Any idea where I can reach him?"

"He used to live over by the college."

"I tried there; he's not home very often. Active social life, I guess."

Her laugh was as purely cruel as only attractive young women can be. "Colin? Social life? Excuse me."

"Do you know a friend of his named Bedford?"

Elmira shook her head. "The only friend I ever heard he had was Broom. Maybe he's at her place."

"Broom what?"

"Broom's all I ever heard anybody call her." Her smile was smug. "Maybe because she was such a witch."

"Where's Broom live?"

"A slum north of Calhoun with a bunch of other punker trash." Elmira wriggled her fingers fastidiously, as if to be rid of the recollection.

"What's Broom do? Is she a student?"

She shook her head. "Tends bar at a place called the Pustule; it's up by the bridge. Guys like to go there to hear her talk dirty."

"Tell me some more about Colin."

Elmira waited till she had something to say. "When I first knew him, which was when we were about twelve, Colin was real popular. Dressed real nice, had *real* nice manners; just like his daddy, you know? But something happened, when we were in tenth grade or thereabouts, and Colin turned upside down—dressed like street trash, swore like a trucker, came on like a *cannibal* with girls. Seemed like he was working real hard at being everything his daddy wasn't; got good at it, too."

"What do you think caused the change?"

She shrugged. "Lots of kids get weird in those years. My friend Sissy lived in the garage for six months."

"Do you think Colin's problem had something to do with being Jewish?"

Elmira was surprised. "Is he? I never knew. I don't think anyone else did, either."

"How about the black kids in school? Did Colin have trouble with them?"

"You mean anything special? Not that I know of. Things got tense every once in a while, but nothing ever happened. Usually."

"Was Colin politically active?"

"Only if metal heads are political."

"Is he violent, would you say? Did he ever get in that kind of trouble?"

Her eyes grew cool and angry. "The *main* trouble he had was keeping his hands where they belonged."

I took a stab. "Are you talking rape?"

Her nose twitched. "Nothing *that* bad. More like coming on too strong and not behaving himself when he was told to. When word got around about his manners, no one would talk to him anymore; no one that mattered, at least. He's *real* angry at something, I know that. And he feels *real* sorry for himself. Colin's a loser, is what it comes down to. No one likes him except Broom. Why I went to the ball with him I'll never know—kids still buzz me about it."

A light on her console lit up. Elmira returned to her business while I went to the waiting room and thumbed through an issue of *Southern Life*. When Seth emerged from his office, his mood was edgy and distracted.

"Come on in," he said stiffly. "But I've only got a minute."

I followed him into his lair and waited while he closed the door. "Have you found him?" he asked on his way to his chair.

"Colin?" I shook my head. "I know where he lives, but no one's been home when I've gone by. But I've made progress."

"What?"

"I managed to talk to the Field Marshal."

Seth's breath quickened. "Who is it?"

"The guy Last told me about: Forrest Bedford. It's likely he's the one you spoke to on the phone. I'm meeting him tonight."

"Where?"

"Hampton Park."

"Why there?"

"ASP is staging some kind of protest out there at six. I'm meeting Bedford afterward."

"I suppose Colin will be there."

"Probably."

Seth placed a hand over his eyes, as if the facts that chilled his mind would melt if he did so. "Can I come along?" he asked.

"Why?"

"I need to understand this, Marsh. I need to know why Colin's doing what he's doing. Maybe if I know what ASP is preaching, I can come up with a way to counter them before it gets out of hand."

As far as I was concerned, it was already out of hand, and Seth's presence would only be counterproductive. "I doubt Bedford knows or cares about your son's inner motivations, Seth. And I don't think it's a good idea for you to get more involved than you are—the only way to get anything out of Bedford is if I'm undercover."

"I can't sit back and do *nothing*."

The expression on Seth's face, coupled with the memory of Alameda Smallings sitting stoically beside me while she endured the slur of the day before, caused me to change my tune.

"Bedford and I are meeting at the entrance to the ballpark out there," I told him. "He's probably going to take me somewhere else before we get down to business—he's paranoid about security. Maybe you could lurk around the park and tail us wherever we go in case Bedford sees through my act and decides to rough me up."

Seth tried for a joke. "I hope you're not trying to pass yourself off as a redneck, Tanner—you don't have the tan for it."

"I'm a white Christian patriot off the plane from Denver. What I want Bedford to think is that if he passes muster, I'm going to pony up ten grand to help him save the race."

Seth shook his head. "This is starting to get spooky, pal."

"It's been spooky for two hundred years," I said, then amended my scenario. "Maybe I'd better find my backup somewhere else. I saw an automatic weapon at Colin's place. Things could get nasty if Bedford gets upset."

Seth slammed a palm on his desk so hard the windows rattled. "This is *my* problem, remember? You're not some mercenary I scraped out of the Yellow Pages, for Christ's sake; you're my *friend*. If there's danger in this, I want to be there."

"You don't need to. Really."

Seth stood and began to pace, then looked at me till I squirmed. "That time junior year? When we got caught swiping food from the kitchen and you got suspended and I didn't?"

"What about it?"

"The reason I stayed in school was because I ratted you out. Someone saw us coming out the window. They knew me, but they didn't recognize you. They went to the dean, and he put heat on me to squeal. I gave you up so I could pitch against St. John's that weekend."

Seth reviewed what he'd said, then edited it. "I wanted to save my ass because I was afraid I'd get kicked out of school and my future would be ruined. I wouldn't get into law school; I wouldn't get a decent job. Plus I was afraid I'd end up in Vietnam."

"That's kid stuff, Hartman. It didn't matter then, and it doesn't matter now. I enjoyed the vacation."

"Of course it mattered—you might have gotten a tryout with the Twins if you hadn't missed those games."

"So you saved me from life in the minor leagues. Big deal."

"It was lousy, Marsh. The lousiest thing I ever did, except maybe my divorce. If I go out there with you tonight, maybe it'll make up for it a little." Seth looked at the law books that crawled across his walls, the ones that defined what we mean by justice. "I never was the person you thought I was, you know."

"Sure you were," I told him. "You were just too modest to believe it."

We shared uneasy silence as we examined the fault lines in our memories. "Something else happened," Seth said finally, his voice tight in the hush of the room.

"What?"

"Another client heard from the Field Marshal."

"Tape recording?"

He shook his head. "Phone call."

"Saying what?"

Seth consulted some notes. "That I was an enemy of the South and an agent of alien interests. If he didn't sever his personal and professional relationships with me, and plead guilty to the crimes he'd committed, he'd be exposed and destroyed."

"Who's the client?"

"Monroe Morrison. A state legislator indicted in the bribery sting. The one who's running for Congress."

"What was his reaction to the call?"

"Fear, I imagine. People ignore the race police at their peril down here."

"Is he bailing out on you?"

"He's on the fence. Hasn't quit me yet, but he's wavering."

"Is he a full-time politician?"

Seth shook his head. "Owns a funeral parlor up on Rutledge Avenue."

"Is he black?"

"Yes."

"I suppose it would hurt your reputation, to have him jump ship."

"Sure it would. He's a respected leader in this town, by both blacks *and* whites; if he discharged me, it would make waves. Plus the reason would eventually come out— ASP and the rest of it; most likely Colin's involvement, too. I *think* I can convince him to stick with me. He's a client, but he's a friend, too. He's the first black man I met when I came south in the sixties."

"What was he doing?"

"He was field secretary for SNCC. Ran the registration drive in South Carolina."

"Does Morrison have political enemies?"

"All politicians have enemies."

"Are any of them White Christian Patriots?"

"That goes without saying, doesn't it? Black competence at *any* level undercuts the concept of white supremacy."

"What I mean is, if he goes to jail or pleads guilty to a felony, someone else would get the nomination."

Seth shook his head. "I know what you're getting at, but the district Monroe represents in Columbia and the one he's running in for Congress are both predominately black, thanks to recent redistricting. If you're wondering who might stand to profit politically if Monroe goes to jail, it will almost certainly be another African-American. I doubt that ASP would be doing them any favors."

The political angle was the only lead I had, so I was reluctant to let it go. "Who's Morrison's main political adversary?"

"A man named Aldee Blackwell."

"Where can I find him?"

"The Panther Bar on Upper King Street. Aldee holds forth from ten to three every night." Seth paused. "I don't recommend you go up there alone."

"Does Blackwell have political ambitions?"

"Aldee fancies himself a kingmaker. Tries to handpick

every black politician in the Low Country, so they'll owe
their jobs to him and be appropriately grateful when the time
comes. He's as determined as ASP and about as ruthless.
Rumor has it he killed a man once—a business partner he
thought was stealing from him—but he never got charged.''

I had more questions, but a buzzer buzzed on the desk
in front of me. Seth twitched at the sound as though it were
a gunshot, suggesting the state of his nerves.

"Sorry, Marsh," he said. "There's someone I've got to
see. Is there anything else you need?"

"Just to borrow the car about five. Can you hunt up
another one for yourself?"

"I'll borrow Jane Jean's. What time's your meeting
with Bedford?"

"Eight."

"I'll be there. Do we need a signal or something? So
I'll know when to move in?"

"The signal is when they start shooting."

TWENTY-THREE

Seth hurried to lunch with his client, apologizing again for deserting me. Uncertain of my next step, I wandered to East Bay Street and browsed some bookstores. While I was waiting to pay for my purchases, I eavesdropped on a conversation between the proprietor and one of his customers concerning the Battle of Sharpsburg. Their description of the carnage couldn't have been more vivid had the men been wounded there themselves.

When I could get a word in edgewise, I asked the proprietor if he had any materials from the Alliance for Southern Pride. When he shook his head without a glitch of recognition, it didn't surprise me.

By the time I'd consumed a salami sandwich and a lemonade at Subway, I was pretty much exhausted. The heat, the humidity, the energetic night with Scar—the combination had rendered me sapped and sluggish. My ideas as depleted as my energies, I trudged my way toward the Home.

Halfway down the cobblestone street that traveled to the rear of my digs, I sensed I was being watched. I slowed to a stroll, loitered to look in the window of a law office that inhabited what looked like a dungeon, then whirled around in hope of taking my nemesis by surprise. The only movement I detected came from the parking lot across the street—

a young man ducked behind a car just before I got a good look at him.

The lot belonged to a bank; the cars belonged to its customers. As I watched from across the street, a woman came out of the bank and got in the car next to the place I'd last seen the boy who seemed to be tailing me.

The car drove off. The young man crouched behind it as long as he could, then took off running toward the door at the rear of the bank, the only means of escape that didn't bring him closer to my post. Since my interest in a footrace was less than avid, I trotted after him as best I could, but not fast enough to alarm him.

When he reached the door to the bank, he dared a quick look back. Although my glimpse of him was momentary, I knew immediately who he was even though his scalp was shaved bald and his eyes were as big as biscuits. As often happens in my business, the mountain had come to Muhammad.

By the time I was through the bank and into Broad Street, Colin Hartman had disappeared. Wondering at his mission, I went back to my room, lay down after removing my shoes, and fell asleep—something in the atmosphere acted on me as a sedative.

When I woke up, I rummaged in my briefcase until I found the reunion materials, then turned to the page in the book for Gil Hayward. Gil was in import-export, his bio said. He lived on Musgrave Street in Jersey City and had a wife named June and children named Rita, Paul, and Gary. I dialed the number.

"Yeah?"

"Gil?"

"Yeah?"

"Marsh Tanner."

"Who? Oh. Tanner. How's it going?"

"Okay. How about you?"

"Glad to be out of the corn country. You, too, right? Frisco probably looks pretty good after a weekend on the farm."

"I'm not in Frisco, I'm in the Low Country."

"Holland?"

"South Carolina. With Seth."

"Oh."

"I called because I've got a question."

"Can't make it," he said quickly. "Sorry. Off to Taiwan tomorrow."

I let his assumption stand. "That's too bad. We could have had a blast."

"Yeah. Maybe next year."

"Right. Anyway, since you can't come down, I've got a second question."

"What about?"

"Aldo Benedetti."

When he spoke again, his voice was guarded and atonal. "What about him?"

"Know him?"

"Not personally."

"By reputation?"

"Sure."

"What is it?"

"What's what?"

"His reputation."

"Tough."

"How tough?"

"Tough enough to retire." Gil's chuckle was raw and clipped. "The story goes that Aldo calls the guys together in Newark—dinner at some dago joint on the water. Everyone sitting around after the cacciatore or whatever, smoking stogies and telling lies, when the waiters sweep in with dessert plates covered with those silver dome things they use when they want to be fancy. Anyway, they wait till everyone's got a plate in front of him, then pull off the tops."

"Then what?"

"The plate's got nothing on it but eyes. A pair of honest-to-God eyeballs looking up at every guy who's been giving Aldo shit about leaving the family business. Aldo goes to the door and says, "*Arrivederci, paesani.* I'll be seeing you." And walks out and keeps going. Ends up down where you are, I heard, living like a potentate. Gets no grief from anyone."

"Where'd he get the eyeballs?"

"Owned an abattoir downstate—had his people collecting them for a month and putting them on ice. And that's all I know about Aldo."

After some closing pleasantries, I hung up—it was time for the rally.

The book indicated Hampton Park was in the north end of the city. What I hadn't noticed until I was driving in that direction was that the park was right next to the Palisade. When I saw the gate was open to outsiders, I opted for a detour.

Inside the fortified enclave, a series of alabaster buildings, topped by medieval battlements, ringed a parade ground whose accoutrements included a viewing stand, some Civil War canon, and even a vintage jet. The interior courtyards of the barracks quads were tiled in squares of red and white on which a handful of students were walking tours of discipline. The cadets striding briskly across the campus in their bright white shirts and service caps were sharp and shorn and stiff and serious—Prussian to the core. Despite their surface solemnity, they seemed happy to be just that.

To an outsider like me, the place looked overly regimented and oppressively restrictive, but not necessarily sadistic. Behind the scrim of rectitude lay urges far less admirable, however, according to the school's more current critics. Still, it was as easy to see why Alameda Smallings found the martial air alluring as it was why men didn't think women belonged there.

After two turns around the campus, I left the school and drove into the broad expanse of the adjacent park, the namesake of Wade Hampton, who had managed to be both a hero of the Confederacy and an enlightened racial healer thereafter, at least according to the guidebook. If Mr. Hampton's history was apt, there wasn't a city in the country that couldn't benefit from his reincarnation.

The park was huge, a series of grassy meadows surrounded by the hulking trunks of oak trees that loomed like brutal bullies above the more delicate physiques of magnolias and azaleas. Its amenities featured fountains and reflecting pools and footbridges, even a gazebo; its fauna seemed confined to ducks and pigeons. Several groups of people were scattered throughout the area, engaged in everything from sunning to soccer, but it wasn't hard to tell where the action was—all I had to do was follow the cops.

There must have been a hundred of them deployed in the park—afoot, on horseback, on motorcycles, in paddy wagons. A police helicopter hovered overhead; a bus full of reserves was stashed behind a hedge in case the day turned nasty. The foot patrols wore visored helmets and carried riot gear, their bearing alert but not provocative. For the most part, they seemed ready for mayhem and hoping for tranquillity, but the black Jewish police chief wasn't taking any chances that ASP would start a riot.

The police presence served as a flexible gasket between the two groups that had assembled in the center of the largest meadow in the park. The smaller was made up of the foot soldiers and sympathizers of the Alliance for Southern Pride, who numbered maybe thirty and were gathered around the gazebo. A hand-lettered banner strung between two trees advertised the event as sponsored by the Purification Brigade of ASP. An equally makeshift sound system buzzed and hummed in the background, whiny proof of its inadequacy. The swastika I'd seen on the door to Colin's apartment and heard in the voice on the tapes was nowhere in evidence, proving that for all its fascist leanings, ASP was not without some savvy.

The ASP adherents were the lesser of the adversaries, however. The larger number of participants were the curious and the counterprotesters, mostly young whites and middle-aged blacks, with a smattering of bearded and braless leftists sporting the clothes and cant of yesteryear sprinkled here and there for spice. The young people seemed more entertained than angered by the occasion, the blacks more sad than outraged; the leftists were content merely to be obvious. The opposition had both the gazebo and the racialists surrounded; the police were a smear of grape jelly between the layers of that unstable cake.

Minutes after I arrived, someone started testing the sound system, and the protesters started singing "We Shall Overcome," though not all of them knew the words. Careful to be perceived as nonaligned, I wandered through the crowd.

The ASP adherents appeared to be mostly what is known as poor white trash—unlovely, uneducated, unhealthy, and conceivably unwanted by anyone but ASP. The women were either fantastically fat or reduced to skin and bone; the men were mostly brown and wiry, with narrow eyes and sullen mouths that bit down hard on cigarettes or leaked the dark brown blood of chewing tobacco. The children wearing camouflage costumes and holding tiny flags were the saddest sight of all—fanatics are best at subverting their kids.

They seemed people from the fringe of the world, lacking the tools to change their station or even understand it. Estranged from everything but their dogs and their trucks and their guns, they must have looked at the families that frolicked on TV and the politicians who courted them every four years as creatures from another planet, or even as blood enemies. Which made it ironic that their anger was directed at the only sect in the nation more outcast than themselves. The subtext was sadly obvious—as bad as their lives might be, at least they were not black.

I moved to the edge of the crowd, leery of assault from any source, including the police. After a while, I spotted Colin Hartman. He was moving through the crowd of allies, taking a collection from the hapless multitude, trying to pay the freight. The collection plate was a Nazi helmet; the pin on his shirt said THANK GOD FOR AIDS; the red letters on the black band around his upper arm read N.G.O.K. His head was shaved bald and his eyes were as bright as a beer commercial—this was as good as it got.

As I neared the gazebo on my second pass, I found myself next to the last person I expected to encounter at a racist rally. She was dressed in slacks and a blouse and was wearing sensible shoes, but her makeup and coiffure were still out of haute couture.

"Ms. Hendersen," I said.

"Mr. Tanner. What brings *you* out on such an occasion?"

"I decided to see what the Klan's been up to since *Birth of a Nation*. How about you?"

She frowned at my flippancy. "My presence is *not* out of sympathy with the cause, I assure you."

"Then what is it out of?"

Her instinct was to resist my prying, but she decided an explanation was called for. When it came, it was entirely lacking in the charm and chatter of lunchtime. "I'm a criminal lawyer, as you know." She surveyed the crowd beyond us with what seemed to be distaste. "It will probably not come as a surprise when I tell you that several of my clients are in attendance this evening. I'm here in case they need me.''

"Preventive justice. I like it.''

"Let's just say I've boned up on the elements of everything from police brutality to incitement to riot, and I'm prepared to offer assistance if called upon.''

"Smacks a bit of barratry, doesn't it?''

For the first time, she exhibited the arrogance of the effective advocate. "Not even close.''

We seemed about to get into a squabble when the sound system produced a squeak and a squeal, and a young man climbed onto the gazebo stage, grasped the microphone, manipulated it with the skill of a crooner, and prepared to begin his lecture.

He was in his middle thirties, I guessed, an emaciated ascetic in army fatigues and combat boots, his hair shorn as close to his scalp as that of the cadets I'd seen just minutes earlier. Even from a distance, his eyes were bright with the ice of true conviction. He looked like one of those guys who hang around a college campus long after their class has graduated, locked in a fit of intellectual effort that has gone beyond all bounds of sense. He wasn't as young as I'd assumed when I'd heard him threaten me on the telephone, but after he'd spoken for a few minutes I decided he might have been smarter.

"White Power!'' he screamed suddenly, to introduce himself and his message, and jolted both groups to silence.

After a moment of recuperation, half the crowd cheered and the other half jeered; the cops looked on with the impassivity that comes from leadership and training. When I looked to see the effect on Jane Jean, I discovered she was gone.

"This rally is a demonstration of the strength and solidarity of the Alliance for Southern Pride,'' he went on, his voice strained and urgent, his face contorted with the effort to make himself heard regardless of recalcitrant electronics or the dissents of his enemies.

"Our movement is for *white people only*—colored are not welcome. How do you know you're colored?" Bedford preened at his rhetoric. "It's simple. If you can't *blush,* you don't have a conscience. If you don't have a *conscience*—if you cannot show *blood in your face*—you Are. Not. White.

"Let me be clear. If you're not white, this rally is not *for* you, it is *against* you. Be on your way, mud peoples, and leave us to our business, which is to rescue the Southern Way of Life from the race traitors who seek to destroy it."

In his audience, pro and con expressions gave way to the rules of quantum physics. Human waves moved toward each other in silent surges, only to be pushed back by the police, who had lowered their face shields and raised their batons and closed ranks against their charges.

After their assault was repulsed, the protestors began to sing "America." In response, the ASP people roared, "White Power!" Onstage, the beaming interlocutor gave each group its head.

"I am Forrest Bedford," he shouted when the singing and chanting began to subside. "I am Commandant of the Purification Brigade and First Field Marshal of the Alliance for Southern Pride.

"I am *white*.

"I am *Christian*.

"I am a *patriot*.

"And I am *mad*.

"Why am I mad? Because the Great White Race is under attack from alien, godless forces who are sworn to destroy it. Who is the enemy, you ask? ASP is here to tell you:

"Your enemy is the traitorous politician who sells the white race down the river in exchange for bribes and payoffs from the investment bankers in Jew York City.

"Your enemy is the shiftless nigger who lacks the intelligence and discipline to do anything but breed out of wedlock and suck welfare money out of the pockets of hardworking white people to finance his drugs and his degeneracy.

"Your enemy is the lemon nigger from Asia who steals the white man's genius to make cars and VCRs with slope slave labor, then insults us from behind a wall of money that was built with white men's blood—maybe we should drop *another* one on them, people, this time in downtown Tokyo.

"Your enemy is the banker who crushes God-fearing white people under a usurious load of debt so he can steal your property to finance the Zionist conspiracy to destroy our race.

"Your enemy is the liberal dupe who shuts down military bases so America will lie helpless in the face of godless foreign devils while white Christian patriots are put out of work. Gorbachev is meeting with the Rothschilds *even as we speak,* people; Yeltsin is huddling with the Trilateral Commission while thousands of Russian Jews invade this country disguised as scientists and businessmen while in fact they are Zionist agents, determined to bring down our Christian nation.

"Your enemy is the race mixer, the baby killer, the liberal, the queer, the tax collector, the debt dealer, the humanist, the environmentalist, the feminist, the peacenik. Your enemy is all around you, people—the niggers want your *women,* the Jews want your *property,* the slopes want your *jobs,* the feminists want your *balls,* and the Communists want your *God.*

"How do we fight back? We fight with the sword of truth. Where do we find the truth? We find it in the Scriptures. The Bible tells us that White Power is god's *will.* God does not *want* race mixing, ladies and gentlemen; God does

not *favor* usury; God does not *support* the Communist Zionist conspiracy.

"We know God is a racialist because we read it in
Acts—'And He has made from one blood every nation of
men to dwell on the face of the earth, and has determined
their preappointed times and *the boundaries of their dwell-
ings.*'

"We know God despises the Jew York moneylender
because we read it in Deuteronomy—'thou shalt not lend
upon usury to thy brother.'

"We know He is sickened by the homosexual, because
we read it in Leviticus—'If a man also lie with mankind, as
he lieth with a woman, both of them have committed an
abomination: They shall surely be put to death; their blood
shall be upon them.'

"We know feminism is evil, because Paul tells us so in
Ephesians: 'Wives, submit yourselves unto your own husbands, as unto the Lord. For the husband is the head of the
wife, even as Christ is the head of the church.'

"*Heed the word of the Lord God Almighty.*

"What can you do to honor God's Commandments?
How can you save the Southern Way of Life? What you can
do is *join* us. Wear our colors. Shave your head in mourning
for your race. Heed the Lord's instruction in Psalm 149: 'Let
the high praises of God be in your mouth, and a two-edged
sword in your hand.'

"The Purification Brigade of the Alliance for Southern
Pride *is* the sword of the great Lord God. With God's help,
we have identified the enemies of the South, and we have
warned them of their peril. If they do not surrender, if they
persist in their evil actions, *we will destroy them*. One by
one, they will fall. Little by little, the South will rise off its
back and retake its place at the head of the bright white ranks
of the warriors of Saxon Israel, the legitimate Sons of Adam,
the *chosen servants of the Lord.*

"Rise with ASP!

"White Power!

"Rise with ASP!

"White Power!

"Rise with ASP!

"White Power!

Bedford's chant was quickly taken up by the ASP adherents, only to be drowned out by counterprotesters singing hymns. The cops remained in the middle, brows knit with worry, bodies the wall keeping the antagonists apart. If an alien had dropped to earth from Mars, he would have assumed that the finest flowering of the master race was a black Charleston policeman with a helmet on his head.

Minutes later, Bedford was losing his voice and the crowd was losing its ire. The counterprotesters began to wander off, satisfied that ASP was not going to become violent, disappointed that the rally had remained peaceful rather than erupting into something rash, which is to say something that would make the nightly news. Casting parting gestures of contempt, congratulating each other on the public proof of their morality, denouncing Bedford's bunch as trash, the outer ring of opposition returned to their cars and drove off.

The ASP supporters were past their peak as well. Bedford seemed to sense it, and his final flourish was an appeal for funds. It was an oddly pathetic request—whatever assets his flock might have possessed, money didn't seem to be among them. When Colin Hartman made another sweep nearby, his helmet was less than half full.

Bedford cast a final curse on the enemies of the South and a final paean to his race, then wrapped it up with a chorus of "Dixie." When the song had ended and the cheers had died, he stepped off the stage to the plaudits of his brethren. He seemed to take them as his due, yet be somehow disappointed.

As Bedford and his minions began to dismantle the

sound equipment, I looked for Jane Jean Hendersen in the thinning crowd. When I didn't find her, I strolled toward the site of my rendezvous with Bedford, still puzzled by her presence. She had said she was there to render legal aid. But if anything untoward had happened, she would have surely been a witness to it, which would have disqualified her from serving as counsel to a participant under the rules of legal ethics I was most familiar with.

TWENTY-FOUR

The stadium was freshly painted, the outfield was trim and lush, the banners were evocative of thrilling triumphs, and the nickname of the Charleston Rainbows frolicked in the mind. Spurred by the silent cheers of the invisible crowd and the pinstriped spirits that passed me on their way to the dugout, I drifted away from my days as a detective and back to my days as a first baseman.

Seth was right—my suspension from school for stealing might have cost me a professional career. I'd been hitting .412 when I left, a dozen home runs, a bunch of RBIs, and I could dig a throw out of the dirt with the best of them. The scouts were definitely coming, not just to see me, admittedly, but I was on their list. And then I was banished for ten days, lost my stroke and my timing, the average dropped to .276 by the end of the season, and I was just another college jock whose athletic future lay behind him. But as with all such disappointments, I wondered if it mattered.

The sound of footsteps crunching in gravel jarred me from my reverie. I turned to see the camouflaged figure of Forrest Bedford advancing on me like a drill sergeant in pursuit of a wayward troop. Swelled with righteousness, stoked by the adulation of his peers, wired by the contretemps he'd provoked, Bedford could have lit the Rainbows' next night game with his eyes, and his stride could have carried him through a revetment.

There was a scar on the point of his chin that suggested at least one object of his wrath might have taken exception. His skin suggested he lived below ground. His walk was stiff and ungainly, although the rolling shoulders and the elbows angled at his sides were an obvious attempt at swagger: Unlike the cadets at the Palisade, he wasn't a congenital Prussian.

He seemed less glad to see me than he should have been, given my imminent largess, so I tried to be ingratiating. "Ever play ball, Mr. Bedford?" I asked, glancing at the stadium at my back.

Bedford would have none of it. "I haven't played games since I read *None Dare Call It Conspiracy* when I was fifteen. Were you at the rally?"

I occupied my role before I nodded. "I'm afraid your rhetoric was more impressive than your audience."

"Not as big as Denver?"

"Not nearly."

"We'll get there."

"I'm sure you will; you've got a way with words, Mr. Bedford."

"I'm just an instrument of God's will, Mr. Tanner."

As we eyed each other in the setting sun, we made a mutual decision to cut to the chase. "You didn't beat up on black people as much as I expected," I said.

"It's time for the South to face facts—niggers aren't the problem. They never were. It's true they're descended from Devil mutants—that's laid out in Enoch, as I imagine you know—and they can no more govern their baser impulses than they can build a rocket. Can you imagine Nigeria with a *space* program? Lord help us. It's the *Canaanites* that are destroying white America. *All* the pre-Adamics must be stopped."

I was fascinated with Bedford's sophistry. "Who's Enoch?" I asked him.

His look was designed to dispatch me to agnostic purgatory. "I was afraid you might not know it; you don't impress me as a religious man."

"Let's just say I draw my inspiration from more discernible sources."

Bedford chose not to probe my frame of reference, probably for fear it would create a moral dilemma: Despite the evidence of the past few years, God may not line up on the side of avarice.

"Enoch is one of the Scriptures suppressed by the Jews at the Council of Nicea," he recited, "when the text of the Bible was established. The books of the so-called Apocrypha—particularly Enoch, Esdras, and Abraham—are where the mission of the Alliance for Southern Pride is grounded. It is there that God's plan of racial separation is most fully suggested, where His blessing on white America is most fully revealed."

Pleased to possess a truth I wasn't privy to, Bedford plunged ahead. "But you don't have to consult the Apocrypha to know God's intentions. Read Deuteronomy. Read Daniel. Read John eight, where Jesus confirms the Canaanites are Devil-born: 'Ye are of your father the Devil,' he says of them. Those are His words, Mr. Tanner. It's pointless to deny them."

I met his message with one of my own. "I'm less interested in words than deeds, Mr. Bedford."

Bedford's look turned crafty. "You should not confuse the Alliance with less sophisticated movements, Mr. Tanner. We are not a hate group. We're not like the skinheads and the original Klan, terrorizing people out of fear and envy because we have no resources to sustain us other than our race. ASP is grounded in *knowledge,* not fear."

"Knowledge of what?"

"Of the Holy Scripture, of course. It is God's *will* that America remain the castle of the white man. But the Devil is too much with us, and God's plan is under siege. ASP is the last defense against the Protocols."

"The what?"

"*The Protocols of the Learned Elders of Zion.* Every white American should know of it."

"What is it?"

Bedford thrust his chest against an invisible assault. "The blueprint for Canaanite domination of the world, the conspiracy that has dogged the Great White Race for a hundred years."

The words were as melodramatic as the blaze in his eyes and the bulge of his jaw. "Tell me about it," I said, though not without reluctance.

Bedford was as primed as the Avon lady. "The Protocols were laid down in 1897 by the combined Canaanite forces of the Jewish High Council, the Sanhedrin, and the Masonic Order. Each protocol is a distinct element of the conspiracy to deliver the world and its riches into alien hands."

"Like what?"

Bedford ticked them off as easily as I used to recite the scouting oath. "Agitation for civil rights for minorities in order to undermine the power of the white majority; creation of corporate monopolies to put economic power in the Devil's hands; Canaanite control of the media; distraction and sedation of the white population with sports and other amusements so it won't be cognizant of its decline; forbidding Creation science and Christian racial history to be taught in the schools; stealing white wealth by means of illegal income taxes and usurious Federal Reserve rates."

He paused to catch his breath and to be sure I was on the same page. "They've been at it for a century—even Hitler couldn't slow them down. I'm sure you know enough about the history of white America to realize they're succeeding." Bedford's voice dropped to a manic rasp. "Some say it's too late; that the Protocols have been too long in place; that Satan will surely triumph. But God will *never* surrender to the slayers of His Son. We at ASP will die to stop them."

"What's this pre-Adamic business you referred to?"

His sneer condemned my ignorance. "Read Genesis, Mr. Tanner; read it carefully. In Chapter One, God creates a male and female in His image. In Chapter Two, He creates Adam and Eve. God created *two* races, not just one."

"Even if you're right, what difference does it make?"

"It's a matter of genetics. The Bible says that Satan raped Eve and she delivered Cain. Cain then mated with the children of the pre-Adamic couple and begat the lineage of Canaanites—Jews and niggers and slopes—the mud peoples. The sons and daughters of Lucifer, Mr. Tanner—*Homo bestialis.*"

"What happened to Adam?"

"After she was raped by Satan, Eve introduced Adam to sex. Adam and Eve produced Abel, and Abel sired the Israelites, the wellspring of the Great White Race."

"I thought the Israelites were Semitic."

Bedford shook his head. "That's a key part of the conspiracy, of course—to persuade the world that *Jews* are God's chosen people. But the *true* course of racial history is set forth in Esdras II, which describes the journey of the lost tribes of Israel across the Caucasus into Northern Europe. The Israelites became *Caucasians*, Mr. Tanner; it's absolute historic fact. The tribe of Ephraim became Great Britain, the tribe of Judah became Germany, and so on. You and I are their descendants—the Anglo-Saxon Nordic and kindred peoples are God's true chosen people, the warriors of Saxon Israel."

"That's good to know," I said, and hoped it didn't register as sarcasm.

But Bedford was on a roll. " 'Adam' means 'to show blood in the face; to be made red.' The white race is the only race that blushes, Mr. Tanner. Adam is our father, and America is the one true home of the thirteen tribes of Israel. Look around you, Mr. Tanner. *This* is the *Holy Land*."

"How do you know it's not Japan? Or Germany? Or Pago Pago, for that matter?"

"It's not Japan or Pago Pago because they're not Caucasians and do not descend from Israelites. It's not Germany because of the signs."

"What signs?"

Bedford answered in the incessant drone of cant. "You may remember from the Old Testament that God made a series of promises to the Israelites, gifts he would confer as long as they upheld the covenant. If we examine recent history, we see that *every one* of these promises has been fulfilled, not for Israel or Germany or Japan or Pago Pago, but for the United States of America."

"Give me an example."

Bedford shook his head. "There are at least a hundred promises; we don't have time to go into it."

"Just a couple."

He shrugged. "It was promised that Israel would become blind to its true identity; that it would change its name; that it would have colonies throughout the world; that it would become the greatest military power on earth. It's clear that while *other* nations may have realized *some* of the promises, only *this* nation has fulfilled them *all*."

I was weary of ersatz theology, so I tried to provoke Bedford onto a subject that might be more revealing. "It seems pretty abstract to me. I like my politics grounded in something more productive than rhetoric."

His smile was Olympian in its condescension. "The

proofs are there for anyone who cares to look for them. You know, of course, that there were thirteen original tribes in Israel and thirteen original colonies in America.''

"That's a bit of a reach, isn't it?''

"Then consider the design of the great seal.''

"What about it?''

"The words 'American Eagle' have thirteen letters. So does 'E Pluribus Unum.' The olive branch the eagle carries has thirteen leaves; in its other claw it clutches thirteen arrows. There are thirteen stripes in the ensign on its breast, and the crest over its head bears thirteen stars. The pyramid on the reverse side of the seal has thirteen courses of stone.''

Bedford grew agitated by my incredulity. "Do you regard this as coincidence? Serendipity? Superstition? Then maybe you can tell me why 'July the Fourth' contains thirteen letters also. Or why the Confederate flag bears thirteen stars even though there were only eleven states in the Confederacy. Fort Sumter was fired upon on the thirteenth day, Mr. Tanner. Open your eyes to the evidence.''

As Bedford paused for breath, I tried to think of a way to steer him in another direction, one that might lead to his leader. But before I could come up with a gambit, he was at it again.

"I see you need more. Then consider the Great War, the single event that more than any other established American supremacy in the world, once and for all time.''

"This is World War One you're talking about?''

"Of course.''

"What about it?''

"The expeditionary force sent to save the world for democracy sailed in thirteen ships, took thirteen days to get there, and fought its first major engagement on Friday the thirteenth. Its commander, General John J. Pershing, had thirteen letters in his name. Surely even you can see that this is not chaos, Mr. Tanner; this is God's will working through His people."

I waited until his attentions were on me and not in thrall to his doctrine, then made an effort to provoke him into an indiscretion. "You sound like you *believe* that shit," I said blandly.

Bedford blinked. "I do."

"Then I think we've got a problem."

"Why?"

"In my experience, fanatics would rather talk than fight. They're too concerned with indoctrination and not enough with agitation. They fail to follow the program because they're too busy ranting and raving to organize for action. I've got neither the time nor the money to waste on lost causes, Mr. Bedford. Even if they *are* God's will."

Bedford struggled to keep his cool. "I assure you, our cause is not lost. Quite the contrary. Now. May I have the funds that we discussed?"

I put my hands in my pockets. "Not yet."

"Why not?"

"This religious stuff disturbs me. It suggests a certain naïveté that isn't conducive to political action."

"I assure you, you're mistaken."

"That may be. But before I write a check, I need to know more about your group and the way it functions. I need to be assured that there is someone in authority who knows something about operational effectiveness."

His reason retrieved from his rhetoric, Bedford crossed his arms and looked away. "We never discuss tactics outside the brigade."

"If I'm going to fund an operation, I have the right to know what it involves. Are you going to proceed in the open or undercover? How many soldiers are in your brigade? Who's been funding you to this point, and at what levels?

Do you include wet work in your plan—are people going to die? If so, who?''

Bedford shook his head. ''We don't reveal the names of contributors. I'm sure you applaud our stance, since you're interested in anonymity as well.''

''I'd still like to know what kind of people I'm associating with.''

''White Christian patriots like yourself.''

''That's as vague as the rest of your doctrine.''

''There's nothing vague when ASP decides to act,'' Bedford proclaimed stubbornly, his former glow now a sullen and suggestive gloom.

''Give me an example of your tactical successes.''

Bedford shook his head. ''I can't compromise security.''

''Presumably you've got some *new* operation in mind. Tell me about that.''

''As I said, we don't discuss tactics outside the Brigade.''

''I was impressed with your speech, Mr. Bedford—you know your racial history. But I won't buy a pig in a poke. Plus, I doubt very much that you're the engineer of all this. No offense, but you're just the Field Marshal. I need to see the General.''

''There is none.''

I shook my head. ''I don't buy it. Someone's pulling the strings and writing the script. Who is he, Bedford? I want to meet him before I hand over ten thousand of my hard-earned dollars.''

Bedford crossed his arms. ''Or?''

''I send my ten grand to Denver.''

Something made Bedford look back at the park. I followed his gaze, hoping I wouldn't see Seth Hartman skulking behind a bush, ready to ride to the rescue if I needed it. But all I saw was the van in which the troops had put the sound system after the rally had ground to a halt. Done up in the same smear of camouflage colors that Bedford wore on his person, the ASP name printed in red letters on its side, the van was moving toward us with the speed and grace of a Sherman tank.

"We need to take a ride," Bedford said stiffly.

I shook my head. "Tell your boss to get in touch with me tomorrow. I don't do business after dark."

Bedford reached in his fatigues and pulled out a Walther P-38 and aimed it at my chest. "That's too bad," he said. "Because I'm beginning to wonder exactly what your business is."

TWENTY-FIVE

The van made a U-turn in the parking lot and came to a stop with its rear doors facing us. Still brandishing his Walther, Bedford motioned for me to climb in the rear. I asked him where we were going.

"Somewhere private," he said.

I looked toward the now-deserted park. "This looks pretty private to me."

"A guy with a directional mike half a mile from here could be taping every word I say."

"Why the paranoia, Mr. Bedford?"

Bedford's eyes were squeezed behind translucent lids. "Those who tell the truth about the race traitors in the Zionist Occupation Government make enemies in high places. ASP isn't going to end up like the Klan, infiltrated by legions of ZOG operatives because we didn't screen our membership closely enough."

"So you think I'm a federal agent."

"Aren't you?" Bedford's smile was sly.

"No."

"That may be, but you're not a Christian patriot, either. I don't know *what* you are. But I'm about to find out."

"You're beginning to sound like you don't want my money, Mr. Bedford."

"We haven't seen any money yet, have we? All we've seen is talk. And talk in the South has always come cheap."

Bedford gestured with his gun. I climbed in the van without a word, and Bedford slammed the door behind me. I felt more than heard him climb into the passenger side up front—the panel between me and the cab plus the rumble of the muffler underneath kept me from hearing what he said to the driver. With a pop of the clutch and a spin of the wheels, we rolled away toward somewhere private.

I tried the inside latch on the rear door, but it was locked. I made space for myself among the car tools and the sound equipment and tried not to imagine my fate. When I noticed a book in a box on the floor, I picked it up. The title was *The Biology of the Race Problem*. It was underlined and annotated, and Bedford's name was scrawled on the title page. I put it in my pocket.

We were on the road for what seemed like an hour but was probably less than half that. Enough exhaust fumes seeped up through the floorboards to make me wonder if I'd survive the experience. At one point, the metronomic thuds of the tires convinced me we were crossing a bridge; at another point, a stink in the air made me think we were going to convene on a shrimp boat; at a third point, we slid to a stop and Bedford got out of the car but returned after a few minutes and we hit the road again: probably a pit stop.

By the time I'd decided we must have been halfway to Atlanta, our journey jolted to a halt. After some fuzzy conversation up front, the cab doors opened and slammed shut. A moment later, the rear doors opened, and Bedford joined me in the van. When I tried to peek beyond him to get an idea of where we were, I couldn't see anything but night.

"Turn around," Bedford ordered, the Walther back in his hand. I did what I was told. In the next second, he slipped a rag across my eyes and cinched it as tight as he could: I was as blind as a bat. Bedford grabbed my arm and tugged me forward. I took a couple of stumbling steps, and then there wasn't anything to step on—I fell out of the van and onto the ground, Bedford laughing as I landed.

My shoulder throbbed and my knee ached as I scrambled to my feet and waited for instructions. With a tug and a nudge, Bedford led me across an asphalt street, then onto a patch of lawn, then over a slab of concrete. At least that's what it felt like through my shoes—I couldn't see a thing.

After crossing the concrete, I was tugged to a stop, then ordered to reach out and grasp a ladder, and then to climb it. When I felt my way onto the rungs, they seemed metallic, crusted, infirm. From time to time, Bedford poked me in the back to keep me moving. All I sensed was that I was out-of-doors and near the sea. A construction site, maybe. Or a boat. Or maybe I was back in the ballpark, climbing to a seat in the press box, the prelude to a twi-night doubleheader.

When I reached the top of the ladder, I stepped off onto what felt like more concrete. I started to walk across it when Bedford grabbed my shoulder to turn me, then shoved me in a different direction. After a few more steps, I heard the grating scrape of sheet metal dragged across cement—the door to a crypt or the lid to a tin coffin. Bedford shoved me forward again, this time with the gun barrel, then stopped me after only two steps.

"This'll do right here." He turned me around, then gave me another shove. I staggered backward until I bumped into something hard enough to hurt me. I rubbed my head and cursed him. His laugh lingered in the stagnant air as if he'd brought me to a dungeon.

A car stopped somewhere nearby, then shut off its engine and waited. Nearer noises suggested there was a third person in the enclosure in addition to Bedford and myself. Given the stench of the place, I guessed I was somewhere used less for habitation than machination, but I wasn't sure of any of it.

"What's going on, Bedford?" I asked when I'd learned all I could by being quiet. "Why the rough stuff?"

"One of my lieutenants has doubts about your bona fides," Bedford answered affably.

"Who?"

"Names don't matter. It's enough for you to know that he's a trusted soldier in the brigade." In contrast to his hectoring back at the park, Bedford's voice had become confident and modulated. Something or someone had changed the script, and quite likely blown my cover.

I started to sweat; there didn't seem to be enough air in the room for my lungs to work with. "What's the deal?" I asked. "You guys don't need money all of a sudden?"

"My lieutenant will discuss it with you. Just to show I'm not prejudiced one way or another, I'm going to leave you two alone. When he's completed the interrogation, you'll either be assassinated or your contribution will be accepted as a generous gift to ASP."

A whispered colloquy somewhere in front of me was followed by the scrape of boots across concrete and footfalls descending a staircase—Bedford had taken his leave.

As with many perils in which I've found myself, my only option was to wait and hope. The main thing I was hoping was that the car I'd heard stop somewhere near the van belonged to Seth Hartman and that he was poised to be my savior should the need for one arise. But in the next instant the hope was dashed. A car door slammed, an engine fired, and a vehicle roared off—Bedford and an aide were making tracks.

I raised a hand to scratch my nose.

"Don't move," a wobbly voice commanded, its forced audacity familiar from the tapes.

"I've got an itch."

"I don't care what you've got. Keep still or I'll dust you."

"What's your problem, pal?"

"My problem is you. For one thing, who are you?"

"The name is Tanner."

"Prove it."

"I can't prove it without moving."

He thought it over. "Okay. But nothing funny."

I fished out my wallet and held it out for him, not the folder with my P.I. license in it, just the wallet. It occurred to me belatedly that the purpose of the entire exercise might simply be to rob me.

I kept my hand in midair after the lieutenant plucked the wallet from it, and a moment later he returned it. It seemed as heavy as when it left, but money doesn't weigh much.

"You're supposed to be from Denver," the voice complained in a liquid whine.

"I am."

"That says San Francisco."

"I've found it's not prudent to carry accurate I.D."

"What do you do?"

"For a living?"

"Yeah."

"I'm an investor."

"In what?"

"In white America."

He hesitated. "Bedford thinks you're a cop."

"What's his problem? I don't have the right accent or something?"

My foe was getting agitated. "*We* don't have a problem. *You've* got a problem."

"Other than that I can't see anything and I'm talking to a nitwit, I wouldn't know what it is."

"I'll show you who's a nitwit." He jabbed me in the stomach with what felt like a fist.

I bent over, fighting for breath and warring with bile.

When I managed to straighten up, it was to confront a heart-felt accusation.

"I already know you're a spy," the voice announced with fresh assurance. "You work for the race traitor Seth Hartman."

Since I couldn't see a way out of my predicament in the direction we were going, I exchanged some subterfuge for truth. "I admit it—Seth is my friend. But he's your friend, too."

His voice rose on a thermal of panic. "I don't know what you're talking about."

"I'm talking about you and your daddy. This is ridiculous, Colin. We both know you're not a killer. I'm going to take this blindfold off so we can discuss it like gentlemen."

His answer was the rattle of a weapon. "I'll waste you if you do."

"No, you won't; you can't afford to kill me yet."

"Why not?"

It was like giving instructions in grave-digging. "You might kiss ten thousand bucks good-bye, and the Field Marshal wouldn't like that."

Before he could fashion a rebuttal, I reached for my blindfold and slipped it off and blinked at the skittish eyes of Colin Hartman. That this tonsured soldier in baggy fatigues and clown-sized boots was the offspring of the debonair Seth Hartman was a jarring disconnect to contemplate. It must have been even more jarring for Colin to have to live with it.

In removing the blindfold, I'd taken the initiative, and Colin didn't know what to do about it. I took advantage of his uncertainty to try to figure out where we were.

It seemed to be some kind of abandoned storage structure—the walls were smeared with graffiti; the floor and low ceiling were slabs of rough cement that were fouled with trash and cobwebs. There was a narrow door at one end of the room, but no windows in the walls except for a slit at my back. For some reason, I had a feeling I'd been there before, though that was clearly impossible.

Suddenly I knew what it was. I was inside a bunker, built of reinforced concrete, embedded in earthenworks on its sides, its orientation toward the sea, its function to repel invasion, like others I had seen in places that felt vulnerable to offshore enemies, such as the Presidio in San Francisco and Fort Worden near Seattle, which possessed installations that could be carbon copies. I paid brief homage to the Field Marshal—it was a good place for conversation and even better for assassination.

While I was piecing that together, Colin Hartman shuffled nervously in the shadows cast by the modicum of light from a distant street lamp that managed to find us through the narrow door. His hands fiddled inexpertly with the semiautomatic pistol I'd seen leaning against the wall of his apartment; it occurred to me that my most likely fate was that Colin would shoot me by accident.

As I moved to where I could see his face, he trained his weapon on my chest. In the dregs of light in the bunker, Colin looked even younger than he was, a bald boy-man with festering flesh, a petulant pout, and the hangdog slump of the outcast. If the father was a man who had never been ill at ease, the son was a child who had never felt comfortable with his life and had surrendered his fate to others.

I gestured at his armband. "What's N.G.O.K?"

"New Generation of Klan. Why are you lying to us?" he continued quickly. "Why were you at Seth's office? Did he send you to kidnap me or something?"

"It seems to me that you and Bedford are the ones doing the kidnapping, Colin."

"We're just defending ourselves," he objected thinly. "From traitors like my dad."

"Your father isn't a traitor; he's worried you're going to get into trouble."

Colin's lips lifted in a pout. "It's a free country; I can say what I want."

"Sure you can. But I'm confused about some things. Maybe you can straighten me out."

I leaned against the wall at my back and watched a spider make room for me. "One thing I was wondering was why an organization like ASP would put a man at the top of its list of enemies, then put his son in a position of power. And then I was wondering why a group that thinks Jews are destroying the world would let a Jewish kid carry their colors."

Colin's eyes grew wide as poker chips as his face gorged with protest. "Are you trying to say I'm a Jew? Because I'm not. It goes through the mother. My dad's a Jew because his mother was, but *my* mother wasn't, which means *I'm not*. It's the way they do it. You can look it up."

I diminished his rebuttal by ignoring it. "I was also wondering if ASP might not be using the young man for something other than a foot soldier."

"Like what?"

"A fall guy."

"What's that supposed to mean?"

"ASP says your dad is an enemy of the South."

"Right. 'Cause he is."

"They've named Seth the enemy, and they've threatened to execute him if he doesn't leave town."

Colin's chest swelled in a defiant strut. "We'll do it, too."

"Let's say your dad is found dead. Because of what's gone down in the past—the tapes and the notice of judgment—the cops will go straight to ASP. Could be trouble for the patriots, unless of course the cops have a reason to suspect someone else, someone like Seth's *son*. They'd buy it, since the son and the father don't get along and everyone knows it, plus I'm sure ASP has collected some physical evidence to plant to point the police in the right direction, including proof that you killed *me* this evening. When ASP gives you up on a murder charge, it gets itself off the hook."

Colin's shell of confidence was eroding beneath an acid bath of fear. "They wouldn't do that."

"How do you know?"

He licked his lips. "Besides, nothing will happen to Dad if he does what they want."

"Which is?"

"Quit helping the race traitors. He's been helping them all his *life,* and he's got to stop." Colin's voice rose to an oily screech. "Guys like me don't have a chance anymore— we're nothing, we're a joke. Niggers get paid for taking drugs and having kids, while guys like me can't even get a decent *job.* White people *built* this country, and it's been stolen by the mud people. The banks, the media, the federal bureaucracy, they're all run by slopes and Jews; they're totally against white people."

"You're being used, Colin. ASP isn't a bunch of Christian patriots; ASP is a hit squad put together to target your father. The question is, why are they after him?"

Colin was sullen and subdued. "Because he's a race traitor, like I told you."

"I don't think it has anything to *do* with race. I think you and Bedford are *both* pawns in this thing."

Colin thrust out his chin and his weapon. "The fuck we are. We're white Christian Americans who aren't going to take Zionist *shit* anymore."

"You're two unhappy young men who are being used to destroy a fine man's life. What I can't figure out is why. Who's behind it, Colin? Give me a name. Let me find out whether ASP is on the up-and-up or whether you're being set up for a frame."

Briefly evangelical, Colin's expression lapsed to a stricken grimace.

"What's the matter?" I asked him.

"Nothing."

"Come on, Colin. What is it?"

"I'm supposed to do something with you. I'm supposed to decide you're all right and make you give me money. Either that or kill you."

"How are you supposed to decide?"

"You're supposed to do something to prove you're a patriot."

"Like what?"

He hesitated, then spit it out like a bite of bad food. "You're supposed to paint a swastika on the door to my father's office."

"When?"

"Tonight. There's paint and stuff in the truck. If you refuse, I'm supposed to kill you. I'm supposed to skin you alive. They took me out in the woods and taught me how. They made me practice on a dog." The phrase was a tremolo of anguish.

I shook my head. "Walk away from it, Colin."

In response to my plea, Colin brandished his MAC-10. It rattled in the concrete cave like the crack of breaking bones. "I can't," he said miserably. "ASP is the only thing I have. ASP is all I am."

In the echo of Colin's anguished essay, I made a final pitch. "What about Broom? What would *she* say if she found out you killed me?"

"She'd be pissed I didn't let her watch."

TWENTY-SIX

Colin toyed with his weapon absently, gazing into the depths of the bunker as though salvation could be found by deciphering the obscene graffiti, which featured pornographic paeans to people named Stephanie and Bryan and a more reverent nod to Mötley Crüe. It couldn't have been more tense had U-boats just been spotted off the coast.

"I'll do it," I said suddenly.

"What?"

"I'll paint the swastika on Seth's office. To prove to Bedford I'm who I say I am. That's the only way we can find out whether ASP is for real or a tool of some conspiracy to destroy your father."

Colin shook his head. "You're stalling. You'll jump me the minute I put down my gun." He squinted at me. "Anyway, I *already* know what ASP is, just like I already know who *you* are."

"Who?"

"The one in the yearbooks. My sister and I used to look at them all the time. Every picture of Dad—what he was doing, what he was wearing, who he was with. There were two pictures of him in the freshman book and seventeen his senior year. That's a lot, isn't it?"

I nodded. "Your dad was pretty popular."

"I'm not."

"I'm not, either. It's not that important unless you're a politician."

Colin didn't find the quip amusing. "I'm not a politician; I'm not anything."

It was time for pop psychology, so I made like Mister Rogers. "Sure you are. Plus you're young. You can be whatever you want to be."

"I don't want to be anything."

"Then you're better off than most—you've already realized your ambitions."

I smiled to show I was kidding—Colin didn't look like someone who'd been kidded very much. Teased, yes—relentlessly. But not kidded.

"I'm going to do it," he said suddenly.

"What?"

"Kill you."

"Why?"

"Bedford said to."

"You'll go to jail, Colin. For a long time. Too many people know you're here."

"Who?"

"Bedford, for one. His boss, for another."

"He doesn't have a boss."

"Sure he does. He's also got friends. One of them is Jane Jean Hendersen. I saw her at the rally—what's Bedford's relationship to her?"

"I don't know."

I fired a random shot. "She's not his mother, is she?"

Colin thought about it. "I don't think so, but I know she gives him money, so maybe she is."

I hoped Colin was wrong about Jane Jean, and I hoped he wasn't going to kill me, but I couldn't count on either. "You can't do it, Colin," I said after a moment.

"Why not?"

"I don't know what the parts of the Bible that Bedford

was quoting really mean, but I know what *one* part really means."

"What part is that?"

"The part of Deuteronomy that says 'Thou shalt not kill.' "

Colin shifted uneasily. "There are millions of exceptions to that."

"Cold-blooded murder isn't one of them."

Colin rubbed his bare skull with his free hand, rapidly and vigorously, as if things were alive in there that he needed to squash. "You know something funny about that weapon you're carrying?" I said casually.

"What?"

"It's a MAC-ten. There's a little lever up by the clip. See it? It's a double safety device. They do that when they convert to automatic firing, so unless it's turned left, the cartridges can't eject and the weapon won't fire. It might even explode."

Colin slid his trigger finger along the magazine, feeling for the nonexistent lever.

"A little farther over."

When he lowered his head to look, I grabbed the weapon and shoved the muzzle skyward as I tried to put my thumb between the trigger guard and trigger so it wouldn't move if Colin pulled it. But instead of rendering the pistol inoperable, I managed to discharge it.

The belch of gunfire was deafening in the concrete sound chamber—Colin was so startled he dropped his weapon and cupped his ears. A ricochet nipped at my shirtsleeve as it whizzed by me on the way back from the far wall; another clanged off the metal doorway.

When the caroms had ceased, I picked up the pistol and ejected the clip. The duct tape around the grip was as warm and sticky as pastry. "These things are awful," I said as I placed it on the floor behind me. "I can't believe the NRA opposes banning them, can you?"

Colin didn't look at me and didn't say anything; he just ran out of the room and straight for the edge of the bunker and jumped off without looking back, hurling himself onto the concrete pad some dozen feet below. I thought he was trying to escape until I realized he was trying to kill himself.

I got to him as fast as I could. Colin lay on his stomach in an unconscious heap, limbs disjointed and akimbo, blood seeping from his ears and nose and from a gash above his eye. My impulse was to carry him to the van and rush him to the hospital, but given the angle of his neck and the nature of his injuries, I decided I'd better not.

The only source of help seemed to be a house whose windows were bright in the night some fifty yards down the street. I glanced at Colin again. He remained a bag of rubber bones, motionless and bleeding. I headed for the nearest phone.

I was into my jog when a figure stepped from behind a bush. "What happened?" it asked me.

When my heart was back in my chest and my lungs had shrunk enough to let me speak, I identified the ghost as Seth Hartman. "Colin's been hurt," I told him.

"How?"

"He fell. Concussion. Maybe worse."

"Where are you going?"

I pointed. "Telephone. I'll be back as soon as I can."

I started to run off, but Seth put out a hand to stop me. "I've got a phone in the car. What do we need?"

"An ambulance would be good."

"A helicopter would be better. What kind of injury?"

"Head and neck, probably. Broken wrist. Possible internal injuries."

Seth ran toward a white Lincoln parked several yards from where we were. In the glow of the dome light, I watched him make the call. "The medical college has a med-evac chopper—it'll be here in fifteen minutes," he said when he returned. "The right people will be waiting when he gets there."

"It pays to be connected," I said, with what might have been a twist of jealousy.

"How about cops?" Seth asked as we started back toward the bunker.

"What about them?"

"Do they need to know about this?"

"Not as far as I'm concerned," I said.

"I've been going crazy down here," Seth went on through labored breaths. "I saw Bedford with the gun, and I wanted to rush in and rescue you, but I was afraid I'd make things worse. What was going on up there? I heard gunfire, didn't I? Colin didn't shoot you, did he?"

I'd been planning what to tell him, off and on, since he'd materialized out of the moonlight, but I still didn't have a story that made sense. So I gave him the basics, most of which he knew already since he'd had me under surveillance, and concluded by saying that when I tried to wrestle his weapon away from him, Colin had fallen off the bunker. I didn't mention murder, and I didn't mention suicide; I hoped I never would have to.

When we reached the front of the bunker, Seth bent over his son, muttering sounds of comfort and assurance, wanting to touch and cradle him but holding back when I warned him not to.

"He's so . . . pathetic," Seth said when I knelt at his side. "Those fatigues, that haircut—he looks like the guy in *Taxi Driver*. He looks like a lunatic."

"If he were a lunatic, I'd be dead."

Seth's weary face was rendered ghoulish by the sterile streetlight. "What's wrong with him, Marsh? Why is he so angry with me?"

"He's not angry at you; he's angry at himself."

"But why?"

"For not being more like his dad."

"But I don't *want* him to be like me. I want him to be *better* than me."

"Colin must have seen that as a pretty daunting task. I ought to know—I wanted to be better than you for quite a while myself."

Seth's sigh was pained and prolonged. "But I never *needed* that from him. I may have wanted it, but I didn't need it. He can be anything he wants; he can be a *bus*boy for all I care. I just want him to be happy."

"He probably thought that when he didn't turn out the way you expected, you divorced him. It's a common reaction, but most of the time they come out of it. Of course, most of the time they don't trade their families for guys like Bedford."

Seth scrubbed his face with his hand, as though to make himself as unsightly as his son. "What can I do now?"

"He may have deeper problems than an inferiority complex, but it couldn't hurt to spend enough time with him so he understands that you're not perfect and he doesn't need to be perfect, either. Hell, tell him about stealing cookies from the college kitchen and rolling over on your friend when you got caught at it. He'll love it."

Seth laughed thinly and looked down at his son once more. "Did he try to kill you, Marsh?" he asked without looking at me.

"No."

"Did you try to kill him?"

"No."

"Did you find out who's behind this ASP business?"

"Not yet."

The sound of the air ambulance split the night. Seth dug a flashlight out of his pocket and began to wave it. In re-

sponse, a light from the chopper shone down on us like proof
of a higher power.

We waited in the wind while the chopper set down in
the street. When the medics were trotting toward us, Seth
tossed me his keys. "I'm going back with them. I'll probably
spend the night at the hospital—bring the Lincoln to the
office in the morning."

"Yours is still at the park, remember."

"I'll send someone to pick it up tomorrow."

The medics strapped Colin to a board as Seth watched
the process with fascination and foreboding. When they were
on their way back to the chopper, I headed for the car. Halfway there, I remembered Colin's weapon was still in the
bunker. After the helicopter had taken off, I fetched it. When
I got back to the car, I stashed the weapon beneath the seat,
then found my way to Charleston, through streets as dark as
drain pipes.

When the telephone cried like a baby in the dark of
night, I barely summoned the strength to deal with it.

TWENTY-SEVEN

When it cried a second time, and kept crying for a dozen more, I stumbled out of bed and picked it up.

"Marsh?"

"Seth?"

"Get dressed."

"What's going on? How's Colin?"

"Colin's fine. Well, not fine, but okay. Bad concussion; broken neck; fractured cheek; broken wrist and jaw. But he'll survive."

"Is he conscious?"

"Yes. But he couldn't talk—his jaw's wired shut. He doesn't seem as hostile as he was. I think something you said scared him."

"Good."

"What was it?"

"Probably that ASP is using him as a scapegoat."

"What do you mean?"

I yawned. "Can't we do this tomorrow? Why do I have to get dressed?"

"Nothing to do with Colin. Pick me up at the hospital as soon as you can."

"Why? Where are we going?"

"Alameda's."

"What happened?"

"ASP burned a cross in her yard tonight. I'll be at the emergency entrance when you get here—the medical college on Jonathan Lucas Street, just north of Calhoun."

I was there in twenty minutes, listless with fatigue, shivering in the clammy night yet hot with the sweat of my rush. Seth came through the sliding doors before I'd come to a stop in the emergency drive-through, and climbed in the Lincoln without a word.

"Where to?" I asked him.

He pointed. "Across the bridge, then take the first left. She lives on Johns Island."

"Was anyone hurt?"

"I don't know yet."

Seth directed me left off the Savannah Highway, then right after we crossed the intercoastal waterway. The signs said we were on the road to Kiawah Island. Since my impression was that Kiawah was an enclave of the rich, I asked Seth if Alameda lived there.

"Not that far down—Johns Island is between here and there; lots of blacks live out this way. After the Civil War, the government split up some of the old plantations into sixty-acre parcels and doled them out to former slaves. A haphazard thing for the most part—land titles are still all screwed up—but there's a substantial black population on the islands left from those times. There are some practical reasons for living down here, too—when they can't get work, people can eke out a subsistence living by fishing and growing crops. Another attraction is that they don't have to deal with white people every day."

The lesson lapsed. I turned on the heater. The too-warm air smelled of dust and dioxide. I drove through the night, leaving the lights of the city, plunging down the corridor formed by the huge live oaks that lined the roadway, a tunnel into the roots of the Southern past.

"Do you know where we are?" I asked after a while; we seemed as removed from civilization as Apaches.

"There's a church coming up on the left. Take the first right after you pass it."

The sign in front of the church read A.M.E. I asked Seth what it meant.

"African Methodist Episcopal. When the black Methodists split off from the white congregation in the early nineteenth century because whites wouldn't let blacks share the graveyard, the A.M.E. was created to fill the void. It's still a powerful force in black lives, politically and socially as well as spiritually, and not only in the South. After the Los Angeles riots, the A.M.E. Church was a healing presence out there as well."

Seth fell silent. The headlights made the trees seem carved from stone, the night seem solid and sacred, a shield from the depression and depravity that lurked beyond it.

"I come out here on Sunday mornings sometimes," Seth mused softly. "I like to see the black people dressed in their Sunday best, piling in their cars and going off to church, joking with each other in the parking lots while they wait for the service to begin. The kids are cute and handsome, and the parents look happy and prosperous in the middle of a thousand reasons why they shouldn't have been either. It's the only thing that gives me hope sometimes," he concluded softly.

I took the next right turn, marveling at Seth's theistic turn. Part of me thought it was apt, and part of me thought it was simplistic and maybe even condescending. There came the South again—no answers; only a store of timeless questions.

Once we were off the highway, the road turned to dirt. We skipped across potholes for a hundred yards, tall pines and high grasses confining our vista to the oval patch defined by our headlights.

Suddenly Seth pointed to his right. "There."

Set back from the road maybe twenty yards was a house, small and square, its roof peaked, its frame raised a foot off the ground by concrete blocks at each corner, its yard unmarked by grass or shrub or sidewalk. The full moon, supplemented by the light from a window, was enough to illuminate the forms but not the faces of the crowd that milled in the barren yard.

They were mostly women, maybe a dozen of them, dressed in simple shifts or housecoats, grouped around one of their own whom I assumed was Mrs. Smallings. The men were less than half that number, separated from the women in a less kinetic cluster off by a clump of cars, hands shoved in their pockets, faces knotted with bottled rage, backs bent like staves under the burden of another insult.

I pulled to a stop, and we got out of the car. When they saw we were white, the buzz of conversation ceased. A moment later, a woman separated herself from the others and came toward us.

She was big and handsome, with padded features and heavy arms and dappled hair pulled back in a bun. "Mr. Hartman," she said, offering a formal handshake.

"Hello, Malavina."

"The Devil come out tonight, Mr. Hartman." The voice was sorrowful and oddly apologetic.

Seth bowed his head. "I know. I'm sorry."

"They kill her next, I expect."

"No, they won't."

"They will if she keeps on."

"We'll make sure she's safe, Malavina."

"Can't keep white folks from doin' what they've a mind to." She looked past the house toward the trees that swayed in the breeze like a line of oafish dancers. "Nothing out here in they way."

"I'll find a place for Alameda to stay in town. Where we can keep watch on her. Where is she? Is she all right?"

Her mother looked at the house. "She inside. Got burnt some trying to snuff it out. Harold across the way had some salve to put on her from the time his stove blew up. She supposed to keep still and rest herself." A smile thinned her lips, a mixture of pride and despondency. "Don't want me to bother you."

"I'm glad you did. Is she in pain?"

"Not so she shows."

Seth looked around the yard, as if he expected it to speak to him. "What happened tonight, Malavina?"

She shook her head to establish the lunacy of it. "I go to bed at sundown like usual. Alameda up with a book, like she do. Next thing I know, there's commotion."

"What kind of commotion?" I asked.

"Alameda fussing at someone. Men whistling and carrying on. Then a gun go off. I go to the parlor, but Alameda not there. I go on the porch, and there it is."

"What?"

"Cross of the Lord Jesus, burning like the bush. Alameda throwing water on it from the rain bucket, but it don't do no good so she knock it down and kick dirt on it. When that don't do, she stomp it like a snake. I tell her to leave it be, it burn itself out, but she pay me no mind. She hurt herself when she shove it over."

"Did you see anyone but Alameda when you got out here?" I asked.

She shook her head. "Not till Harold come over."

"Did Alameda see anyone?"

"Says she was fixing to go to bed when she heard a car pull up. Then some scraping and pounding. Then come the fire." Malavina shook her head. "I thought that Klan foolishness be done with, Mr. Hartman."

"Not yet, I'm afraid," Seth said.

"I reckon it's to do with that fuss at the army school, don't you?"

"Probably."

Malavina crossed her pillowed arms. "I wish she'd let go that dream, Mr. Hartman. Some things ain't meant to be."

Seth patted her shoulder. "Alameda's a bulldog, Malavina. Just like her daddy."

Her eyes rose toward the silver globe high in the night sky. "Her daddy don't want her dead."

"I don't, either," Seth said. "If she wants to stop, we'll stop."

"Have you had any trouble like this before, Mrs. Smallings?" I asked.

"Men drive down the road a time or two. Hollering like fools."

"Hollering what?"

Her look branded me a dolt. "Expect you know."

"Did it get worse after Alameda filed her suit against the school?"

Mrs. Smallings nodded.

"How often did it happen?"

"Saturday nights, mostly. Liquor talking."

"Any idea who they were?"

She shook her head. "I don't even look no more. Most nights I don't even wake up."

"Do they ever do anything but yell? Leave signs, or pamphlets, or anything?"

"Not that I seen."

"Any crosses before tonight?"

She shook her head.

"Can we go see Alameda?" Seth asked her.

Mrs. Smallings glanced at the house. "In the bedroom. Likely asleep."

"If she is, we won't wake her," Seth promised.

Mrs. Smallings stepped aside to let us pass, and we

started for the house. To our right, the group of men parted so that one of them could emerge to challenge us. "You the lawyer?" he asked Seth.

"That's right."

"I'm Hitchens from 'cross the road. What you gonna do about all this?"

"Call the sheriff."

"Already called him," Hitchens said bluntly.

"Good," Seth said. "I'll make sure Alameda has a safe place to stay for a while."

"Sheriff ain't going to do nothing. Soldier boys too much to mess with."

"What else can I do?"

"Call out the state police. National Guard, if need be. Only way to root these crackers out."

"I'll see what I can do, but since no one was hurt, they probably won't . . . " Seth shrugged to demonstrate his helplessness. "Is there anything else you can think of?"

"Tell Alameda to let go this notion she got. Army ain't no place for a black woman."

"If she tells me she wants to stop, we'll stop."

"You got to tell *her*."

Seth shook his head. "I won't do that."

"She keep on keeping on, she be dead, Mister Lawyer."

"I'll do everything I can to keep that from happening."

"See that you do. Meantime, the motherfuckers come again, I take *another* shot at they military ass."

"Another shot?" I said.

He pointed. "I'm on the porch with some sippin' whiskey when I hear them rootin' around over here, doin' I don't know what. Then when I see the fire go up, I fetch my bird gun and let fly when they drive off. The wife grab my arm so my aim drifts, but I *hear* that buckshot ding they fenders. Next time I pepper they *ass*."

"What kind of car was it?"

"Nothin' special. Chevy, maybe. Blue."

"How many men were there?"

"Two. Maybe three."

"How were they dressed?"

"Just regular."

"Were they shouting? Did they say anything about white power or southern pride?"

He shook his head. "Quiet as snakes till they drive off, then they singing 'Dixie.' I wouldn't have noticed, 'cept I don't sleep good when I eat tripe."

"Did you see anything else that might help identify them?" I asked. "Either this time or the times before?"

He shook his head. "These not the usual bunch. These more serious; serious as death. You get Alameda out of here, Mister Lawyer. 'Fore they lynch her."

We thanked the man for his help and went inside the house. It was small and tidy and surprisingly well furnished, with several upholstered pieces, a newish stereo and TV, and some rugs to soften the rasp of the rough-hewn floor. The pictures on the walls were of Christ, King, and Kennedy, as well as Sergeant Smallings, whose life insurance had presumably paid for the furnishings. Homage to men long dead, with no new heroes to replace them.

We made our way to the bedroom in silence, but we could have blown a bugle. Alameda Smallings lay flat on her back in the center of a narrow bed, wearing cutoffs and a red halter, her arms and legs splayed to form a black angel on the white bedclothes. Staring at the ceiling, her eyes wet with pain or fear or both, she didn't know we were there until Seth pronounced her name.

She blinked and turned our way. "Evening, Mr. Hartman. Mr. . . . ?"

"Tanner. We met in Seth's office."

She nodded. "I remember."

"How are you, Alameda?" Seth asked.

"Fine."

"Does it hurt?"

"Some."

"Do you need a doctor?"

She shook her head.

"Have you been able to sleep?"

"Don't want to."

"Is there anything you need? Food. Medicine. Anything?"

She shook her head. "I'm fine."

Seth dragged a chair beside the bed and sat on it. "We should talk for a minute."

"I'm not going anywhere," she said. Her small smile seemed to hurt her.

"Maybe we should pull the plug on the Palisade business," Seth said bluntly. "You've made your point. The issue is out there, and the courts in Virginia are dealing with it in the VMI case. Sooner or later, the Supreme Court will decide. Maybe we should let it pass."

Her eyes objected more loudly than her words: "If they scare me off, there'll never be a black woman at that place doing anything but mopping floors."

"You don't know that for sure. Someone else will come along."

"I should let *her* bear the burden, is that it?"

"The timing's wrong, Alameda. Maybe feelings will have calmed down in a year or so. Maybe the next woman won't have this kind of problem."

"They burned a cross, Mr. Hartman. Those kinds of feelings haven't changed for a hundred years. They never will."

"But they have, Alameda. Things are better now. Not nearly enough, I admit. But some."

Her lips were thin as wire. "I can't let it go, Mr. Hartman. I couldn't keep reading my letters if I did."

Seth closed his eyes against the ghost of her sainted father. "Just think about it. Okay?"

"What do you think I've been doing for the last hour? I'm going ahead. If you won't help me, I'll find a lawyer who will."

Seth took her hand. "If you're sure you want to proceed, I'd like to represent you. If you'll have me."

She turned her head to meet his look. "I will."

"Fine. But at least let me move you to someplace safer. In case they come back."

Alameda shook her head. "They want some more of me, they know where they can get it."

"That's foolhardy, Alameda."

"It may be, but I stay right here till they let me in that school. You want to help, take Mama to that safe place."

Seth kissed her on the cheek. "We know what she'll say to that, don't we?"

"I'm afraid we do," Alameda Smallings agreed, and laughed like a child around her pain.

TWENTY-EIGHT

Back in the yard, we decided to wait for the sheriff. When he arrived, it was in the improbable person of Deputy Gurton Cawl, who displaced three hundred pounds and emitted a drawl as thick as a gumbo. His flesh was as cumulus as clouds; his uniform fit the way rind fits melon. He rumbled through the yard as though he hoped its occupants would genuflect but suspected they would laugh.

When they didn't do either, when they didn't even acknowledge his presence, he coughed and bellowed and scratched and wheezed. "Listen up, y'all. We had a report of some kind of tussle out here. Now what I need is to see a . . ." He consulted his notebook. "Mr. Hitchens or a Mrs. Small-ings."

No one moved an inch. "Well? What the sam hell went on out here tonight? Ain't no one gonna tell me?"

Seth walked up and introduced himself. "There was a cross-burning here tonight, Sheriff."

"A what?"

"A cross-burning."

"Who done it?"

"We don't know."

"This here cross, it didn't have, like, a human bean attached to it, did it?"

"It wasn't an execution, Sheriff."

"Then what was it?"

"I think that's for you to determine."

"You saying it was Klan business or some such as that?"

"Quite possibly."

The deputy surveyed his surroundings. "Why they messing with folks way the hell out here?"

Seth told him about Alameda, and her lawsuit, and the reaction it had produced.

"You figure this is about that?"

"I do."

"Anyone hurt?"

"The girl who put it out."

"Bad?"

"No."

"Any idea who done it?"

"No."

"But you think the Klan?"

"Possibly. Or possibly ASP."

"Who?"

"The Alliance for Southern Pride."

"What's that?"

"A hate group."

"Who they hating?"

"Anyone not white and poor and Christian."

The deputy glanced nervously at the assembled crowd, confirming that except for me and him, everyone fell into at least one of the hated categories. "Political, huh?"

"In a way."

"Guess I should take some statements."

"Maybe you should call in Sheriff Leadwell."

Cawl sucked in his gut. "Sheriff don't like to be disturbed at this hour. He's up at a parole hearing in Aiken anyways; won't be back till Friday."

"Then I guess you should take some statements."

"Where's the girl? The one what's hurt?"

"Inside."

Cawl nodded, then hoisted his pants higher on his belly, then lumbered toward the house. As he passed the group of men, someone muttered something only the deputy could hear. Cawl stopped in his tracks, grasped the butt of his sidearm, and twirled toward the surly crowd—when Seth started to intervene, I held him back. After a moment of silent stalemate, Cawl shrugged his sloping shoulders and continued with his mission.

"Maybe you should go with him," I said to Seth.

He frowned. "Why?"

"She's black and he's white. This could get nasty at some point. Who knows what he'll say she said if push comes to shove?"

Seth nodded. "I'll head him off." He turned away, then stopped. "Thanks, Marsh. The thing with Colin has made me goofy."

Seth hurried toward the house, and I strolled around the yard until I was standing by the cross that had been aflame only hours before and now lay flat on its back beneath a heap of dirt and ashes, its sole surviving potency a carboniferous bouquet. It was about six feet high, built of two-by-fours that had been wrapped in rags, then dipped in kerosene. Not a terrifying object in normal context, but for black people in South Carolina the context had never been normal. I suppose I was feeling somewhat smug, until I remembered the last cross-burning I'd read about had happened in Iowa. And the one before that in Seattle.

I continued around the house, past the clothesline and vegetable garden and the chickenless coop near the mattress with box spring that was slung by its corners from the branch of a weeping willow. It looked so comfortable I almost lay down on it, but just then I heard a car drive up, so I went back to the front.

The car was a big Chrysler, and the man who got out of it was as black as his vehicle; although it wasn't quite dawn, he was dressed in a suit and tie and showed no sign of fatigue. Despite his cane, there was prance in his step and pomp in his bearing; the eye that wasn't covered by a patch glowed hot with the glint of a zealot.

He went past me as though I wasn't there, on his way toward the knot of black men, each of whom greeted him by name. Which made him Aldee Blackwell, political ward heeler to Charleston's black population and rival of Monroe Morrison, Seth's client who stood accused of being bribed.

I eavesdropped as much as I could, and what I heard were varying versions of what had happened and who had done what about it. After listening to the ornamented strains of melodrama, Blackwell issued a matching burst of outrage, which made his audience even more demonstrative. By the time he marched toward the house, I was afraid his disciples might regard me as a handy source of retribution, but thankfully it didn't happen.

When I caught the eye of the neighbor, I motioned for him to join me. "You mentioned the men were military," I said when he'd walked to where I was.

"That's right."

"You mean they wore fatigues? Jungle boots? That kind of thing?"

He shook his head. "I mean those swords like they use at that school."

"Are you sure?"

"When I fire at the car, they stick one out the window and whoop and holler like hooligans. Who else got shiny swords beside the boys at that army place?"

I thanked Hitchens for the information and made another trip around the house. This time I peeked in the chicken coop, lit a match for light, held my breath against the stench, lit a second match to take a closer inventory, moved some stuff around and peeked inside some other stuff, then backed out into the fresher air. On my way back to the front, I stopped by the cross a second time, took *The Biology of the Race Problem* out of my pocket, and wedged it under a nearby stone, far enough from the cross to be overlooked unless someone knew it was there and searched for it, close enough to be considered evidence when they found it.

By the time I got back to the front, Deputy Cawl was in his car, and Seth and Aldee Blackwell were arguing. "She'll do what she has to do," Blackwell was saying. "She's come too far to turn back."

"She can turn back anytime she wants to, Aldee."

"You hear her say anything about wanting that?"

"No."

"Then do like I said—press on."

"I intend to proceed unless she tells me otherwise."

"That's fine then." Blackwell made sure his triumph had been witnessed by his constituents. "Tell me, Seth," Blackwell went on with elaborate ease. "How's your man Morrison holding up?"

"Just fine, Aldee. And he's *your* representative, not mine."

"He going to resign his seat?"

"He's going to establish his innocence at trial, then serve out the balance of his term in Columbia and stand for Congress in the fall."

"District's changed a bit, you know."

"I know."

"Some folks feel another brother might best advance out interests."

"Be a shame to pit two good men against each other, Aldee. Especially two good black men."

"Be a shame for one black man with a corruption charge over his head not to step aside and give another black man his turn."

"Be a shame to toss six years of experience and effectiveness out the window for no reason."

When Aldee smiled, he exposed a golden tooth. "I imagine we'll discuss this again."

"I imagine we will."

Aldee drove away, and Seth gestured and I followed him to the car. We traveled several miles before he spoke. "Hard to believe anyone would do something like that in this day and age."

"This is the day and age of Howard Beach and Bensonhurst. It's lucky there wasn't a lynching."

"Who do you think was behind it? ASP?"

"Possibly. Except it seems odd that ASP didn't leave a calling card. Don't the hate boys usually want credit for their outrages? To help with the recruiting?"

"I don't know. I'll ask Rick Last about it."

"Plus, I doubt that Bedford was planning any more missions this evening. My guess is he was inclined to cool it till he saw whether the scene with me and Colin was going to make trouble for him."

Seth looked at me. "If not ASP, who else could be behind it?"

I hesitated. "Maybe Alameda."

"What do you mean?"

"Maybe she did it herself."

Seth looked at me so quickly he almost drove us off the road. "Why would she do something like that?"

"Watching her with you, hearing her talk about her father, imagining what's gone on between her and people like Blackwell, all suggest that Alameda's been under a lot of pressure to pursue her Palisade admission. Maybe that's the reason she's doing it—other people's expectations, including her dead daddy's dreams. Maybe the pressure got to her, and this was the only way she could think of to get out from under—fake a Klan attack. No one would fault her for not going up against them."

Seth was shaking his head. "That dog won't hunt, Marsh. Alameda's been behind this all the way."

"White people have been sure they've known what blacks are thinking since the slave ships landed, and they've been wrong for three hundred years. There's kerosene in the chicken coop in back of the house, and scrap lumber. If the lab got called in, it could prove it one way or another."

"How about the car Hitchens saw?"

"Maybe she just used it to her advantage—torched the cross after they'd gone."

Seth shook his head. "I don't buy it, Marsh. Not for a minute. But assuming you're right, which you're not, what are you suggesting we do?"

"Nothing."

"But—"

"The law isn't going to pursue the cross thing too strenuously, so you can leave it where it is—Alameda can go ahead with her lawsuit or stop, whatever she decides."

"You're letting this Southern stuff get to you, Marsh," Seth said with an uneasy laugh.

"Maybe, but there's one more person we need to talk about."

"Who?"

"You. Everything that has anything to do with ASP seems to have at least as much to do with hurting you as it does with Christian patriotism or racial purity. Who's out to get you, Seth?"

"Lawyers have enemies; I've already told you some of mine. Plus, I haven't exactly been a saint in my private life."

I took a breath and let fly. "Lots of arrows point to Jane Jean in this."

The heat of his anger warmed me from across the car. "What do you mean? *What* arrows? She *loves* me, for Christ's sake. Hell's fire, man."

I believed he believed it, but I still had my doubts. Or maybe I just wanted to be dubious—Scar Raveneau would have said that Jane Jean had flummoxed me.

"Tell me about her ex-husband," I said.

"Bilbow? What about him?"

"He's a Palisade man, I hear."

"Everyone who's been within ten yards of him has heard that—it's all he talks about."

We stopped at a light, and I pointed. "Isn't his dealership down that way?"

Seth nodded. "What about it?"

"I've got a hankering for a used car."

"You're kidding."

"Nope. Take a left."

Seth started to object, then shrugged and made the turn.

The highway was blessedly dark and eerily unoccupied at that hour, which was a few minutes after 5:00 A.M. By the time Seth pulled into the dealership drive, his ire at my slur on his inamorata had rendered him mute.

A chain barred the road into the sales lot, so we had to reconnoiter on foot. I bypassed the new cars and headed for the used, with Seth a sullen shadow in my wake, hugging himself for warmth.

Most of the cars in the lot were spick-and-span, covered only with a spray of dew, but a few were still dirty, recent arrivals presumably, proof that Bilbow had done new business. It was the dirty ones I paid attention to.

What I hoped to find on one of the half-dozen cars that were soiled enough to have been driven to Johns Island that evening was a broken taillight or some chipped paint or other evidence of the sting of a round of birdshot from the gun of Harold Hitchens. But nothing I found would pass for proof.

As I started back the way we'd come, Seth grabbed my arm. "What are we doing here?"

"I thought maybe Bilbow used one of these to drive out to Alameda's and torch the cross."

"He's not that stupid."

"Are you sure?"

Seth swore. "No."

I started to climb back over the chain, then had another idea. I hurried back the way I'd come and made another pass at the dirty vehicles, this time running my fingers along the rear of the cars at the point where the metal body met the plastic bumper. I found what I was looking for on the fourth one I tried, a blue Celebrity that was salted with dirt and sand.

I held them up for Seth to see.

"What's that?"

"Birdshot." I sniffed. "And that smell you smell is kerosene."

Seth shook his head. "Jesus. I wouldn't have thought he had the guts."

"It's the guys with no guts who like to play bully. I'll bet Bilbow was one of the biggest hazers at the Palisade in his day, trying to make the new guys as terrified of the place as he'd been."

Seth nodded. "I've heard that about him, as a matter of fact. So he takes it on himself to preserve the school's manhood and beat back the invasion of the female hordes. I can see that. But someone put the idea of the cross in his head."

"Any connection between Bilbow and anyone else in your life? Except Jane Jean?"

"Not that I know of. And lay off Jane Jean. She's not involved. She couldn't be."

"Who owns the dealership?"

"It's not public knowledge, but a guy named Benedetti has most of it."

"Aldo? Of the Newark Benedettis?"

Seth frowned. "How do you know about that?"

I told him I was psychic.

TWENTY-NINE

$\mathbf{W}$e drove to Hampton Park under the siege of a heavy silence. Fatigue made words a chore; the incident at Alameda's made reality anathema. In the forefront of my mind, I was pleased that by linking Bilbow to the cross, I'd foreclosed Alameda's complicity in it. In my deeper recesses, I was confused and contradicted over the role of Jane Jean Hendersen in ASP and its enmity toward Seth—it seemed possible that contrary to what Seth saw, she carried some deep-seated seethe for him. But my brain had baked too long that day to piece such peculiar parts together, let alone make sense of an entire puzzle, so I postponed deduction until daylight could lend assistance and leaned my head against the seat and tried to soothe my alkaline eyes.

When we reached the lot where I'd parked his Thunderbird some dozen hours earlier, Seth pulled next to it and stopped. I yawned and stretched and got out of the Lincoln. "Go home and get some sleep," Seth advised after buzzing down the window.

I asked where he'd be the rest of the day, in case I needed to reach him.

"I'm going to stop by the hospital to see Colin, then go straight to the office. I'll probably be there all morning—Monroe's coming in to discuss whether he should change his plea on the bribery charge."

"Tell the hospital people I'm cleared to see Colin."

"Sure. Why?"

"He's still the only link to ASP I've got. Maybe his adventure this evening has scared him enough to talk to me. Also, you might want to consider putting some private security in there, until he's released."

"Why?"

"Bedford and his troops might worry that Colin's telling tales out of school."

Seth met my eyes. "Which is precisely what you want him to do."

I nodded. "More or less."

Seth sighed and rubbed his eyes, as though exhaustion were as removable as makeup. "He's my only son, Marsh."

"I know that, Seth. But innocent people have been hurt by this ASP business, and more will be until we shut it down. At this point, Colin's the only wrench I've got."

"Use it wisely," Seth said levelly, then drove away in a troubled huff. I got in the Thunderbird and turned the key. It started the way I felt—irritated and enervated and reluctant to do what it was designed for.

Although I was tired from a lack of sleep and sustenance, my sag had a more elemental source. The cross-burning was one of those moments, like riots at ball games and lootings at earthquakes, that remind us we are not what we think we are, not what we ought to be, not as different as we should be from the Visigoths and Huns: Evolution notwithstanding, proof abounds that what we love above all else is a good excuse to kill each other. Or so it seemed as the sun slid toward me across a compliant sea on a steamy Southern morning that was far too congenial to contradict the smudge of the night before.

I maneuvered the Thunderbird out of the park and drove toward the heart of the city. When I reached a little beanery near the medical college, I paused long enough to down four slices of French toast and enough coffee to reprise the tiff between the *Merrimac* and the *Monitor* while I formulated a plan of action. After my fourth cup of coffee and my second trip to the bathroom, I doubled back to the hospital.

Because health care is the only booming business left in this country, it took almost an hour to get where I was going—find the right building, the right wing, the right floor, and the right nurse to pitch my plea to. After I evoked Seth's name and cited evidence of our friendship, I was accepted as his emissary and allowed to see his son.

Colin was under observation in the neurology department, presumably because his head injury was more ominous than his orthopedic problems. By following some indolent instruction, I found his room and peeked inside.

The nearest bed was empty; Colin lay propped up in the other. The woman sitting beside him was crooning words of solace as she stroked the back of Colin's hand. Her sepia skin contrasted sharply with its vesture, which was the antiseptic trappings of a nurse. In contrast to his attendant's assiduous demeanor, the patient sported the glistening cheek and spongy nose of someone who'd just been crying.

His right eye was bandaged; his left eye was black; the jaw beneath it was swollen and discolored. His right wrist sported a cast. His shaved head was now imprisoned in a halo—one of those metal cages they screw into your skull to make sure you can't do damage to your dislodged brain. Removed from Bedford's entourage and its studied puffery, deprived of his fatigues and jump boots, Colin Hartman seemed merely a kid who'd fallen off a swing and been skinned up in the school yard.

As I lingered out of view, the nurse murmured something soothing, and Colin responded with a mumbled blurb that suggested he had trouble moving his jaw: I remembered it was wired shut. When I shifted position, I made a noise, and Colin and his nurse turned my way in mutual resentment at the interruption.

When he saw who it was, Colin turned toward the woman with an expression that could not have been more needful had she been his private angel. I smiled at the incongruity of the alliance—no atheists in foxholes; no racists in intensive care.

The nurse patted Colin's hand once more and told him she had to go; Colin did something to show he didn't want her to leave. I waited while they worked it out. As she passed on her way out of the room, she asked me to be brief and to try not to upset him. I claimed it was no problem. The name on her tag was Bunting.

She started to move on, then stopped, her look distant and distrustful. "He can understand you, but because of the facial fractures he can't form words yet. Don't try to make him do so."

I glanced at the halo and the barren head trapped within it like a possum, then lowered my voice to a whisper. "Is there brain damage?"

"We don't think so, but we'll need to do more tests to make sure." She held up two fingers. "Two minutes. Then I come back and kick you out."

I took the seat Nurse Bunting had vacated and smiled to spiff up my intentions. Despite my outsized chumminess, Colin closed his unbandaged eye and arced his head and his halo back into his pillows, as though he hoped they would hide him.

When I said his name, he winced. When I asked how he was doing, he grunted through a pulpy lip and a fence of broken teeth. When I told him I needed some information, he closed even tighter his good eye, which extruded a tear in its clouded corner. He was in pain, and I knew it; I was hoping to use it to my advantage.

"You need to talk to me, Colin," I began easily. "You need to tell me some more about ASP."

Nothing, not even a grunt. Since time was of the essence, I opted for tough love.

"You're between a rock and a hard place, son. You didn't kill me like you were supposed to, so ASP will suspect you've rolled over and sold them out. On the other hand, if I talk to the cops, I can get you indicated as part of a criminal conspiracy, so your goose is cooked either way. Lucky for you, one side is still willing to ride to your rescue."

His grunt was probably a curse, but I chose not to decipher it. To give him time to think, I strolled to the window and looked out. At least six steeples pricked the morning sky like carrots sprouting through the clods of city soil. I wondered which church Beau Bilbow attended, wondered if any of them would turn him away if they knew what he had done that evening. I began my pitch without bothering to turn around.

"You and Bedford kidnapped me. And falsely imprisoned me. And assaulted me with a deadly weapon. Big-time felonies, Colin; kidnapping's a capital offense in most states. Even if they only stick you in jail, you're going to wish they'd executed you, because jails are full of people you and your buddies call 'Homo bestialis.' When word gets around about your waltz with white supremacy, you'll have a shank in your neck in a week. And as far as I can tell, you dad is the only one on earth who'll give a shit."

I finally turned and looked at him. What he was trying to show was stoicism, but all he succeeded in showing was an abject blanch of terror. As his tethered jaw bulged with the effort to make some sound that would release the explosive vapor of his fears, tears coursed down his cheeks as though he were a block of ice in the Southern sun.

"The good news is that there's still time to pull this out," I went on. "I haven't told the cops about the business at the bunker yet. Your dad knows we had a spat, but he doesn't know you tried to kill yourself, and he doesn't know you tried to kill me. If I get what I want from you, he never will.''

I met his look, which still struggled to be defiant despite the lapse of a moment earlier and the tune I was tapping on his mind.

Since he couldn't talk to me, I tried to bridge the gap. ''You played a big game, so you have to pay a big price, Colin; if you're man enough to wear combat clothes and carry automatic weapons, you're man enough to take the consequences when you fuck up. The consequence for *you* is, if you don't tell me what I want to know, you're going to do some time. Long time; scary time. So what's it going to be?''

His response was a guttural curse, succeeded by a moan of pain.

''I can tell it hurts to talk, so here's all you have to do. I'm going to ask some questions. They can be answered yes or no. Move your thumb for yes, your index finger for no. Your index finger is your trigger finger,'' I added when he seemed puzzled by the instructions. ''Okay?''

He blinked his single eye.

''If you lie to me, I'll find out about it. And I'll go to the police and tell them what went down at the bunker and file charges against you and Bedford both. You might as well face up to the fact that ASP is history for you, Colin; you're going to have to choose sides, and only one side still wants you on its team.''

I gave him a minute to extrapolate from the bare bones of my projection. ''Your dad's a nice guy,'' I went on as his lip trembled for an instant, ''but I'm not. As far as I'm concerned, you're either with me or against me. If you're with me, I'll walk through hell to help you. If you're against me, you fly solo, and no one's around when you crash. If you don't open up, I'll call Bedford and give him your room number, just to make sure he knows where to look. Get the picture, Colin?''

Hesitation. Then thumb.

''Good. Here's the first question. Do you know who Alameda Smallings is?''

Hesitation. Thumb.

''You sent her a tape, didn't you?''

Thumb.

''Whose idea was it, Bedford's?''

Thumb.

''Is that why you talk to Elmira once in a while? To keep current with your father's cases so you can tell Bedford which people to target?''

Thumb.

''Was Bedford planning to do anything else about Alameda? Was he going to try to stop her from going ahead with the Palisade case in some other way that you know of? Something besides the tape?''

Finger.

''Did Bedford ever talk about a cross-burning?''

Thumb.

''At Alameda's?''

Finger.

''Just in general?''

Thumb.

''Were they planning anything like that for tonight?''

Finger.

''Fine. Just a few more. Do you know Beau Bilbow?''

Finger.

''Did you ever hear any talk that ASP got some of its money from a car dealer?''

Finger.

''Do any of the ASP people have connections with the Palisade?''

Finger.

"How about Ms. Hendersen? You told me she gave
Bedford money. Is she involved with ASP in any other way
that you know of?"

Finger.

"But you've seen her with Bedford?"

Thumb.

"Did you hear what they said?"

Finger.

"Were they friendly?"

Finger.

"Angry?"

Thumb.

"About what?"

Shrug, then wince.

"How about Aldee Blackwell? Does he have anything
to do with ASP?"

Finger. Twice.

"Does Monroe Morrison?"

Finger. Twice.

"How about Montgomery Hendersen?"

Finger.

"Your sister? Your mom? Your stepdad?"

Finger. Three times.

"Did Bedford ever say who was providing the money
for ASP?"

Finger.

"Is ASP planning anything violent in the future?"

Thumb.

"What?"

Nothing.

"Are they planning to kill someone?"

Nothing.

"Come on, Colin. Have they talked about killing someone?"

Hesitation. Then thumb.

"Who?"

Nothing.

"Is ASP really going to kill your father? Is that what it's come down to?"

For a long moment, he didn't respond. A fresh seep of tears wet the bandage on his covered eye and trickled to the cheek below it. His body convulsed in a painful writhe; the cry through his teeth was feral.

"I have to get to Bedford before he goes ahead with this," I said, as urgently as I could manage. "Where is he?"

Colin moved his head a millimeter.

"Come on, Colin. Nothing's changed, except that in addition to your other crimes, you can add conspiracy to commit murder. You've got to help me stop it."

I went to the bed and grasped his arm. As he twisted away in protest, Nurse Bunting banged through the door behind me, as lethal as a murderess herself.

"What do you think you're doing? I'll *not* have you causing this man discomfort. If you don't leave the building immediately, I'll have security remove you. This boy is in critical condition; I thought you were a friend."

"I'm the best friend he's got," I said, and closed the door behind me, sad that it was true.

THIRTY

Stymied by Nurse Bunting, I set my sights on Bedford; the only road I knew that might lead to him passed through Colin's quondam girlfriend, Broom. The phone book didn't list that name, but the bleary voice that answered the phone at the Pustule told me she lived somewhere in the Ansonborough District, near the corner of South and Drake.

After checking my map, I drove east on Calhoun, left on East Bay and again on South Street, then cruised the neighborhood till I found a house that matched Elmira's prim description of the cultivated sloth in which Broom and her buddies lolled. Prepared as I was for squalor, it took me a while to absorb it.

It was as though they'd snatched one of the grand mansions from south of Broad, airlifted it north of Calhoun and dropped it onto a vacant lot, then subjected it to a series of stress tests to see how it would stand up to the twentieth century. Every foot of paint festered with a peel or a blister. Every shingle was curled, every column was tilted, every gutter was flopping loose, every piece of trim and siding was either warped, buckled, rotted, or tugged from its anchors by the strains of postmodern existence. The effect would have been comic had the house been sitting on a back lot, waiting for the sequel to *Psycho,* but the idea that people actually lived in there wasn't conducive to levity.

The sign beside the door was scripted in rough calligraphy: ABANDON HOPE ALL YE WHO ENTER HERE. The *H* in HOPE had been crossed out and replaced by a hand-scrawled *D*. Next to the sign, an arrow pointed to a bucket placed precisely below it. In the bucket were several flattened roaches and some glassine envelopes of what looked like crack but was surely a sucrose imitation.

Although exhaustion was as much a drain on me as influenza, I summoned the vigilance to keep from tripping on the front step and falling through the hole in the porch and being cut by the shards of glass that had fallen like snow from somewhere. When I banged my fist on the door, the roof above the porch began to creak and groan; a bird appeared from within its recesses and began to scold me. I began to wonder if Broom was worth the risk.

The kid who opened the door was male: The reason I was certain was that he was naked below the waist. His T-shirt was a billboard for Nirvana, his hair a testimonial to General Custer. The void in his eyes was a by-product of illicit medication.

"Yeah?" was all he was able to say, and he managed that only after he'd massaged his temples with the heels of his hands till the color went out of his wrists.

"Broom here?" I asked him.

"Who wants to know?"

"A friend."

"Broom don't have friends."

"What does that make you?"

"Her slave."

"How did *that* happen?"

He yawned. "I needed bread, you know? So Broom, like, gave me some and stuff, and now I got to work it off. It's not so bad—most days I don't even notice, 'cept when she makes me suck her toes. Who're you?"

"A business associate."

"Like, from the bar?"

"Like that."

"You look like a cop."

"Would a cop own a place like the Pustule? Where is she?"

Fortunately the flaw in the dialectic didn't register. "Asleep, probably."

"What time does she get up?"

"What time is it?"

I looked at my watch. "Seven-fifteen."

He frowned, then looked beyond me at the diluted dawn. "In the, like, morning?"

"Bingo."

"Then she probably ain't gone to bed yet. Is today Wednesday, or was it yesterday? I got to get my unemployment if it's Wednesday."

"That's today. You've got about sixteen hours to work with it."

"Cool."

Broom's slave stepped aside to let me enter the domain of his mistress, then gestured to the hallway off the foyer to his right. "Scope the kitchen," he mumbled. "Last I saw she was, like, doing something with ice cream."

"Like, eating it?"

He fished for memory, then shook his head. "Something else."

Sure enough, Colin's old friend Broom was doing exactly that. Dressed in a bodysuit that blackened her from neck to ankle, with white silk panties and a white lace bra worn on top as guideposts to her erogenous zones, she was crouched over an old-fashioned ice-cream maker, cranking as fast as she could.

Her teeth were clenched like clamps; oval stains of sweat darkened the valley between her breasts and the caves beneath her arms. The tune she hummed was "Happy Birthday," but she made it sound like "The Volga Boatman."

After a few more turns of the crank, she grabbed a paper bag and added salt to the ring of ice. The top of her head was a bristly hair ball that was dyed to match her outfit; her left eye was ringed in black like a parody of the Rascals' dog. Her nostrils and ears and lips were pierced by so many silver circles it brought to mind a Slinky. Her skin was as piebald as bad teeth.

She didn't know I was there till I said her name. When I did, she put down the salt and looked at me with disinterest. "I know you're not the landlord, so I can't even *begin* to persuade myself that you've got a right to be here."

"My name's Tanner; your slave invited me in."

"That's a relief; last I saw of him, he was asleep in the bathtub. You figure someone could drown that way, or you figure they'd wake up?"

"I figure they'd wake up."

"So did I." She was as blasé as a meter maid.

I tried to earn some points. "Apparently I woke him in time to collect his unemployment. I figure that earns me a favor."

She looked at me suspiciously. "What kind of favor?"

"I'm looking for Forrest Bedford."

Broom stopped cranking. "The Bible junkie? Haven't seen him in weeks."

"Where did you see him last?"

"Used to come around the bar trying to recruit more rockheads for the cause. If I see him again in this century, it'll be too soon."

"I was hoping you might know where I could find him."

She shrugged. "Only thing I know about Bedford is, he makes the Scriptures sound too much like *Mein Kampf.*" She wound the handle again, this time as fast as she could.

Sweat bloomed on her brow and dripped down her cheek and fell onto the ring of ice. After a moment of puff and pant, she stopped turning the crank and lifted the lid on the canister and inspected the mix. "Shit. This stuff is as bad as Johnny—it won't get hard no matter what I do." She shook her head and looked at me. "What's your rap, mister? What are you pushing? Dope? Porn? What?"

"Salvation, maybe."

She shook her head and laughed. "I'd have never pegged you for a Bible beater. Sorry to break the news, but you're out of your jurisdiction. The only god I worship is sleep." She put the lid on the canister and cranked with renewed ferocity. "I got to get this done," she muttered through clenched teeth.

"My kind of salvation is pretty focused; a boutique evangelism, you might say."

"What the fuck does *that* mean?"

"I'm out to save a single soul. Its name is Colin Hartman."

Her eyes jumped off the ice and onto me. "What's he got to do with anything?"

"He's in trouble. And he's scared."

"He's got lots to be scared about."

"Like what?"

"The same thing we're *all* scared of."

"Which is?"

"That there's no place to hide." She brushed a lock of greasy hair away from her shiny forehead. "What I don't get is what difference it makes to a white-body like you."

"You know about Colin and Bedford and the Alliance for Southern Pride?"

She shrugged. "I know about Bedford the way I know about diarrhea."

"He tried to set Colin up for a fall last night."

"What kind of fall?"

"Bedford tried to get Colin to commit a major crime, so he could use it as leverage against him."

"What kind of crime?"

"Murder."

She coughed. "Who was he supposed to murder?"

"Me."

I walked to her side and nudged her out of the way and took the crank from her hand and turned it. The ice rattled against the sides of the wooden crock like a carcass passing through a pulverizer. When I looked back at Broom, she was crying.

"What's the matter?" I asked.

"Nothing."

"You might as well tell me—I'm not leaving till I get some of this."

"It's not your problem."

I shrugged. "Whose birthday is it?"

She hesitated. "My mom's, I guess."

"How old is she?"

"How the hell should I know? Forty-five, maybe."

"Where does she live?"

"Battery Street."

"When's she coming by?"

"Never." She bit her lip and swore.

"When's the last time you saw her?"

"Two years yesterday."

"I didn't think Charleston was that big a place."

"It is when you want it to be." Broom cocked her head and watched me work. "I still don't know what you're doing here," she said as I warmed to my task.

"I'm trying to get Colin Hartman out of trouble."

"How?"

"By putting Bedford out of business. To do it, I need to know who's bankrolling him. Any ideas on the subject?"

She shook her head.

"Is that true? Or are you one of the Israelites?"

"As far as I'm concerned, the Israelites are all in Israel. Or maybe Scarsdale. I still don't see how this is my problem."

"I heard you and Colin were friends."

"Emphasis on were. Once in a while, I let him cry on my shoulder."

"Why?"

She paused to watch me crank. "'Cause I owe him."

"For what?"

"For being there for me when I needed him."

"When was that?"

"In school."

"Bishop England?"

She nodded. "Some heavy stuff went down for me at home. Colin was the only one who understood what I was dealing with. One of the few good things I've managed to do with my life is not forget that."

"That doesn't sound much like the Colin I know, to be so sympathetic."

"Yeah, well, Colin's a little fucked up."

"Why? What makes him so unhappy?"

"Because he cares what his daddy thinks, and his daddy thinks he's straight."

She'd said it without thinking, then quickly wished she hadn't. "Fuck," she breathed. "I'm so tired I don't know what I'm doing."

"Colin's gay? Is that what you're saying?"

She tried to be offhand. "I don't think Colin's all that involved with the issue, actually. I'm not sure he's ever been laid."

"He attacked the girl he took to the senior prom. Wrecked her dress and everything."

"Maybe he does that for a reason."

"Which is?"

"So they'll put a fence around themselves, and he'll have an excuse to bail out. So he won't have to face whether he is or isn't."

"Is or isn't what?"

"Queer," she said dully.

"He's still in the closet?"

"He'd better be."

"Because of Bedford, you mean?"

"Bedford, his old man—on that issue, they're coming from the same place."

I kept cranking while we measured each other. When she reached some sort of decision, Broom relieved me on the handle. "Hey. This is getting *real*. Way to go." She paused long enough to give me a high five.

"Tell me about Jane Jean Hendersen," I said as she turned the handle furiously. "What's her connection with Bedford?"

"She's his lawyer, is all I know."

"What does he want with a lawyer?"

"Advice."

"About what?"

"How much trash he can talk before he gets busted, I suppose."

"Is Jane Jean a racist?"

"She's a lawyer. She's whatever she gets paid to be."

Broom opened the ice-cream canister, ran a finger through the mix, nodded in satisfaction, then found a spoon in a drawer and offered a bite to me. The icy nugget was slick and peachy on my tongue.

After I complimented the chef, we exchanged some weary smiles. "I got to go to bed before I die," Broom said.

"Where does Bedford live? Just give me that. So I can get to him before he does any more damage."

"Why should I care *what* he does?"

"Because we both know Colin doesn't belong with

those people. And because right now I'm the only one who has a chance to shut them down.''

It took her a while to decide. ''Folly Beach,'' she said finally. ''Squats in a concrete house that got squished in the hurricane and left for dead by whoever owned it. Lives down there with his pets.''

''Dogs?''

''Guns,'' she corrected. ''He's got about fifty of them. Just in case you think he'll go easy.''

THIRTY-ONE

It felt like midnight, but it was only 7:45 A.M. Folly Beach was a long way away. Because I doubted Bedford would be up and at his lunacy this early, I decided to make a stop before I went after him. A phone book told me the Morrison Mortuary was on Rutledge Avenue, and my map told me it was just north of Sumter Street. I got there in ten minutes, a counterweight to the morning rush.

By the time I pulled to a stop, I had come off my high of the ice-cream social and was feeling morbid myself. The world seemed diseased and deformed—Colin Hartman was a mess both physically and psychologically; Broom missed her mother to the point of deep despair and belabored symbolism; Seth had been oblivious to his son's religious and sexual confusions for years; the ugliness of ASP lingered in the morning air like pestilent dust that invades your pores and poisons you through your flesh.

The mortuary and its environs only curdled my mood. The dour brick structure was so wounded by time and the winds of Hugo it had sprouted a tangle of vegetation in order to hide its scars. The gutters in the street were piled high with scrap and rubbish that had been waiting too long for collection. The people walking down the block seemed reluctant to get where they were going. If Morrison had a spare coffin around, I might decide to rent it. The front door was open behind a concave screen; I walked through it tentatively, bewaring not the dead but those they'd left in charge.

The foyer was large and high-ceilinged, ringed by a line of folding chairs broken only by a coatrack and an urn of flowers. Beyond it, a formal parlor preened like a Victorian diorama behind a pair of sliding doors. The furnishings were an eclectic collection of solid antiques arranged in an irregular circle to ease the act of consolation. The music in the air was a fugue from a recorded organ; the book lying open on a stand beside the door was a place to prove my presence. Since it was early for a visitation, the room was empty of all but portent.

I returned to the foyer and followed the hall that led to the rear of the house and knocked on the first door I came to. When nothing happened, I turned the knob.

In the center of the room was a coffin, its lid raised to display the earthly remains of a man wearing a blue suit and a big smile. Arranged around the oaken box, as though the currency of some strange contest, were scores of floral tributes, ferns and blossoms so abundant they threatened to engulf the woman who sat in a straight-backed chair in the center of the displaced nursery. Gowned in black satin, veiled in black net, gloved in black leather, she was throwing something at the man who lay in state atop the white lining of his sculpted bed. I guessed she had been there all night; the things she was throwing were pennies.

Despite my misgivings, I repeated the procedure at the next door I came to. This time I was invited to enter, by a voice that was more piqued than grief-stricken.

The room was less a public parlor than a private sitting room, with more clutter on the surfaces and less grandeur in the furnishings than in the professional chambers up front. A man wearing white silk pajamas and a black silk robe sat in front of a large bay window, sipping coffee and reading the morning paper in the carbureted light that squeezed through the white gauze curtains at his back.

In keeping with the decor of the establishment, a number of floral bouquets shared the room as well—voluptuous arrangements of everything from orchids to mums to iris, stuffed into vessels that ranged from cut-glass carafes to galvanized milk cans. I expected to sneeze or at least have a need to, but when I looked more closely, I discovered the plants were plastic.

The man on the love seat lowered his paper and scowled at me. His features were fine and handsome, his eyes dark and direct, his hair cut close and splashed with trails of gray. He reminded me of a darker Belafonte, except the pinch in his forehead and the squint in his eyes hinted at a status somewhat less transcendent.

He was in need of a shave and some peace and quiet, but he wasn't going to get either for a while. "These are private quarters," he grumbled in a reedy chord. "If you're part of the Prideaux party, wait out front until the service. If you need bereavement counseling, I won't be available till nine."

"My name's Tanner," I said. "I'm looking for Monroe Morrison."

"For what purpose?"

"Information."

"Concerning?"

"Seth Hartman."

"Why come here? Why not go to Seth?"

"I've already been to Seth. I'm working for him, in fact."

He raised a brow. "In what connection? My trial?"

"Indirectly, at least."

"What's that mean?"

"It means that what I'm directly concerned about is the

Alliance for Southern Pride. If I'm not mistaken, you're concerned about them, too.''

Morrison folded the paper and placed it at his side. ''You seem to know more about my affairs than you should.''

''I'm an investigator in hire to your attorney; the work-product and attorney-client privileges say that without your permission I can't disclose any information I might uncover to anyone but Seth.''

He looked at me for a long moment. The breeze through the window was cool and sharp, the light in the room was watery and insubstantial, the man who loomed across from me was formidable and aloof; I felt as if I'd entered a cloister.

''I may want to call Seth to confirm this,'' he threatened suddenly.

I gestured toward the phone on the table beside him. ''Feel free.''

After we traded appraising stares, he motioned for me to take a seat. As I tried to get comfortable in a wing chair, Morrison sipped his coffee. ''Does this have to do with what went on out on Johns Island last night?''

''Not directly. Unless you know something I don't.''

''I only know what I hear,'' he said.

''Which is?''

''That Bedford and his bunch finally went too far.''

''Maybe. But don't bet on it.''

''Why not?''

''Because I don't think ASP was involved.''

He bristled. ''What you think doesn't matter.''

''It does if anyone's interested in justice.''

''No white man has anything to tell *me* about justice.''

His look damned both my judgment and my lineage. I cast about for a rebuttal but was too tired to frame one that didn't amount to an exchange of insults.

"What do you want from me?" Morrison continued roughly, in the tone of a man who had spent too much time feeling subservient and had sworn to redress the balance.

"What does *ASP* want from you?"

"Same as the FBI."

"What's that?"

"Get me out of politics and into jail."

"By FBI you mean the sting operation."

He nodded. "Part of the deal Reagan and Bush cut with the evangelicals was that after they got elected, they'd set about putting the black judges and politicians behind bars, just like the preachers wanted. They got Hastings; they got Barry; now they're after me. But this time they'll come up short."

"From the newspapers, it sounds like they have some potent proof. Videotapes and all that."

"They got no kind of tape on *me*. I drank their liquor and ate their food, but when they tried to lay some walking-around money on me, I'm out the door."

I shifted gears. "Do you have any idea who's behind ASP?"

"Bedford."

"You think he puts up the money?"

Morrison shrugged. "Plenty of money for racism around. Guy like Duke holds out his hand, and it fills up fast."

"Why do you think ASP is after you and not any of the other black politicians in the state?"

Morrison became evangelical himself. "My body's been on the line for black people for thirty years: Selma; SNCC; Freedom School; legislature; black caucus. I make more money in a month than a cracker makes in a year— I'm the scariest thing they've ever seen in a suit, and they've got to move against me now because by November I'll be too big to break."

"Because you'll be in Congress."

"That's right."

"But isn't it true that even if you resign your seat and get out of the race, another black man is almost certain to take your place?"

"Just because he's black on the outside doesn't mean he's black up here." Morrison pointed to his head. "Or in here." He pointed to his heart. "Man who'll front for Blackwell got nothing on his mind but graft."

"What kinds of pressures are being put on you?"

"Tax man's into my business records; election man's into my campaign records; U.S. attorney wants me in jail for selling votes. Pressuring me, pressuring my lawyer."

"ASP wants you to drop Seth, right?"

He nodded. "Call him a traitor to the South."

"Are you going to? Get another lawyer, I mean?"

"Depends."

"On what?"

"On what they got on him. Seth a good man, but if he's going down, I can't let him drag me with him."

"What could possibly bring him down?"

Morrison shrugged. "Man with that much money got to have stumbled once."

"How did this sting thing originate?"

"FBI got an informer."

"Who?"

"Man named Keystone."

"Who was he?"

"Used to be a lawyer around town. Lately a lobbyist for the gaming people."

"The bill to build a casino on the island?"

He nodded. "Bill comes out of committee, Keystone starts spending money to line up votes. Not the first time it happened, but no one took a fall before, so they belly up to the trough again. Only this time they get caught." Morrison smiled faintly. "Entrapment, they claim."

"Was it?"

"Not for me to decide."

"Seth thinks this ASP thing may go back to something that happened the summer he worked for SNCC."

"Don't see how it could."

"I don't either, but do you mind talking about it?"

Morrison sighed impatiently. "You're like that man with his book, all the time picking at the old days. Me, I never found it profitable for a black man to look back. Nothing behind him but misery."

"What made you get active in SNCC?"

"What made me? South *Carolina* made me."

"How?"

"Failure to obey *Brown* versus *Board of Education* ten years after it supposed to; keeping black people from voting by poll taxes and numbered place laws and acts of violence; trying to get the Voting Rights Act of 1965 ruled unconstitutional. That's how they *made* me."

"When did you get active politically?"

"When the freedom riders got beat bloody up in Rock Hill back in '61. Opened my eyes: Prayer and patience weren't going to get it done. Black man had to *demand* his rights, not wait for the white man to *give* them to him. Went to Mississippi to work in Bob Moses' Summer Project; hung with Forman and Lewis and them, stayed close to a year. Made it to Selma in time for Bloody Sunday." He smiled wryly. "Got my righteousness activated by one of Sheriff Clark's police dogs. Came back and helped Septima with the Freedom School. Enrolled at Benedict College the fall of '65 and opened a SNCC office in Columbia to coordinate the registration project. When my daddy died the next year, it was see his business buried with him or come back and run it myself. So I came home. Worked in the Hollings campaign. Got the business in shape and made some money. Decided I'd get political myself when the time was right.''

"So this is the family business.''

He nodded. "In Daddy's time, only way for a black man to make money was preach or teach or bury the dead. Since he couldn't read, and didn't see all that much in Charleston that was holy, he went to Atlanta and learned embalming from a black mortician over there, then opened his own parlor in a chicken shack up the river. Bought a new car every year of his life after he opened the doors.''

"Tell me about the SNCC project,'' I said.

His smile implied both irony and a faded passion. "I was field secretary. Paid ten dollars a week.''

"What were you doing, primarily?''

"Convincing black people that voting was worth getting shot at, or fired from their job, or burned out of their homes. Finding lawyers to file papers to make the crackers in the courthouse put them on the rolls once they got there. Trying to keep my staff from being hunted like skunks while they were out canvassing the community.''

"How was Seth involved?''

"Came down from up North for the summer.''

"What did he do when he got here?''

"Same as the others—went to every store and shanty and church in the backcountry to persuade folks it was worth risking everything they had to use the rights we'd fought for.''

"Was Seth the only white person on your staff?''

Morrison shook his head. "Seth wasn't on staff, he was a volunteer. Had a dozen of them. Shitwork, mostly—young and sappy and sorry for black folks.'' His voice betrayed a hint of hurt. "They didn't turn tail, I'll give them that.''

"How did the blacks and whites get along? The ones that worked for SNCC, I mean.''

His lip stiffened. "Got along good, once they saw who was the chief and who was the Indians."

"How was Jane Jean Hendersen active in all this?"

He shrugged. "Same as Seth—drove her Mustang down every road in Clarendon County, bringing folks in to register. Helped her daddy some, too."

"Monty was helping with the lawsuits? Getting writs and stuff?"

"That's right."

I took a quick tack. "Did Jane Jean and Seth have a romantic relationship that summer?"

His face was impassive. "None of my business if they did or didn't."

I waited till he looked at me. "Did *you* have a relationship with her?"

He clenched his teeth and uncrossed his legs—for a moment I thought he was going to hit me. "What right you have to come to my house and say something like that?"

"I'm trying to find out if anything happened that would cause Jane Jean to carry a grudge from those days."

"She was a volunteer. That's all I know about it."

"How about now? Do you have much contact with her?"

"Only when I need campaign contributions," he said roughly.

"How about Seth? Did he have any *other* relationships while he was down here? With a black woman, maybe?"

"You're talking to the wrong man again."

I'd gone too far; Morrison stood up and walked to the door and waited for me to go through it.

"One last thing," I said. "Is there anyone still around from those days? Anyone prominent in Charleston who worked for SNCC that summer?"

"Only one I know is Aldee."

"Blackwell and you were colleagues?"

"Till he got more interested in pussy than civil rights."
The contempt in his tone was palpable.

"You fired him?"

He nodded. "After I whipped his ass."

"The cane and the eye patch?"

"That's right."

"So sex was a problem in the group."

"For some it was; for most it wasn't. You need to excuse me now." He adjusted his gown. "I got to get dressed and comfort people."

THIRTY-TWO

Folly Beach was a charmless waterfront community just south of James Island, a pedestrian venue of seaside living for those who couldn't afford the price of admission to Kiawah or Hilton Head. It took half an hour to get there, but in my state of benumbed exhaustion it seemed as if I were driving for a day.

The town had been badly battered by the hurricane, and some of its residents apparently lacked the wherewithal to reclaim their property from the leavings of the storm. I took a left when Highway 171 dead-ended at Arctic Avenue and another left on Fifth Street. In the second block from the corner, I came across a forlorn structure that fit Broom's description of Bedford's illicit hideout.

Befitting the Field Marshal's militaristic bent, the house was built of concrete blocks and encircled by a Cyclone fence that the storm had transformed into concertina wire. The house had originally rested on six stone pillars that raised it some four feet off the ground, presumably to avoid sea surges during high winds, but Hugo had been so strong— up to 180 miles an hour, Seth had said, blowing over a period of fourteen hours—that it had been shoved off its stilts. It lay where it had fallen three years back, crumpled on one corner, elevated on another, off-center, off-kilter, and abject, as though it had jumped from its perch in an act of self-destruction of a mate to Colin Hartman's.

The yard was a match to the house in degree of neglect, and seconded the message scrawled on every surface and pasted across the boarded windows—KEEP OUT. For their part, the three front pillars still stood guard over the crippled structure, a trio of stiff-backed sentinels who were hoping they wouldn't be blamed for the calamity that had befallen their charge.

There was no sign of Bedford in or around the place. I circled the block and drove by again, this time inspecting more closely. What I thought I saw in the wooden windows were some ventilation slits cut in the plywood, and what I thought I saw running through the scruffy yard were some wires that could have been fallen phone lines or could have been the trip wires to a booby trap. I drove two blocks north and parked, then spent some minutes planning an assault on Bedford's ersatz fortress. The tactic I finally opted for was brilliant—I walked to the front door and knocked.

When nothing happened in response, I banged the door again, this time with the heel of my hand. Although silence reigned in and around the building, my sixth sense told me someone was inside and I was being observed and evaluated, although for the life of me I couldn't see how. After a third knock produced the same result, I turned my back to the house, sat down on the stoop, leaned against the door, and urged the sun to improve my pallor.

Cars drove past, slowed when they noticed me, measured my intentions to see if they seemed honorable, then hurried on when I appeared benign. I took out my notebook and reviewed the scribblings I'd made since Seth first told me of his tiff with ASP. Nothing took shape, no patterns emerged, the incidents and information remained stark and disconnected, even though my conversation with Monroe

Morrison had given me an inkling of the provenance of the problem.

I was stuffing the notebook back in my pocket when something buzzed at my back. I stood up and knocked at the door. Again, no answer. But when I tugged on the knob, the door swung toward me after a lengthy groan of protest, as though I were the first visitor in years.

I expected to enter a foyer or even the living room, but what I confronted was a second door, this one made of sheet steel, as were the walls of the cubicle that encircled me. It was a mudroom of a sinister sort, a security system similar to the fortified entrances to crack houses I'd seen in San Francisco. Behind the cold steel doorway, Bedford doubtlessly had his evil eye on me. I waved and waited and wondered what he would do.

A moment later the steel door slid to the side and Forrest Bedford materialized in the inner doorway. He was dressed in a camouflage outfit of the type that he'd worn to the rally, his pistol nestled in a shoulder holster beneath a smirk of amused contempt that brought to mind the lubricious sneer of Goebbels. "Good morning, Mr. Tanner," he said with smarmy friendliness. "Welcome to the Field Headquarters of the Purification Brigade."

I looked into the claustrophobic cavern at his rear. "The Vietcong had better dayrooms than this," I told him.

"The brigade doesn't rely on material allure, as you well know; the riches I offer are spiritual in nature."

"Right. I was particularly moved by the 'Thank God for AIDS' signs at the rally."

"God smites those who flout his law. The fates of Sodom and Gomorrah forecast the consequence of buggery."

I looked at the flag on the wall behind him. "How about the fate of Hitler? What did that forecast?"

His lip crested in a curl of scorn. "You will come to regret your flippancy, Mr. Tanner. The battle lines are drawn.

Tolerance and compromise have brought us to the brink of spiritual destruction. From now on, it is God's white warriors against the forces of darkness and degeneracy. Be white and be right—it's as simple as that.''

"I think I'll pass, thanks all the same. The god you speak of isn't anyone I'm familiar with.''

"That's because you're ignorant. A student of the Scripture has no choice—we do as the Word commands us.'' His expression was a heady mix of moral rectitude and pagan pleasure. "Who told you where to find me, by the way? Colin, I presume.''

"Colin's not talking at the moment. About you or anything.''

"How wise of him.'' Bedford crossed his arms. "Well? Why are you wasting my time?''

"I think we should chat for a minute. About matters of mutual interest.''

He thought it over. "Normally I don't allow civilians to enter the headquarters, but in your case I'll make an exception. How *is* Colin, by the way?''

"Alive.''

"That's too bad. I was hoping you might have taken him out.''

"To save you the trouble?''

Bedford only sniffed. "Please come in. I'm sorry I can't provide refreshment, but my larder is rather Spartan. Without electricity the options become limited.'' He stepped aside and let me enter his Carolina version of Berchtesgaden. "Take either chair you choose.''

The alternatives were a padded barstool and a faded director's chair; I opted for the latter. After sliding the door to his lair into place, Bedford faced me at parade rest, his expression cool and imperious. But the corner of an eye was twitching with tension, and the flap on his holster was unbuttoned.

The only light in the room came from a Coleman lantern that was screwed into a propane bottle and set on top of an ammo can. What it illuminated was a bunker almost as impregnable as the one Bedford had taken me to some dozen hours earlier, but this time the walls weren't concrete but sheet steel.

The room was lined with more than a score of steel plates, half an inch thick, the width of plywood sheets but longer. Propped along the walls of the house, they seemed capable of repelling everything from rocks to rockets. Eventually I realized what they were—Bedford had appropriated the lids the street and water departments use to cover the holes they dig and used them to feather his nest.

Stacked in front of the steel, in a series of precisely defined piles, were a cube of numbered boxes along with a score of plastic containers, some as large as rain barrels, others the size of milk gallons, filled with water and perhaps a cola—a wet dream for squirrels and survivalists. I guessed the barrels held bulk and dried foods, and that there was sustenance to last six months. I also guessed that the disaster Bedford was determined to withstand wouldn't originate in nature.

The rest of the furnishings were minimal—two chairs, sleeping bag and foam pad, dented file cabinet, Coleman stove, plastic plates and spoons. The only concessions to the century were a transistor radio and a cellular phone.

"You could hold out for quite a while," I said affably. "Let me guess. You've got sensors outside, to tell when someone's coming. And Claymores in the yard—I saw the wires. I'll bet you've got a tunnel out of here, too. In case they try to burn you out, the way they did with the SDS."

His smile was arch and lazy. "Surely you don't expect me to reveal *all* my secrets."

"Plus you've got that." I gestured toward the wall opposite the makeshift pantry, where Bedford had arrayed his arsenal. Propped against the steel were everything from Glock revolvers to Remington trench guns, MP-5 assault rifles to government-issue RPGs, even a long green thing that must have been a missile. Stacked to the side were crates of appropriate ammunition, two of which served Bedford as a desk.

I shuddered and looked away. "When do you expect them to try to take you?"

The light in his eyes was a clone to the light from the lantern mantles. "When we are poised to take control."

"Of what?"

"The political process."

"When do you expect that will be?"

"After the uprising."

"By whom?"

"The Great White Race, to reclaim its birthright from the mud peoples."

"Like *The Turner Diaries,* you mean."

"*Much* worse than that, I hope. Mr. Pierce's imagination was rather limited." Bedford strolled to the weapons rack and looked over his store. When he turned to face me, he seemed to quiver with anticipation. "What brings you here, Mr. Tanner? Another bogus offer of support? Or are you the advance party for the forces of darkness?" He could hardly restrain his rapture.

"Sorry to disappoint you, Bedford; I'm all by my lonesome. I just came by to clip your wings."

His eyebrows rose like gulls. "Really."

"Afraid so."

"How will you manage that? You aren't even armed."

I smiled and crossed my legs. "What do you know about Johns Island?"

He shrugged. "It's about an inch away from Borneo. Other than that, not much."

"By Borneo I take it you mean that a lot of black people live out there."

"Take a drive someday—you'll think you took a wrong turn and ended up in Kenya."

"I took the drive about five hours ago."

He blinked and frowned. "Why?"

"We'll get to that momentarily. For now, the thing you need to know is that as of this minute, you're to lay off the Hartmans. Colin and Seth both, as well as Seth's clients. No more tapes, no more phone calls, no more notices of racial judgment, no more setups like the bunker. The Hartmans are off-limits, to you and everyone else in ASP."

Bedford was laughing by the time I finished my spiel. "You seem confused about the balance of power, Mr. Tanner. Perhaps another look at the weapons along the wall will serve to remind you. The firepower I can bring to bear is stupendous."

My eyes stayed locked on his. "You're behind the curve, Bedford. Power doesn't come from guns, power comes from information. I've got it, and you don't. That's why you're going to do as I say."

"What information?" For the first time, his swagger seemed to tilt.

To leave time for his nerves to sizzle, I stood up and strolled around the room. The stack of numbered boxes near the door contained something called the Gourmet Survival Pack, with a shipping label of a company called Health and Survival Products. In a separate crate were a variety of items that included several army MREs, packets of Mountain House freeze-dried foods, bottles of a potion called Colloidal Super Concentrate, and several jars of Food Tablets.

The box next to the survival pack was a library of books and pamphlets. The authors ranged from Henry Ford to Ezra Taft Benson; the subjects ranged from the effective use of plastic explosives to the origins of the Masonic Order; the titles ranged from *Bible Law on Money* to *The Bondage of the Free*.

I turned and leaned against the cold steel door. "I've spent the last two days trying to get a line on ASP," I began. "Who's behind it; what makes it tick; what it's really after. And do you know what I've discovered?"

"What?"

"That you're keeping such a low profile, no one knows much about it. You're not taking on the system, not in any way that might upset the powers that be; mostly all you toss around is rhetoric. As far as I can see, other than the puff stuff in the park last night, all you're really doing is making life miserable for Seth Hartman and his clients."

"You know nothing about our field operations. When the time is right, the potency of ASP will become apparent to all that stand in the way of the New Confederacy." His words were fervent, but his expression was as bloodless as the gray metal that surrounded him.

"You haven't done anything but whine," I said nastily. "You and the person bankrolling you are being very careful not to do anything that would justify a police investigation. Smart, I guess. Safe, certainly. Cowardly, some would say. But safe. Definitely safe." I took two steps toward him and stopped. "But I'm about to blow you out of the water, Mr. Field Marshal. I'm in a position to cause the law to come down on you like a pile driver on a post."

"I don't know what you're talking about."

Bedford wiped his brow with a camouflage hankie and rubbed his gun for comfort.

I walked to the wall at a leisurely stroll, then snatched up an automatic pistol from the end of the line of weapons and fiddled with the magazine. When Bedford drew his Walther and pointed it at me, I held up a hand in peace.

"Don't worry," I said. "I'm not going to shoot you."

I lowered the weapon to my side. "There was a cross-burning out on Johns Island last night."

Bedford was relieved at the new direction. "Good."

"Do you know anything about it?"

"I know white people would be better off if there was a cross-burning *every* night."

"I thought you said blacks weren't the problem."

"It's not laying down some terror on the blacks that's important, it's activating the anger of the whites. Once they're mobilized, we can direct them to more fruitful targets."

"Such as?"

"The Canaanites."

"Who are?"

He shrugged. "Jews, lemon niggers, Arabs. Whoever stands in the way of white supremacy will fall."

"The Jews and Arabs will be pleased to learn they're on the same side for a change."

Bedford's cheeks broiled with insult. "I hope you're still laughing when we decide to cut your throat. I'll be sure to reserve you a body bag."

I shook my head. "You're not going to touch a hair on my head; the big boss wouldn't like it. What you *are* going to do is lay off the Hartmans."

"You're in no position to dictate terms, Mr. Tanner. I believe it's time for you to leave."

I shook my head. "The target of the cross was a young lady named Alameda Smallings. She's the black woman who's filed suit to be admitted to the Palisade. She's also the woman you had Colin send a tape to."

"What does that have to do with anything?"

"Alameda is young, she's smart, she's politically prominent, and she's not about to be intimidated. Which means the law-enforcement people in Charleston are going to be under pressure to shut down whoever was responsible for harassing her, especially after I give them the tape you sent. This is a tourist town. They don't *like* people who do things that make folks from Cleveland and Chicago decide to go to Disney World instead. The black Jewish police chief will put you and your brigade out of commission so fast it will bleach the stripes out of your tiger suit."

Bedford frowned. "I don't get it. What does any of that have to do with me? *I* wasn't on Johns Island tonight."

I waited until he was eager for an answer. "I can prove you were."

His brow ignited as the glow of the lantern light blazed across his forehead. "Impossible. After I left the bunker, I came straight here."

"I can prove you were on Johns Island, setting fire to a homemade cross."

"How?"

"*The Biology of the Race Problem.*"

He frowned. "I've read it, and it's persuasive. But what does it have to *do* with anything?"

I stayed silent and let him twitch.

After a moment, his frown of worry evolved into a grin of conquest. "It doesn't matter anyway. The Supreme Court just ruled cross-burning isn't a crime. Even if they *do* think I did it, there's nothing they can do about it."

I tried not to show my concern over the likelihood that his sense of the law was accurate. "You don't have it quite right, Mr. Field Marshal. Talk to your lady lawyer. Ask her what the court *really* said in that case. Ask her if it was anything that will keep you out of jail for what happened on Johns Island last night."

His cockiness shrank to the size of a pea. "You're lying," was all he said.

"It's a simple deal. Let the Hartmans alone, and I keep the proof to myself. I'm not saying you have to close up shop entirely—the Canaanites and the pre-Adamics are going to have to hire their own P.I. I work for the Hartmans, and as of now they're off your list.''

''I don't know. I need to talk to . . . '' He stopped himself before he blurted the name I no longer needed.

''You're concerned about the money man. Well, don't worry; I'm going to shut him down, too.''

I gestured with the weapon in my hand, the one with the duct tape wound around the grip that was etched with the shapes of my fingers. ''The next time you send someone out on an assignment with this thing, be sure to show him how to use it first.''

THIRTY-THREE

All I intended to do was stop by my room and take a shower and make some calls. I got the first part done in good order; but somewhere between drying off and getting dressed, I managed to fall asleep. By the time I woke, it was late afternoon, and someone had come in while I was sleeping and draped me with a cotton blanket. The Southern samaritan also left a note: *Stop up when you're aroused, Sleeping Beauty.* I finished dressing as fast as I could, made the calls I needed to make to be sure the people I needed to reach would be where I could reach them when I needed to, then followed instructions.

Scar Raveneau's entire attire consisted of a surgeon's shirt, a butcher's apron, and a pair of bikini panties. Each item of clothing was coequally spattered with paint—yellow and green and red, mostly—which combined in a particularly interesting pattern on the backside of the panties, a phenomenon I only became aware of after she'd kissed my cheek and squeezed my arm and led me to the core of her studio.

"Hey, stranger," she said as she offered coffee from an airpot. "You seem to be getting into this Southern thing full time. I stopped down to see you at a pretty ungodly hour, but no one was home. If I didn't know better, I'd say you've been on the prowl all night."

"Not quite *all* night," I said. "Thanks for the blanket."

"I'm glad to know there's something going on around here that's interesting enough to lose sleep over. I don't come across that kind of action myself." She dropped her pixie pose, walked to the window and opened it, and stared across the veranda to the park. The paint on the panties suddenly seemed bathetic.

When she spoke again, her voice held a tremor of regret. "I've been wondering how much longer you're going to be around."

"I'm leaving tomorrow."

"Tomorrow?"

"Afraid so. Would you like to have dinner tonight?"

She sighed, once and deeply, then turned to face me with a plucky smile. "Won't Seth and Jane Jean want to give you a Southern send-off?"

"I don't think they're going to be in the mood."

"You sound like something bad is going to happen."

"Something bad has already happened."

"To Seth?"

"To lots of people."

"You sound like a good cop in a bad novel. You're not going to tell me about it, are you?"

Without waiting for an answer, she walked to the couch and sat down heavily, creating a cloudlet of dust in the process. "I don't know what to say. About tonight, I mean. You already know I like you. Maybe even more than like. But a long good-bye might be too ... masochistic, don't you think?"

"Why don't I call when I wrap up my business and see how you feel about it then? If things go the way I hope they will, I'll have done all the damage I'm going to do by seven."

"You're not going to come back, are you?"

"To Charleston? Probably not."

"Which means it would be foolish to try to make this into something."

"If something is better than nothing, it wouldn't." I went to the door and waved back at her with far more nonchalance than I felt. "I'm off to hunt down a historian."

"A what?"

"Some guy who's down here researching a book on the civil-rights days."

"You mean Stan."

"Stan?"

"Professor Mickelson. The guy doing the book."

"You *know* him?"

"We met in a bar one night."

"When?"

"Couple of weeks ago."

"And?"

"We talked."

"And?"

"We had some laughs. *I* had some, at any rate; Stan's wrapped a little too tightly to be real good at horseplay."

"And?"

"We went our separate ways."

"You don't happen to know which way was *his* way, do you?"

"Quality Inn."

"What room?"

Her look was as pointed as a tusk. "How should I know?"

I held up my hands to surrender the implication. "What did you and the professor talk about?"

"What he *wanted* to talk about was Seth and Jane Jean. When he saw that was my least favorite subject, we talked about the war."

"The War of Northern Aggression, I assume."

She was pleased I'd remembered the euphemism. "We

agreed that contrary to two hundred years of Yankee propaganda, it wasn't about slavery at all.''

"What was it about?"

"States' rights."

"The right to own slaves, you mean."

"The right to be free from federal interference."

"To be free to own slaves, you mean."

She thumbed her nose. "You Yankees have a one-track mind," she said, then joined me at the door.

"You're right about that," I said, and flipped up her apron and slapped at her buttocks. "But the war *we're* obsessed with didn't end at Appomattox. And the uniforms are much more attractive."

I kissed Scar on her forehead before she could laugh or cry, then went to my room and called the Quality Inn. When they rang the professor, he didn't answer. The operator asked if I wanted to leave a message. I was still debating the point when she said, "Are you Professor *Lawton*, by any chance?"

The lie came easily. "Yes, I am."

"Then I have a message from Professor Mickelson. He says you can reach him at the Panther any time after six."

"The what?"

"The Panther. That's a bar. On Upper King? You all *might* want to take someone with you."

Since I had some time to kill, I drove back to the hospital. When I peeked in Colin's room, it looked like he was sleeping, so I went off in search of his nurse.

I found her in another hallway, strolling beside a woman whose body was so curled and twisted she needed a walker to keep from falling over. "I'd like to speak to you when you have some time," I said. "It's about Colin Hartman." I pointed. "I'll be at the nurses' station."

Nurse Bunting joined me five minutes later, her face gleaming from the heat of her ministrations, her eyes hostile with the memory of my prior visit.

"I got carried away when I was here before," I said as she sat on the couch beside me. "It won't happen again."

"Your name is Tanner, right?"

"Right."

"You're a friend of Mr. Hartman's."

"Right."

"Colin claims he tried to kill you last night. Is it true?"

"Does it matter?"

"It might."

"To whom?"

"His therapist, for one. It might help Dr. Gilman understand how . . . *extreme* Colin was feeling when he got here."

"Extreme's a good word for it. Colin's seeing a psychiatrist?"

"Yes."

"At whose request?"

"His. And mine. I take it you object."

"On the contrary, it's one of the reasons I'm here—to make that suggestion."

Her nod was approving, but her eyes were remote and cautious. "There's a man standing guard by Colin's room," she said. "How necessary is he?"

"Less so than he was this morning."

"But not totally redundant?"

"No."

She shook her head with skepticism. "I suppose it's too much to ask for you to tell me what's going on."

"I work for his father. My report should be ready this evening. How much of it he thinks you should know is up to him."

She wasn't pleased with the brush-off. "That leaves Colin a bit in the lurch, doesn't it?"

"I hope not, but I don't have any say in the matter. Seth

and the therapist should talk; I'm sure Seth will be cooperative. In the meantime, I have a suggestion that might help.''

"What kind of suggestion?"

I hesitated, wondering for the millionth time if I was doing the right thing in bending the rules of my profession to satisfy the needs of my person. "I wouldn't want this to become public knowledge," I said, "and I wouldn't like it traced back to me."

"You need have no worries on that score."

It was easier to accept the assurance from her than from most people I've dealt with. "I think Colin's underlying problem has to do with sex."

Her look was sardonic. "Doesn't everyone's?"

I tried a dash of mirth. "Speak for yourself, Ms. Bunting."

Her lapse was only momentary; she rebuffed the reference to her private life by crossing her arms across her breasts. "You're speaking of his sexual orientation, I take it," she said stiffly.

"You know about that?"

"We've discussed it."

"How? I thought his jaw was broken."

"The swelling has been reduced to the point that he can form some words without moving his mandible. It's not a problem, really; many of my patients are victims of abuse. I have quite a lot of experience communicating with people who have that difficulty."

"So Colin told you he's gay."

"He's indicated his sexual orientation is sufficiently confusing to disturb him. Yes."

"His father doesn't know about it."

"I know."

"Neither does anyone else that I know of, except his buddy Broom. Has he mentioned her?"

"No."

"She's been his friend since high school. She's known he was . . . confused for a long time. She might be of help if therapy gets difficult."

"Thank you for telling me."

"No problem. Well, I guess I'll take off. I thought I was going to point you in the right direction, but I see you're already going that way."

I made a move to leave, but Nurse Bunting wasn't ready. "Why did you come to me with this? Why not go to his father?"

I shrugged. "Colin's been hanging around with a hate group of late. I figured if he's reached the point where he'd let a black woman hold his hand, he might let her into some other corners of his life as well. The group is homophobic as well as racist, by the way. Strange that he'd hang out with them, given what he knows about himself."

She shook her head. "Over the years, I've discovered that for some people in Colin's position, particularly males, there's a period of rather intense self-loathing that occurs before an understanding and acceptance of their sexual status is achieved. Based on the button he was wearing, I'd say Colin's urges in that regard were being met quite well by indulging in this organization's rhetoric."

I reached in my wallet and handed her a card. "I'm leaving for San Francisco tomorrow. If you think of any way I can be of help from out there, don't hesitate to call."

"Thank you for your concern."

"And the same for yours," I said. "Tell Colin I said good-bye. Tell him the brigade is standing down, and Bedford's been relieved of command."

THIRTY-FOUR

I drove to Upper King Street accompanied only by an inchoate sense of what lay behind the travails of Seth Hartman and a more explicit urge, one that had blossomed before I realized it existed, to exchange the brume of the Southern sump for some San Francisco summer fog.

The neighborhood got increasingly black, increasingly decrepit, increasingly kinetic. Pocket crowds were gathered next to minimarts and liquor stores to pass the evening sharing bluster and bullshit and bottles in brown bags. Rakish vehicles crossed my path on uncertain errands made ominous by the smoked-glass windows that masked the intents and purposes of their drivers. Children romped in grassless yards; broken vehicles were stacked like cordwood around the husks of abandoned buildings; police cars lurked in peculiar places.

Half a mile north of the freeway overpass, I came to the Panther Bar, which occupied the ground floor of a weather-beaten clapboard structure in the middle of an empty block. The black enamel paint job had peeled with sufficient frequency to make the Panther's skin look more like an ocelot's. The roof was tin; the doors and windows were masked with iron bars. In the lot next door, the vehicles ranged from soft-top Cadillacs to pockmarked pickups that seemed to have survived a war. I parked next to a low-slung Honda and went inside the bar.

The room swelled at its seams with merrymakers and the noise spun off by their frolic. The neon lights that laced the ceiling were so dimmed by smoke and grease that the gender and age of the occupants was indeterminate except for the waitresses, who wore short black skirts and revealing white blouses and stockings with seams up the back. The fan in the ceiling was tasked to shoo the stench of cigarettes and fried foods through the vent in the roof, but it was too puny to get the job done. The music from the jukebox was loud and primordial; the dancers matched its abandon.

With one exception, the faces in the room were black—I headed his way like a freighter for a channel marker, slow and steady and alert for floating obstacles. Along the way, I passed a lot of people who didn't like it that I was there, and nary a one who welcomed me.

My destination sat alone at a table near the back—the only clearing in the bar was the four-foot perimeter around him. He was clasping and unclasping his hands, crossing and uncrossing his legs, trying to look composed and carefree but not getting within miles of it. His eyes darted around the room like bees, hopping on and off the source of every outburst to make sure it wasn't perilous. When I sat in the chair across from him, he was more relieved than surprised by the encroachment.

"Professor Mickelson, I presume," I said.

He acknowledged the reference with a bow. "At your service."

"My name's Tanner. I'd like to speak with you a minute."

"About what?"

"The Columbia Field Office of the Student Nonviolent Coordinating Committee during the summer of 1966."

He waited for his surprise to subside, then glanced

briefly toward the door. "I'm expecting someone to join me momentarily, but I suppose we can talk till he gets here."

"Aldee," I said.

He raised a brow. "Do you know Mr. Blackwell?"

"We've met."

"In what connection?"

"In connection with a crime."

He licked his lips. "He's a criminal?"

"I wouldn't know."

"I don't understand."

"You don't need to."

He frowned and squirmed and squinted. "Then what is it you want from me?"

It was time to end the dance. "I need to know what happened back in 1966 that would give someone a motive to destroy Seth Hartman."

"I see." To gain time to review the bidding, the professor licked his lips and looked toward the bar but didn't catch the eye of a waitress. If Blackwell didn't show up soon, he'd be having the same problem an hour from now.

"I'm not sure it's in my best interest to discuss such matters with you," Mickelson said when his campaign to order a drink had collapsed.

"Why not?"

"As you may know, I'm doing a book on that very subject. There's been lots written about SNCC in Mississippi and Alabama during those years, but not much about the South Carolina project—I'm trying to fill that void. I've got a grant from a foundation and a promise of tenure at Duke if I finish by the end of the year."

"What does that have to do with talking to me?"

His smile was precious. "I believe the book's reception will be more . . . *dramatic* if my findings remain confidential until it appears. In all candor, it would be to my personal and professional advantage if it made something of a splash."

"Fine with me," I said. "But I don't have time to wait till it's written."

"Why not?"

"People have threatened and attempted murder because of what happened back then, Professor, and I've been hired to put a stop to it. What you've learned may help me do it."

"I . . . you're not saying I have any *legal* reason to co-operate with you," he said, with the smugness of the seasoned Socratic.

I leaned toward him with a smile on my face and spoke without moving my lips. "I'm saying that if you *don't*, I'm going to take you out to the parking lot and feed you your teeth. And then I'm going to take you to the cops and charge you with compounding a felony."

When he tried to swallow, he had trouble with the mechanics. "I believe you're serious."

"You're a good judge of character. I'll keep what you tell me confidential if I can, but there are other people involved, and raw emotions, so no guarantees."

"I don't know. I have to—"

"I don't have time for dilemmas, Professor. If you want to scurry back to Durham with a cast on your face, keep stalling."

He licked his lips once more and glanced toward the bar for an ally. When he didn't see anything but glares and cold shoulders, he looked back at me. "What do you want to know?"

"What happened between Seth Hartman and Aldee Blackwell that summer?"

"Hartman got Blackwell fired."

"By Monroe Morrison."

"Right."

"For having sex with white women."

Mickelson scratched his nose. "You seem to know everything already."

"One thing I don't know is why you've gone into the sex business in the first place. It doesn't sound scholarly."

"On the contrary, it's a key part of the history of those times. *Lots* of romances developed between the male leadership and the female volunteers in movement groups like SNCC; I'm merely the first to chart the sociology from an interracial perspective. Was the relationship secret or public? What did black *women* think about it? What did white *men* think about it? There must have been tension, so how did it manifest itself? What effect did it have on the underlying mission? I'm also interested in what happened to those relationships later on—were they only summer flings, or did they continue into later life? What were the repercussions? Are any of the parties still together? If not, does the current mate know about the former lover? That kind of thing fascinates me. My editor, too."

I withheld judgment on the weight of his academic pursuit. "You've outlined your syllabus, so what have you found out? What happened back then that's still causing a ruckus in Charleston?"

He rubbed the sweat off his brow with the back of his hand. "I don't know. Truly. Every interracial relationship I'm aware of ended when the project did. Several of the *intra*racial couples stayed together, but I've yet to unearth repercussions. I'm sorry if that's not what you expected, but . . ."

"Who did Aldee Blackwell have sex with that got him fired?"

"That's part of what I'm here to find out."

"Do you have any indication it was Jane Jean Hendersen?"

My question didn't surprise him. "At this point, I have

only suspicions. She has refused to talk to me, as has Mr. Hartman, at least on that subject."

"Were Seth and Jane Jean lovers in 1966?"

"I don't know for certain, but I don't believe so. Not that he wasn't interested; every man who *knew* her was interested, apparently. But my guess is that Hartman was denied her favors."

"Then who was the lucky guy?"

"You're assuming there was one."

"Aren't you?"

As the professor basked in uneasy conceit, a hush fell over the bar and a breeze freshened the fetid atmosphere. I looked toward the door in time to see Aldee Blackwell, complete with eye patch and cane and the shiny black suit he had sported on Johns Island that morning, enter the saloon the way the Windsors enter Albert Hall. The denizens seemed surprised to see him, presumably because of the early hour. He fended them off with waves and nods as he moved toward the bar like a prizefighter advancing toward the ring. Behind him, an entourage of three was ready to make sure no one lodged any complaints against management.

After a brief conversation with the bartender, Blackwell exchanged some earthy repartee with two women at a nearby table, then casually looked our way: We must have been as conspicuous as snowdrifts. When he saw that we saw him, he said something that made the bartender laugh, then strolled leisurely toward our table, bringing every eye in the place along with him.

"Evening, gentlemen," he said in a stentorian monotone that made his hauteur a halo. "Welcome to my drinking establishment. May I offer some refreshment?"

"I'd like a beer," I said. The professor said likewise, but only after due consideration. Blackwell snapped two fingers, and a waitress who had been studiously ignoring us headed for the bar as though it were on fire and she were the one with the hose.

The professor introduced himself and held out his hand. Blackwell ignored it and turned toward me instead. "You were on Johns Island this morning."

"That's right."

"Seth's man."

"Seth's friend."

He nodded once and pointed toward the professor. "This one called for an appointment. *You* march in without any by-your-leave at all. The lack of respect is distressing the brothers and sisters."

"I was under the impression that this was a public accommodation."

His patch hopped and his eye flashed. "As public as the accommodations on East Bay Street."

A murmur in the vicinity confirmed his estimation of dram-shop parity. "I need you to answer some questions," I said easily. "Then I'll get out of your way."

"Ain't no *white* man been in my way for thirty years." Some people near us laughed; others muttered oaths; the waitress brought the beer. "What kind of questions you got?" Blackwell continued casually.

"About the SNCC days."

He pointed to the professor. "Same as him."

I drank half the beer before I answered. "Not quite. He's going to go into a lot of detail about who did what and when and why. Then he's going to put it in a book. The best I can do is keep you out of jail."

Blackwell's wrought-iron scowl suggested the advent of mayhem. "What call you got talking about jail?"

"Someone's threatened to kill Seth Hartman. If you tell me what I think you know, I can prove it wasn't you."

"Why would they think it was?"

"Because Seth had you fired from the SNCC staff thirty

years ago. The man who did the firing has become Seth's client and friend and your political enemy. Lots of motive lying around—enough for the cops to make a case.''

''*Fuck* your motive. Seth Hartman don't have anything to *do* with me.''

''He got you fired for messing with white women.''

''Messing with *his* white woman, you mean.''

''Was it true?''

''Didn't matter.''

''Why not?''

''Reason Monroe cut me was I was pushing to put the program with the *Panther* party. Get rid of the nonviolent shit, and cocktail Negroes like Monroe; white women and college boys, too. Plus anyone else who thought Martin Luther candy-ass going to get something done. Only way to *get* something is to *take* it. True then; true now.''

''You're saying the problem between you and Morrison was political.''

''Right on, it was. Monroe part of the *old* way—days when we say please and thank you and shuffle in the dirt like chickens. But times change. Stokely take over SNCC; brothers from the Revolutionary Action Committee come down from Philadelphia preaching power and pride. Panthers say buy a piece and use it; get weapons like the crackers got, then shove the movement up they ass. But Monroe wouldn't go 'long with the program.''

''So your dispute had to do with tactics.''

''Damn straight. In summer, Monroe the boss, so he makes the rules. No confrontation, he says. No weapons; no sexuosity, either. Come fall, Stokely toss Monroe out on his gravediggin' ass and send the college kiddies back where they come from.''

''And SNCC?''

''SNCC's time passed. Black *Panthers* where it at.''

''How was Jane Jean Hendersen involved in all this?''

Blackwell scowled thunderously. "Who says she was?"

"The people who think you were having sex with her."

"Shit." Blackwell glanced around to see who was listening. "White bitches all the time trying to show how *unprejudiced* they was, rub they sugar against the black man's ass. Got no time for it, myself."

A woman at the next table said, "Amen."

"All I know is this," I said. "If you're getting back at Seth for something he did back then, I'm going to find out about it. And if you're using the Alliance for Southern Pride to do your dirty work, I'm going to find that out, too." I waved toward the room. "The brothers and sisters aren't going to like it if they find out you're financing a hate-monger like Forrest Bedford just to serve some private vendetta."

Blackwell checked to see how widely my speech had been overheard, then grasped my arm with fingers that were powered by melodrama and despotism. "You go 'round claiming I'm behind some kind of *supremacist* bullshit, that's the last tale you *ever* tell. Got it, white man?"

As I smiled with as much unconcern as I could muster, the professor piped up. "You don't have to deal with this man, Mr. Blackwell; cooperation is not in your best interest. *I'm* the one who can put those days in historical context. *I'm* the one who can tell the world of the evolution of the new black militancy in which you played such an important part. *I'm* the one who can put you in the perspective you so richly deserve."

Blackwell made a fist and raised it. "Right on, motherfucker. Context. Got to know my *context*." Blackwell looked at me and grinned, then poked me in the chest with his cane. "Get on back to Broad Street, spook. Here on Upper King, context for you ain't worth *shit*."

THIRTY-FIVE

I left the bar and drove back to the center of town. The city that had seemed so pristine and delightful when I arrived had tarnished in the interim, become a tired old whore made up to look her best while disease and degeneracy festered beneath the latex sheen of commerce. But that wasn't the truth of her, either. Like everyone and everything I'd come across in Charleston, from Seth Hartman to Scar Raveneau to the social and political climate I'd encountered only vicariously, full definition lay beyond me.

When I got to his office, the door was unlocked and the receptionist's chair was empty—Elmira had gone off to an evening of fun and frolic, or maybe just to do her laundry. Seth was sitting behind his desk, face propped heavily on his hands, eyes sightless and boggled, essence isolated and bemused.

When my features found a match in his memory, his smile was reminiscent of the corpse being bombarded in the mortuary. "Are you bringing me bad news?"

"What makes you think so?"

"Because everything in my life is turning inside out all of a sudden." His voice was timorous and contrite. "Nothing seems to stop it. Not even you." He lowered his hands from his chin and picked up a pen from the desk and started scribbling on the yellow pad in front of him. "It's only fair, I suppose. Things went my way for a long time. It had to even out sooner or later.''

When he was free of his ontological musings, he looked up from his doodling. ''Want some dinner? Jane Jean is coming in; you're welcome to join us.''

I shook my head. ''I'm having dinner with Scar Raveneau later. I just stopped by to tell you I'm leaving tomorrow.''

Delayed by the state of his nerves, his reaction was argumentative, then apologetic. ''But you just *got* here. You haven't met my daughter yet. You haven't gotten to know Jane Jean. Hell, you haven't even been out to the house.'' He shook his head miserably. ''Jesus, what a total *shit* I am.''

''Maybe next time, Seth.''

''You won't be back and you know it. You wouldn't have come *this* time if I hadn't . . . '' The pen fell from his fingers. ''You're upset with me, aren't you?''

''I don't know. Am I?''

He nodded. ''You're mad because I didn't turn out the way you thought I should.''

''Maybe a little. If I were you, I wouldn't let it bother me.''

''But it does. It always has. I spent four years trying to earn your respect.''

''Well, you got good at it.''

''Then why are you so peeved at me? Because of Colin?''

I shifted uneasily, uncomfortable with attitudes I didn't fully understand. ''I'm not sure. Maybe it's because you had so much going for you, you don't have an excuse for screwing up as much as you have.'' I reheard my words, then diluted them. ''I'm not being fair, I suppose—life isn't perfectible; at best it's a fragile accommodation. All we can do is all we can do, and I have no reason to think you haven't done that.''

"I'm not sure I have, actually."

I smiled. "Me, either."

We shared the blemish for a moment. "I'd like to give it another try, Marsh," Seth continued quietly. "Get together again, maybe in San Francisco, after the ASP business is over, and Monroe's trial and all. Make it more like the old days."

"That would be nice."

His look turned downcast. "You don't sound optimistic."

"It's just that I'm not sure the old days are what we need. I think what we need are some *new* days."

"What do you mean?"

"We should go forward, not backward. Make a new friendship based on what we are now."

Seth nodded. "We can do that. Can't we?"

"I don't know."

"We should find out, at least. Shouldn't we? I mean, friends are a rare commodity. And new friends aren't quite the same as old friends. Do you know what I mean?"

"That's why I'm here."

Seth regarded me with quiet appraisal, looking for a blanket acquittal that I couldn't bring myself to give him. "Is this it, then?" he said finally. "You're off to the airport in the morning?"

I nodded.

"You'll let me take you, won't you?"

I shook my head. "I'll grab a cab."

He nodded miserably, as though my refusal were symbolic. "I'm sorry about this, Marsh. I really am."

"About what?"

"Begging you to come down here. Not really . . . being with you since you arrived. It was unfair to burden you with my problems; to think you could do anything about ASP and the rest of it."

"As a matter of fact, I *am* doing something about ASP. If things go the way I hope they will, they'll be out of your hair by the end of the evening."

Seth started to stand, then sank back so heavily his chair tipped against the wall. "What's happened? What are you going to do? How can you be certain it will end it?"

"I'm not certain, but I'm hopeful."

"But what have you learned? Who's behind it? How are you going to make them stop?"

"I haven't learned that much, really. Just some things about the SNCC days."

Uncertainty scrambled his features and made his confusion comic. "I don't . . . What about them?"

"You know more about it than I do, Seth. You were there."

"I know, but I don't understand what those times have to *do* with anything." He sagged back in his chair, burdened by a murky past and the sudden need to translate it. "I don't understand," he repeated dismally.

"It's better that you don't. I just need to confirm some things, then I'll be on my way."

"Where are you going?"

"Here and there."

He blinked back a tear. "Don't tease me, Marsh. Please. Does it have to do with Jane Jean? Just tell me that."

"No, Seth. You tell me."

"What?"

"About Jane Jean and the black man."

"I don't—"

"Yes, you do," I interrupted rudely. "And I need to know about it."

Dazed by a potent brew of past and present, Seth looked longingly at the law books, but none provided refuge. When he finally spoke, his words amounted to a requiem.

"We'd been in McClellanville for a week. Walking

down dusty roads, climbing onto sagging porches, begging people to go to town and register. Asking them not to be afraid, urging them to be brave, hoping we weren't adding to their misery or sending them to an early grave. People who worked dawn to dusk for next to nothing. People who couldn't read. People who'd been told we were infidels and Communists and people who thought we were the Second Coming of the Apostles, there to deliver them from evil.''

He paused to rethink and remember. I kept quiet and let him do it.

"It was the end of the summer. Hot as Hades. Humid. It was like Milton's 'bottomless perdition'—I'd never lived in such weather before. We'd spent the week with families out in the countryside, sleeping on floors or cots but not really *getting* much sleep because every noise in the night might have been rednecks coming around to run us off or worse. We were exhausted, and exhilarated. Some days were depressing, but other days were glorious. People *were* coming out, people *were* signing up, people *were* being magnificent. The South was about to change. We could *feel* it."

He leaned back in his chair and closed his eyes and laid his arms across his chest in the manner of a corpse. "It was Friday night. I finished up early and drove back to the rooming house in Columbia the SNCC people shared. I was determined to make one last plea to Jane Jean. To show her how I felt; to say or do something that would make her feel the same way about me. I showered and changed and went to her room. She wasn't there, so I waited. I was reading— *An American Tragedy,* I remember. It got late; it got dark.''

He stopped talking and listened, as though an ancient noise were traveling to him through walls of time and space. "After a while, I heard her drive up—her Mustang had a click, valves or something. I'd read eighty-three pages, I remember. I went to the window and looked out and saw her in the car, talking to someone sitting next to her. A man. A black man. I couldn't see their faces, but I could certainly see their bodies. I could certainly see what they were doing to each other.''

He sniffed and cleared his throat. ''She was the aggressor, almost from the second she stopped the car. She put her arm around his shoulders and pulled him toward her. Her hands roamed his chest and back, then slid to his lap—it was obvious what she wanted. I was disgusted and aroused simultaneously—the thought of her stroking his cock was . . . anyway, after a while she unbuttoned her blouse, and he began to fondle her in turn. She put her hands on his and showed him how to please her: Rough black hands roaming soft white flesh—it was like something out of a stag film. It drove me crazy, Marsh. For the only time in my life, I was capable of murder. I screamed, I cried, I called them every vile name I could think of. If I'd had a gun, I think I would have shot them both, point-blank, and be relieved when they executed me for it.''

''But you didn't,'' I said softly.

''No, but I did something just as bad. The next day I went to Monroe and demanded that Aldee be fired. For reasons of principle, of course—compromise of the movement and all that. Monroe did as I asked, though not because of my tantrum, I realized later, but for reasons of his own.''

Seth sat up. His eyes met mine momentarily, then ducked away. ''I've spent the rest of my life living with the fact that I'm just as prejudiced as the crackers I'd been fighting that summer, creatures I'd despised as being less than human, people I'd regarded as craven cowards. The minute a black man took something I wanted, I became a raging bigot, too. It's been hard to live with that over the years. Close to impossible sometimes.''

''We all have feelings we're not proud of, Seth. The question is what we let them do to us.''

He waved away my essay. ''I avoided Jane Jean the rest

of the summer, went back to school, and failed the course in forgetting. I didn't come back here to work for civil rights; I came to be near her.'' He waited for his mind to switch to a more current track. ''Is she involved with ASP, Marsh?''

I hesitated before I answered. ''No.''

''I'm going to *marry* the woman, for God's sake. You have to tell me if she's *responsible* for this.''

''Nothing I've learned should affect your plans, Seth. But I need to know one thing.''

''About her and Aldee?''

I shook my head, then said something I'd sworn just minutes before I wouldn't say. ''It wasn't Aldee.''

''What do you mean?''

''The man in the car. It wasn't Aldee Blackwell.''

''But it *had* to be. I'd seen them together that morning— he was wearing the same shirt. Besides, by that time the only black men on staff in Columbia were Aldee and . . . '' His eyes ballooned. ''No. Impossible. It *couldn't* have been.''

''I think it was.''

''I don't believe it. I *won't* believe it. She *told* me it was Aldee.''

Seth looked to be in shock, then moaned from the rip in his soul. ''God. It almost killed me then, and it's almost killing me now.'' He regarded me with the hot hurt of new wounds. ''I can't deal with this anymore. I have things to do.'' He searched the room for a diversion, then snatched a file from the corner of his desk and opened it without looking at its contents. ''I'm busy. What is it you need to know?'' he asked inanely.

''Does Jane Jean have children?''

His perplexity approached delirium. ''Children? I don't . . . What does *that* have to do with—''

''*Does* she?''

My intensity shoved him toward composure. "No. She doesn't."

"Why not?"

"I . . . she can't. An infection or something; her tubes are blocked with scar tissue. One of those loop things, I think. But what does that have to *do* with anything?"

"Ask her tomorrow," I said, and stood up. "Two more things."

"What?"

"I need the tape Alameda brought in."

He opened a drawer in the credenza behind him, extracted the tape, and handed it to me. "I'll want it back," he said. "In case the ASP thing blossoms into a harassment suit."

I put the tape in my pocket. "The Lincoln you drove to the park last night. The one we took to Johns Island later on."

"What about it?"

"You told me you were going to borrow it from Jane Jean. But you didn't, did you? You got it from someone else."

I was already out the door by the time he uttered the name of the man I was on my way to see.

THIRTY-SIX

The house was new and sumptuous, rebuilt since the hurricane the way nearly all of its neighbors had been, a bright new seashell washed upon the shore of Sullivans Island by the winds of a tropical depression. The flagstone path to the entrance was garlanded with flowers and shrubs and shaded by a row of stunted palms; the facade was a pleasing mix of clapboard and limestone and glass brick; the door was a copper-sheeted rectangle already beclouded by the elements.

The woman who opened it was wearing short white shorts, a scarlet tube top, and white mesh sandals, redundant accessories to her organic allure. Her shoulders were brown and bare, her hair was loose and licentious, her lips were barren of all but a pucker of puzzlement when she saw who had come calling.

"I'm here to see your daddy," I told her.

Her forehead folded with uncertainty. "Are you in some kind of trouble?"

I shook my head. "Social call. I thought he might be in the mood for a chat."

"What is it you want to talk about?"

"Old age, mostly."

Jane Jean frowned and looked beyond me. "Is Seth with you? Are you picking me up for dinner? I don't understand what you're doing.'' As the sequence neared its end, her voice rose to the realms of panic.

"Seth is still at the office. It's like I said—I need to talk to your father.''

"But what *about*?''

"Life.''

"*Whose* life?''

"His and mine and yours and Seth's.''

She shook her head sharply, as though to relink a short circuit. A drop of sweat rolled down her neck, ducked between her breasts, and disappeared beneath the expanded band of elastic. I'd have been happy to crawl in there myself.

"Daddy's resting,'' Jane Jean managed finally. "Plus, he's with someone. You'll have to come back tomorrow.''

"I'm leaving town tomorrow. Maybe it will help if I list some of the people I've talked to today: Monroe Morrison; Aldee Blackwell; Forrest Bedford; Professor Mickelson. Tell that to your daddy. Tell him if I don't see him in five minutes, I'm going to hunt up a reporter and tell my tale to her. It won't be as lyrical as Faulkner or Eudora Welty, but I think she'll hear me out.''

She had an urge to slam the door and shut me out, but in the end all she could manage was to stand in place and fidget. I took her hand to keep it from flying about her person like a butterfly. "We both know what this is about, Jane Jean.''

"I have no idea what you're referring to.''

"I know what he's been doing and so do you. He needs to know I know, and he needs to know what will happen if he doesn't stop it.''

She looked in my eyes long enough to see that I was serious, then withdrew her hand and stepped back, her charm and proficiency reduced to the mundane by the genesis of my demands. The shorts and top seemed suddenly too large for her, the house a cheerless cell.

"Do you have to do this?" she asked, grasping my arm with red-tipped fingers to plead her case with the aid of her best weapon. "He's not well, you know. He has heart trouble."

"I don't know about his heart, but in his mind he's a tough old bird. You know that better than anyone. He's not going to stop unless I play my trump."

"Play it now. For me. I'll make him understand what he has to do."

I shook my head. "You're his darling daughter, and you've been trying to shut him down for months, but you haven't been able to manage it. Then you tried to buy off Bedford, but that didn't work, either."

Her lips firmed with naked loathing. "You . . . you *foreigner*. You come down here and poke around for a few days and think you know what we're about. But you don't know *anything*. Yankees are dumb as stumps."

I laughed. "I may not know everything, but I know enough to know that R. Montgomery Henderson isn't going to stop using ASP as his personal puppet until I call in some shock troops. If you're as smart as I think you are, you won't make me talk with the feds."

The evening darkened a shade before she spoke. "He's out back," she said resignedly, as though the coil of her life had unkinked. "With his new friend."

"I know," I said.

She canted her head. "How?"

"Just a guess. She said some things."

"*Seth* doesn't know, does he?"

"I don't think so."

"Will he have to?"

"Not from me."

She sighed from deep despair. "That's part of it, too, you know."

"I know."

"By both of them, I mean."

"I know."

"Poor Seth."

With a twitch of resolve, she thrust back her shoulders and threw back her hair, then marched down the hall to the kitchen and pushed through the doors that led to the porch that skirted the rear of the house. I had to trot to keep up with her.

The porch was a kaleidoscope of flowered fabric and painted wicker atop a vinyl flooring that borrowed the colors of custard and used brick. The evening breezes were undisturbed by the silvered screens that were the only barriers to the sea beyond them. The hollow knock of wind chimes made it seem as if we were going to have fun, but like the rest of life in the Low Country, the indications were misleading.

I looked beyond the dunes and marsh grasses to the waves that sidled toward us. Their edges glowed in the twilight like jagged lines of neon, sparkling hues of luminescence that advanced in easy eddies, then shattered on the sand and sank to some subterranean sinkhole. At the moment, they seemed metaphoric of a fractured friendship.

Dressed in shorts and thongs and nothing else, R. Montgomery Hendersen was sitting in a padded wicker chair watching the pulse of the ocean as though he were its court-appointed guardian. On a chaise to his right, her left hand entwined in his and her other clasped negligently around a cocktail, Chantrelle Hartman reclined like a bikinied odalisque, her eyes not on the surf but on her man. In contrast to Chantrelle's firm and burnished body, Monty's bloodless flesh sagged off him like loose linens.

"Daddy?" Jane Jean said from just inside the door. "Mr. Tanner is here. He needs to talk to you a minute."

He didn't move his eyes from the vista that had clearly bewitched him for a lifetime. "Who?"

"Mr. Tanner. Seth's friend? You met him at Saracen the other day. Chantrelle, have you—"

"We've met." Chantrelle flashed a proprietary glance to her left, then curled her long legs under her. "Are you looking for *me*, Mr. Tanner? Has Daddy hired you to make me come to my senses and stop *fucking* this dirty old man?"

"The only thing I want you to do is leave the room for twenty minutes."

She bristled. "You don't have any right to march in here and—"

"Mr. Hendersen and I are going to be discussing matters that neither you nor Jane Jean need be privy to."

"What kind of matters?" Chantrelle demanded.

"Biblical matters."

"What?" She wouldn't have been more surprised if I'd said we'd be singing some two-part harmony, then lip-syncing to the Platters.

"Pre-Adamics," I went on. "Canaanites. The Lost Tribes of Israel. Old Testament stuff."

Chantrelle looked left. "He's deranged, Monty. Do you want me to call the sheriff?"

Hendersen shook his head a single time. "Go." He looked back at his daughter. "You, too, darlin'. Mr. Tanner and I need to set a spell."

"But . . . " The women sputtered the same word at the same time.

"You heard me."

I looked at Jane Jean. "Is there a phone out here I can use?"

She pointed toward a cordless unit on a table beneath a bouquet of fresh flowers.

"How about a sound system?"

She frowned, then pointed to some compact Sony components stuffed in a cabinet near the door, then turned to her daddy. "Don't let him upset you. You know what the doctor said."

"Yankee hasn't been made who could put a kink in my line, sugar lump. Now run on." He looked to his right. "Chantrelle, sweetheart, it's time to find a new toy." He pointed to his chest. "Ticker won't stand up to another ride, I don't think; takes more out of me than boatin' a marlin. Not that I don't appreciate it."

Outrage embossed her eyes. She started to say something, then swore, then drained her drink and threw the glass at my face. As it shattered against the wall behind me, she gathered her clothes off a chair and ran for the door without looking back.

After a moment of indecision, Jane Jean started after her. "I'll be in my room," she said on the way.

"Seth deserves to know what happened," I said to her bare back. "All of it, I mean."

She paused, then nodded, then was gone. The only residue was her scent, a hint of rose and lilac that was soon swallowed by the winds that swept in from the beach and occupied the porch with the assurance of a lifelong neighbor.

"Liquid refreshment?" Montgomery asked me calmly, his eyes still on the surf. "There's beer in the cooler. Imported." He pointed toward an Igloo on the floor beside him.

"No, thanks."

"It'll get chilly in a minute; if you want, I can hunt up some cognac."

I shook my head.

"Then I guess we're off the high ground and down in the ditch. What's on your mind, Mr. Tanner?"

"Seth Hartman."

"Known Seth for a long time." His squint turned sadistic. "Hated his guts for *almost* as long."

"I've known Seth a long time, too; he doesn't deserve what you're doing to him. Lots of other people don't deserve it, either. Including Monroe Morrison."

Hendersen chuckled like the chug of a loaded dump truck but didn't offer a response. I sat on the chaise Chantrelle had just vacated and trained my eyes on the sea as well, but its message was indistinct. It didn't trust foreigners, either.

"I got into this when I met Seth at our college reunion," I said as preamble, "and he told me about his troubles with the Alliance for Southern Pride. But before that, I'd been doing some thinking. Not about Seth—just about life. And one of the things I realized was that even twenty-five years after the fact, I still carried around resentments from my college years. Resentments against the school, and the faculty, even against some of the students I'd been close to back then, because I thought somehow they'd diminished my life. I was wrong, of course—my life is what I made it as it went along, not what someone did or didn't do back then—but I still harbored resentments."

"I'm not a head doctor," Hendersen said when I paused for breath. "I'm just a country lawyer. You're going to have to tell me how your troubles up at some Yankee school have anything to do with me."

"The relevance is that you've got resentments, too. They've come to the surface not because of a class reunion, but because you're getting old. In particular, you resent Seth Hartman and Monroe Morrison because of something that happened in the SNCC days. As you see it, they betrayed you, lessened your life forever, and their treachery is all the more painful now that you're thinking about your legacy. The pain eventually got so bad that you decided to strike back, at people who took a large part of that legacy from you. There *is* something Biblical about it—you're playing

God, and Bedford is your archangel, dispatched to do battle with transgressors who have wronged you.''

Monty exchanged his stereotyped persona for the gravity of an oracle. ''I'd say Beelzebub is a closer analogy, wouldn't you?'' The cornball went out of his voice. ''Now maybe you can get to the point.''

''The point is that your gripe against Seth comes from two sources. The minor provocation is that Seth has displaced you as Charleston's Clarence Darrow.'' I paused. ''It's ironic, in a way.''

''What way?''

''You're the man both Seth and I wanted to grow up to be when we were younger. Champion of the oppressed; defender of the weak and powerless; fearless advocate for truth and justice.''

''Cut the bullshit.''

''I wasn't being sarcastic. The way Seth tells it, you were all those things, and I have no reason to dispute him. What I'm trying to say is that I admire you for what you were, and I'm sure you justifiably reveled in it. But righteous causes don't *come* to you much anymore; most of them go to Seth. He's made you irrelevant, and you can't stand it. If he gets Morrison acquitted in the bribery trial, while your client goes to jail because you advised him to cop a plea, you'll never see a major case again; they'll say you're past your prime. Which is why so much of ASP's effort has been to frighten Seth's clients into changing counsel—so you could take over his cases and get back on the fast track, jurisprudentially.''

He was shaking his head before I finished. ''It's bull pucky. Hell, man, I'm the next thing to retired. Been wishing I was dead for twenty years.''

''Which brings us to your *real* grievance.''

Monty wriggled in his chair and made it creak at its

joints like a sloop in a storm. "I don't know what the sam hell you're talking about."

"Sure you do," I said. "Your *real* gripe against Seth Hartman is that a quarter-century ago, he wasn't man enough to keep your daughter out of the arms of Monroe Morrison."

THIRTY-SEVEN

His voice took on the hard, hot crust of molten lead; he looked at me with naked hatred. "You're in the wrong part of the country to be singing that song, boy."

I reclined on the chaise and clasped my hands behind my head, prepared to stay till doomsday. "I'm not telling you anything you don't know, Mr. Hendersen. When Seth and Jane Jean and Monroe and Aldee were up in Columbia registering people to vote, your daughter had a fling. Idealistic young white girl working side by side with a committed young black man, coming in from a day of getting spat on and cursed and threatened with mob violence to find solace in each other's arms—a fertile field for romance. But in this case, it didn't end there. There was fallout, as there often is with sex. Some of it got Aldee Blackwell fired, because Seth thought Jane Jean was having the affair with Aldee. And some of it hit you."

"You're not making sense. I barely remember my bird dog's name, let alone who was funning who in those days."

"You remember your daughter got pregnant," I declared. "With Monroe Morrison's child. I don't think Seth knew, and I'm not sure Monroe did, either. But you did."

His look was meant to melt the circuits in my brain. "There's no way on God's green earth you can prove that."

"You're probably right, since you got rid of the evidence."

"What's that supposed to mean?"

"Instead of having the child, Jane Jean had an abortion. I'm sure you paid for it, and you probably found the doctor, too, since back then abortion was not only expensive and illegal, it was also dangerous."

Monty swelled with indignation. "You're saying I'm perturbed because my daughter didn't give birth to a *mulatto*?"

"I'm saying that as a result of the abortion, your daughter couldn't have children. Which meant you couldn't have *grand*children. Which means when you've gone to your Maker, the Hendersen line will die. They stole your immortality, Monty, and now that you're pushing seventy, it's preying on your mind. The fact that the man who'd seduced and abandoned your daughter was about to be elected to Congress made it all the more insupportable that his sin was unavenged."

Hendersen reached in the cooler, took out a beer, and twisted off the top the way he would have liked to twist my neck. "There's no one alive who will open his mouth about any of this."

"I'm not sure about that; you cast your net pretty wide. It wouldn't surprise me, for example, if you were the one who suggested to Mr. Keystone that he turn double agent and set up Morrison on the bribery charge, just to make sure that when he fell, he fell all the way to the bottom."

Monty drained half his beer, then looked at me. "If you think you'll be doing anyone a favor by bringing this out, think again. Monroe's career would end in a New York minute; he couldn't be elected poultry inspector. And Aldee would be gutted like a grouper by those hoodlums he hangs out with."

"Quite possibly," I admitted. "The problem for you is, I couldn't care less."

Monty decided to track his options. "Have you talked about this with anyone?"

"Not yet."

"Fixing to?"

"Not if you shut it down."

"Shut what down?"

"The Alliance for Southern Pride."

"Never heard of 'em."

I got Alameda's tape from my pocket and walked to the Sony and started it. As Colin's words spun into the dusky air, they seemed even more rancid than before, a mate with the stench of rotting fish that seeped at us from the nearby shore.

As the tape wound to a close, I looked at Hendersen. "Proud of yourself?"

His expression was ashen and unhealthy, but he was determined to bluff it out. "What makes you think I got my foot in *that* boot?"

"Because I took a MAC-ten assault weapon away from Colin Hartman last night, and stashed it in your car and forgot about it. This morning, Seth returned the car to you. A few hours later, that same weapon was leaning against the wall in Forrest Bedford's bunker, down on Folly Beach." I smiled. "It may not be enough for a D.A., but it's enough for me."

He thought it over so long I knew he was going to stonewall. "If you know Bedford, then you know he doesn't fish that lake for money," he said. "He won't turn tail even if I pinch off the teat."

"He doesn't have to turn tail; he just has to lay off the Hartmans. And I think I've persuaded him to do it."

"How?"

"None of your business."

He finished his beer in a single gulp. "Damn. Seth's baby girl almost fucked me dry." He hoped I'd be insulted by his vulgarity; when he saw that I wasn't, he erupted.

"Even if this shit storm was true, what do you think *you* can do about it, you California sumbitch? Folks in Charleston owe me; they owe me big. You go to anyone with this, you won't float out of the swamp till a year from Thursday."

I walked across the room and picked up the phone and dialed a number I got from my wallet. As it rang, I returned to the chaise and lay back like an heir to a small fortune.

"Some of my cases have ended with gunplay," I mused easily. "And some with a brawl, some with a confession, and a few with a raid by the cops. This one's going to end with an aria."

Monty helped himself to another beer.

"Yeah?"

"Aldo Benedetti, please."

"Who's this?"

"A friend of Callie's; I called an hour ago. If Aldo doesn't want to be on the front page of the Charleston newspaper tomorrow, he needs to talk to me a minute."

The phone banged and the background buzzed and another voice came on the line, simultaneously intimidating and restrained. "What's this shit about Callie? I talked to her ten minutes ago—she never heard of you."

"I needed a way to get to you, so I used her name."

"She's got nothing to do with it?"

"No."

"I don't like people who mix family with business."

"It's lousy; I apologize."

"Then what's the problem?"

"Your car business in Charleston."

He hesitated. "Who says I've got a car business in Charleston?"

"I do."

"If I do, what about it?"

"Your manager has been playing games, and they're going to get you in trouble."

"Games? What kind of games?"

"Burning crosses on black people's lawns."

"What?"

"You heard me."

"Like the Klan and that shit?"

"The same."

"You're saying fucking Bilbow is in the fucking *Klan*?"

"I'm saying he's working with a group called ASP. The Alliance for Southern Pride, they call themselves."

Monty Hendersen coughed and choked and spit a mouthful of beer across his naked chest.

"Bilbow and this outfit burned a cross?" Aldo asked.

"Yep."

"Cops know about it?"

"They know about the cross; they don't know about Bilbow."

"They going to?"

"Not if Bilbow and ASP give up the race games."

"What makes you think they'll do that?"

"Because you're going to tell them to."

He thought it over. "Bilbow, okay. He doesn't wipe his ass unless I provide the paper. But this other outfit. This ASP. How do I get in touch with them?"

"The headman is right beside me. Tell him who you are and what will happen if ASP and Bilbow don't leave innocent people alone."

"What's his name?"

"No names for now. Just tell him why he should cease and desist. Tell him about the eyeballs."

I held out the phone to Hendersen. "It's a tenor, not a fat lady, but the rule still applies—it's over, Monty."

He took the phone from my fingers, but his hands were so wet he dropped it.

THIRTY-EIGHT

When I got back to the Home, I knocked on Scar Raveneau's door. When she didn't answer, I went down to my room and called her home number. When she came on the line, I asked if I could take her to dinner.

"I don't think so," she said huskily, the words a throaty buzz in my ear.

"Why not?"

"I've had enough pain in my life for a while." She sighed. "It's not your fault. It's just that I've got all this *love* in me, and what I want most in the world is to *give* it to someone, but the only men who come along are the ones who can't use it."

"It's not that; it's just . . . logistical. It might be different if I lived down here."

"I doubt it."

"Don't beat up on yourself that way. The other night was great—one of the best times I've ever had."

"Really?"

"Really."

"That's something, I guess."

"It's almost everything, isn't it?"

"Not even close." Her voice turned raw and defensive. "You said I should decide whether I wanted something or nothing. Well, I decided to settle for nothing."

"Why?"

"Because it doesn't hurt as much."

She hung up in the middle of my ungainly attempt to rebut her.

I took a deep breath, fixed a strong drink, and dug another number from my wallet. "I don't think I'm going to make it," I said when she came on the line.

"I didn't think you would."

"Are you mad?"

"No."

"Sad?"

"Yes."

"Me, too."

"Then why don't you come up?"

"I will someday. I promise. But not now."

"Why not now?"

"I need to recuperate a bit."

She hesitated. "That sounds ominous; what on earth happened down there?"

"The old days crawled out from under a rock and sort of made a mess of things."

"They have a tendency to do that." Her laugh was dry and distant—defense mechanisms fully engaged. "Are you all right? How's Seth?"

"I'm fine. Seth will be fine, too. But it's going to take a while—we cut each other up a bit."

"Not literally, I hope."

"Close enough."

"But why? What did he do to you?"

"A long time ago, I decided he was perfect. When he proved I was wrong, I got mad at him."

"And what did you do to him?"

"I shined a bright light on the people he loves most in the world and some scars showed up."

"I still don't understand, but I have a feeling I'm not

supposed to. I've been wondering if you answered the question."

"What question?"

"Whether you're a success or a failure."

"I guess what I've done is decide it's irrelevant."

"Why?"

"Because all I *really* need to know is that I enjoy what I do, and I'm good at it, and I do it better than I'd do anything else. And that once in a while I help more than hurt. It's difficult to keep it in mind sometimes, but if I do, I think I can live with the situation."

"What makes it so difficult for you to feel successful?"

"Because my work is a zero-sum game. When a doctor heals a patient, another patient doesn't die; when a pilot lands an airplane, another aircraft doesn't crash. But when I solve a problem for one person, I tend to make a problem for someone else: The client goes to dinner; his nemesis goes to jail. Usually it's an easy exchange—help the good guy; lock up the bad. But sometimes the trade-off isn't comfortable. In Seth's situation—"

"I didn't know Seth *had* a situation," she interrupted.

"Well, he does. Or did. It's taken care of, pretty much—the bad guy was a frightened old man who was afraid the world was going to forget him, a nobleman who became a thug because he couldn't abide his own mortality."

"Is he going to jail?"

"Just purgatory."

"And you're okay with that?"

"I think so."

As far as I could tell, it was true. Seth's burdens had been lightened, Alameda would have her chance to attend the Palisade, Monroe Morrison would have a fair trial, and Colin Hartman would be pried away from ASP. I'd done what I'd been hired to do, and more. If someday South Carolina honors Monty Hendersen the way it ought to, the damage I'd done wouldn't be permanent.

"Anyway," I said, "I wanted to tell you that I enjoyed our time at the reunion."

"Me, too."

"San Francisco probably could use a good caterer, you know."

"I doubt it. But I'm sure Baltimore could use a good detective."

"If I run into one, I'll let him know."

"I never did like false humility. I don't know if I mentioned it."

I laughed. "I'm sure you did. Well . . . "

"Well . . . "

"See you, I guess."

"Yeah. See you, Marsh. But where?"

"There's always another reunion."

ABOUT THE AUTHOR

STEPHEN GREENLEAF is the author of the John Marshall Tanner novels and two other works, *The Ditto List* and *Impact*. Prior to writing, he practiced law in Monterey and San Francisco and taught trial advocacy. He now lives and writes in Seattle.